I would like to dedicate this novel to Sebastien De Castell, one of my favourite authors.

Without him taking more time with me than he needed to, the world of Hybrid wouldn't feel nearly as alive as it is.

From a fellow Canadian author, Thank You!

Cover illustrated and designed by Miblart

I also can't start the story without thanking

YOU

For supporting small authors. Every time you read one of our books you're taking part in fulfilling our dream.

Thank you

Chapter 1

The sky turned a deep purple hue as the sun began to descend on the Scarlet Sands. A desert known for the dull red tint of its earth, as well as containing one of the most powerful kingdoms on the continent. It was in the castle of Arid Retreat, what was once a small military outpost many years ago turned into a full-on trading community, that princess Anachorita felt her disappointment at the setting sun. She had spent her day reading war stories and wished to continue. The desert night wasn't one to shine brightly in lieu of a full moon, and according to her governess, a lady wasn't to spend the midnight hours awake. This made things more problematic as one lit candle in her tower, and the whole door frame would light up like a bonfire.

She sighed as she marked off the page of her book by bending the corner and put it back on the shelf. Looking at the bookcase reminded her again of being chided for reading such nonsense made up of military strategy and historical events. She was getting tired of being told to leave such things to her brother Kasbiel, as he was the firstborn and in line for the throne. Ana felt like she was only around to show up to parties. She wasn't even allowed to leave the castle without an escort. Not once in her full seventeen years of life had she been able to roam around on her own. At least not without anyone knowing.

It was a lazy day for Ana, though. She had no plans to sneak out in the middle of the night and just wanted to make it through to the next day so she could have some natural light again. She crawled into her soft down bed, a rarity in the desert, and covered herself in a heavy layer of linens. At the very least her window had a good view of the night sky. If she had her brother's room she would be staring at a cliff face, as the back end of the sprawling castle left nothing but mountains. That and the fact his tower was shorter were the only things she could hold over him.

Everything had felt normal. Crawling into bed, getting cozy, watching the sky turn its way from purple to a dark red, and finally, into the clear black night. Ana wondered how she didn't have enough light with how the stars twinkled so clearly. Something was different, though. An odd feeling. One that felt like something was left undone. It wasn't something she wasn't used to, as most chores were completed by servants. Too often did they take care of how she dressed and acted. There was nothing that she could have forgotten about that someone else wasn't already paid to do. She disregarded the feeling and tried to get a good night's sleep.

Ignoring the problem didn't seem to fix it. There was something out there Ana needed to do but had no idea what it was. She had no idea where it was. It was just out there, and it couldn't wait. She managed to get a bit of sleep before waking up again with the same feeling, but amplified. The dark room was barely visible even to Ana's adjusted eyes, but she felt she had to get up.

Her rise from the sheets didn't come with the same protest she usually had first thing in the morning. Sure, her long brown hair was all tangled in a mess, but that was nothing new. She felt her way around the room and toyed with the idea of lighting a candle but knew better. It would be much easier to sneak through the castle halls without a light. Without knowing why, she began her escape in the dark.

Once she found her way to it, Ana knocked on the inside of her door. There was no response. This was from experience, as she knew her father would place a guard outside on some nights. Sometimes it was due to a foreign power being hosted that might want to take her for political reasons, but it was usually for fear of doing exactly what she was now. Sneaking out at night.

The door opened with a soft creak. Not enough to hear far down the stairwell, but enough to make her head dart around to ensure no one was nearby. The coast seemed clear as she pushed the wooden slab closed behind her. Unfortunately, the stairwell was darker than her room. Having a taller tower was suddenly disadvantageous as she used her bare feet to feel the end of each stair. She kept inching her foot forward until her toes could curl around the lip and then moved her foot down to the next smooth stone surface and repeated the process.

It was gruelling, but the last thing she wanted to do was fall. Her hand felt its way along the sandstone bricks that made up the wall, and eventually the path became lighter and lighter. She kept some distance back as the torchlight was finally close enough to make out the dull browns and greys that made up the main hall. The last thing she wanted to do was cast a long shadow into the hall. The faint sound of footsteps confirmed her paranoia was worth it. The guards were soon to pass by on their rounds.

While Ana stood and waited, she had to make a choice. The two easiest ways out from here were the kitchen and the dungeon. The dungeon was always the easier one, but much creepier. Especially if they were hosting "guests". The kitchen came with its own troubles, including more staff, but it was easier to pass off getting caught as just looking for a midnight snack. Though if the guards believed her anymore was to be determined.

As she heard the footsteps get closer, she paid attention to the shadows that flicked their way into her stairwell. She couldn't peek out enough to see which way they were going for fear of getting caught, but their shadows told her exactly which way was safe. They were walking from the south side, and this let Ana breathe a sigh of relief as that meant the kitchen became the easier path. Her last trip through the dungeon came with too much spit and unwanted comments.

The moment the shadows gave way to the torchlight, she began to make her move. There wasn't anything in the castle requiring high security today, so she knew those would be thc only guards on this floor. As her feet touched the light brown stone slab of the main hall a chill went up her spine. Mostly from how cold the floor was, but partially due to how scary this bit was. She needed to be fast and quiet if she was going to make it through without getting caught. As she walked south with a brisk pace, the thought crossed her mind that one of her tutors might be up for a midnight snack and prayed to the gods of the sands that they weren't.

The floor was cold and hard on her feet. Since the castle was initially built as a fortress, none of its owners, including the current King Rolfe, spent much on luxuries. Some wanted to keep the structure's historical value, and others just wanted to pretend they were still at war even though no battle had been fought here in a long while. Ana wasn't entirely sure which side of the scale her father sat on.

The path forward was winding and filled with three more small staircases downward. The whole castle was built to keep the higher floors from being invaded. This meant small corridors that led to wider openings to defend. The small passages were always to Ana's advantage. She smoothly snuck past another pair of guards after her second descent. The third was a bit more clumsy, as she heard nothing on her way down and almost stepped directly into a guard at post. It made the trip a bit trickier, as she had to wind her way back up a floor, through some more halls, and down once again.

She began to question all this effort and pain in her feet, but anytime she did, the feeling to leave got stronger. There was even a thought her clumsiness could be linked to this senseless urge. It wasn't going to stop her. Even if the feeling was nothing, she'd at least get some fresh desert air. It was a straight shot through the next flight, and it put her even closer to the kitchen than the previous path she took, so things were looking up.

At least until she got to the next floor down. There was a light from behind the kitchen door.

It was nothing irregular, but it did mean someone was in there. It all depended on who that someone was. If it was a guard, she could pass off getting a snack until they left. If it was an intelligent guard, they wouldn't leave the princess alone. If it was her father or brother, they'd know exactly what she was doing, and if it was her governess... She didn't even want to think about that.

Well, she had come too far now. It may have been the urge talking, and it was definitely what made her next move for her, as she didn't even check for a patrol before briskly walking over to the door. She confidently pushed open the door and closed it behind her as if she was meant to be here. It was strange she had to act like that, considering the whole royal title and all.

Upon scanning the room, she found the candles burnt for Seamus, a short, stocky man that worked the kitchen. Ana breathed a sigh of relief, as this man could care about nothing more than cutting and seasoning vegetables.

"Good evening Seamus." She greeted, making her way over to a pantry mostly full of raw ingredients, acting as if she was looking for a quick snack. Seamus grunted in response and kept working away. "Just here for a midnight snack." She kept wandering around the kitchen pretending to be browsing, though it turned out to be unnecessary.

"If you're going to go, just go," Seamus responded in a high-pitched annoyed voice. "They don't pay me enough to keep you from escaping." He inspected a slice of prickly pear he had just chopped. Dissatisfied with its size, he gave the princess a glare as if it was her fault. It likely was.

Ana breathed a sigh of relief and grabbed a leather cloak and a pair of sandals from beside the kitchen's back door. The staff used them when stepping outside in the night or the rain, usually to smoke some leaf on break. It was musty, but it was much better than dealing with the freezing air of a desert night. She opened the back door, which in turn hit her with a chilling wave of cold air. She turned to thank Seamus before she left. There was no response save from slightly louder chopping, which was her cue to leave.

Ana always loved the desert night. Stepping out into it was a breath of fresh air from inside the stuffy stone walls. Even the castle courtyard would suffice her need for an open sky above her head, but apparently it left her "too vulnerable". The only problem with the castle ground was the lack of reality. Sure, it was beautiful, with its lush grass and the man-made stream that flowed around the keep, but it wasn't the desert.

The desert was a beautiful yet unforgiving landscape. The sands staining your very eyes from their bright shimmer, and the sharp rocks being the only break in the horizon. If you were lucky, you'd find a plant or an oasis and cherish them and their beauty all the more when all you've seen for miles were dunes and deadly creatures. Living the lush castle life made it easy to forget that.

The only thing Ana wanted to forget was this force that kept pulling her forward. Like a whirlpool it sucked her in deeper the closer she got. Fear sank in her heart as she could tell where she was being pulled; Out into the dunes, and somewhere along the mountains. She could see it now, though she was still at the castle, a picture appeared in her head. One of a cave. A small one, off to the east side of the kingdom. It was quite a ways out, but it was more interesting than reading the same book the hundredth time in a row. She pulled her cloak tight around her trying to ignore its musty smell and pressed onwards.

Again, Ana took less care in how she moved the more the urge got to her. She knew nearby there were some jutting stones on the outside wall she could climb up to get over, but she made it there with haste. Too much haste, as the guards that patrolled the grounds saw her the moment she grabbed the first ledge.

"Who goes there?" The call came. Good, they didn't know it was her yet, which means the worst they'd do is kill her. That would be slightly better than getting scolded the same way by about five different people. Since neither outcome was positive, she climbed as fast as she could over the fifteen-foot wall.

The sounds of clamouring and screaming to stop came from behind her as she rushed her way up. Ana nearly lost her footing right near the top but recovered. It wasn't the first time she had done this. None of the guards had followed her up, and being part of the royal family, had a good feeling they weren't going to. She knew how much they got paid, and it wasn't enough to jump down fifteen feet on the other side of a brick wall. For her, it was usually a breeze, and she climbed down as quickly as she went up. A bit too quick, as she lost footing again near the bottom and hit the paved ground with a thud. Rubbing her knee as she got up, she knew that would still hurt in the morning.

A quick jog and push through some decorative bushes, and she was out on the town. It was easy to blend into the desert night, as the number of market stalls open at night was still enough to draw a crowd in the higher end. It was just a matter of slipping out of town since it wouldn't take long for someone to check her room and realize the intruder that was scared off was actually the princess.

The best way into the desert wasn't a long shot, luckily. A jaunt down the main street, a sharp left turn, and out to the sands. All she had to do was make sure she wasn't distracted by something on display or get pickpocketed. The latter wasn't as much of an issue this time out since Ana wore nothing but a nightgown and a hastily thrown on cloak. The problem was the stall that caught the corner of her eye, selling what looked to be old rusted weapons. She slowed as she walked by, trying not to meet the shopkeeper's gaze. The items on display seemed to be relics from a war long past. One of the ones she read about. Perhaps the war of oil and fire from days long gone, or even the very war that gave The Scarlet Sands their name. Though there were plenty of those relics in the castle, Ana wanted some for herself.

On a typical night, her judgement would have been clouded. Likely she would have stopped at that stall and been caught by the guards while browsing. Tonight was different, as the moment she thought about stopping, a throbbing pain hit her head as the image of that cave came back. The moment she tried to think about turning around and maybe *not* going out into the untamed dunes, her feet were already on the move for the exit. She couldn't stop them. They were already at a jogging pace. It was as if she had lost control of her body, and though she felt if she pushed hard enough she could stop herself, her curiosity was too intense.

The rest of the market didn't interest her. It could have been from lack of wares, but it was more likely from this sense of urgency that came over her. Ana couldn't even tell what half of the stalls she passed were selling. There was one goal in mind. A cave buried in the side of a mountain. A cave she had never seen before in her life and had never heard of. It wasn't some strategic outpost like the many she had read about. Most of those were within the city walls. This was likely just some cave. So why was it so special?

Before she knew it, she was out of the city walls and into the desert. The night became darker as the torchlight faded behind her. She didn't even know if her destination was real or if it was just a hallucination. This was likely a dream, something she would wake up from and not worry about ever again. Though it was the most realistic dream she had ever set foot in, as she could feel the cold sands between her toes as her feet dug their way into the dunes.

The clamour of the town was far behind her, and without knowing it, Ana was in a full-on sprint. She felt like a passenger in her own body as it took her where it wanted to go. The only thing she consciously did was keep her cloak pulled around her tight to keep warm. Even this far out, there was already fear that someone would find her and know who she was.

These anxious feelings quickly washed away as she found herself in front of her destination. The cave was wide-mouthed, definitely natural, and if the night was black, she was staring into the void. She managed to stop her feet for long enough to view it with a careful eye. It was nothing special, but something told her that her whole life was leading up to this moment. Although that was crazy. It's not like she had been building her entire existence just to visit this place. Or was she? The line between reality and whatever this was had been drawn in the sand and taken away by the desert wind.

Ana cautiously approached the mouth of the cavern, expecting some kind of ambush or animal. There was nothing initially, and the only problem to contend with was the transition from the soft sand onto hard rock as she made her way inside. She broke her urge to just rush in and took a quick look back at the city before she entered. It was a surprising distance away. If she didn't know any better, she'd guess that she did more than an hour of running.

Though the cave gave way to no light, she quickly felt her way around, not knowing what she was looking for. There was the occasional ambient echo that gave her a jump back into reality but nothing too special. This was feeling more and more pointless as time went on. Then, something strange happened.

The sound of a chirp echoed in the distance. A distinct chirp, not like one of a bird but more like a rodent. It was a quiet sound, but an important one. It burned Ana's ears to no tomorrow, but in a good way. It was like hearing the voice of a friend you hadn't seen in months or even years. There was a warmth to that chirp. She made her way towards it.

The cavern quickly got smaller as she crawled her way through. There wasn't an easy way of telling how small aside from feel. Though she did begin having to duck her head. The chirp kept coming, and it kept getting louder and louder. Eventually, she found the source, and though she couldn't see it, she knew exactly what it was.

A bat. She had come all the way out here for a single bat. It was infuriating. All of this escaping and running into the desert, and all she was after was a damn bat. This didn't answer the question of why but instead made it so much worse.

Giving up on any rational reasoning, Ana decided to keep moving forward, no matter how claustrophobic the cave became. The chirps were more frequent as if the creature knew she was getting closer. Even though she couldn't see it, she could picture it in her mind, similar to how she saw the cave. It was a small creature, very fluffy with pointy ears and beady eyes. Even for a bat, this thing was tiny, perhaps a child or the runt of a family. It was good that she could see it with her mind, as the cave was pitch black, and it was right in front of her. She knew it was, and could somehow see the rodent and nothing else.

It came closer to her immediately, flapping its wings quickly but moving forward cautiously. Ana instinctively held her finger out for it to land on. If she was coming out this far to see the damn thing, she might as well give in to it. It floated in the air in front of her for a second and seemed to sniff her finger. Once it was content, it took its perch and hung upside down.

Something was wrong. The moment it landed on her, she knew it. The once pitch-black cave was now lit, and the source was this thing's talons. Right where they met her finger, they began to glow a blue light that crawled its way across her hand and up the bat's leg.

She tried to fight whatever was happening, but it was quick. The light kept spreading, and the cave fell dead silent. She couldn't move. The last thing she could remember was a flash of light, then back to the pure darkness the cave once was.

Chapter 2

Ana was first roused by the soreness covering her body. It was as if she had slept on solid rock all night long. As her eyes opened, it felt like they were still closed. The night in the desert gets dark, but not quite this dark. The last warning sign was the temperature. It was cold. It was never cold in the morning.

She lifted herself up and realized that this wasn't her bed. There was stone underneath her, jagged and unforgiving. Every bone in her body cracked as she lifted herself up, even ones she didn't know existed. She could feel at the very tip of her hair there was a ceiling above her and was happy she didn't jolt to her feet. She might have wound up with a swift concussion, or worse. It began to register that what she went through the night before wasn't a dream. She really did escape into a cave and pass out. There was a short mental debate about whether or not she should even go back, as the guards were probably looking for her left and right. There would be no leaving her room for at least a month, and that's if she was lucky.

She was undecided, but at least she would get out of this cave. Even if she was going to live among the snakes and scorpions instead of going home, the first thing would be to get up and search around her new territory. Trouble was she could barely see a thing. It wasn't as dark as the night before, but Ana quickly attributed that to the sun winding its way through the labyrinth of stone. It was hard to believe it was reaching this far back in the cave, but regardless, it was enough to get by.

It was just as unpleasant leaving as it was coming in. The claustrophobic environment felt even smaller than before. Ana could swear her every breath was bouncing off of the cave walls. Not only that, but her hair was a mess, sticking straight up only to be pushed back down by the low ceiling. Luckily this cave was not a huge system. It was a relatively straight shot in and out.

Her whole time crawling was spent thinking up excuses for how much of a mess she was and why she escaped that night. The truth was out of the question, as it was far more unbelievable than a well-thought-out lie. They'd probably believe her if she said she just went out for a walk and went too far. It wasn't a good reason that would avoid punishment, but it was something. Maybe she could throw in that she wanted to feel what living like a peasant was like, to be more attached to her people if she ever came to rule.

She already heard the laughter from her father. There was no way she would take over instead of Kasibel. He was already captain of the guard. He was more studied in strategy and had seen combat, even if it was just a few bandits. Meanwhile, she was unable to do any of that, and it wasn't her fault. It came down to those damn rules he implemented. Just because she was a princess didn't mean she couldn't fight.

Though with that double standard, it was hard to tell which one of them he cared for more. Ana didn't have a chance to experience what Kasibel did, but she was always kept out of harm's way while her brother was thrust into life-threatening situations. Whenever she went too far on this train of thought, she always tried to imagine how he felt, and it wasn't any better.

The sun began bouncing off the cavern walls the farther she made it. It was a relief to know she wasn't lost and that the sands were soon to stand before her. It was brighter than expected, and her eyes had an unusually tough time adjusting even at the first sign of light. This made some sense since she spent her night in the darkest cave she could find, and it wasn't unlike the many times she had spent in her room with the blinds shut and being shunted out into the street on some royal showing.

It wasn't long before things started feeling different, though. As Ana crawled her way to the cave entrance and tried to witness the sands before her, she couldn't. It was too blinding. The pitch-black cave was easier to navigate than the desert was going to be. It was like a ball of pure white shining into the mountainside. It made it impossible to distinguish even land from sky.

Ana figured she'd just sit at the entrance for a while with her back turned to the scorching sun until her eyes adjusted. She chalked it up to sleeping in the darkest place she ever had. It wasn't every day the princess escaped to go spend her night on a rock floor. Something had felt strange about this whole thing, though. Not just the feeling that brought her out here, but this morning was different. It was likely the cave itself, but the sun had never bothered her eyes so. It became even more suspicious when it took more than a few minutes to get to a point where she saw more than just blinding white. It felt like at least an hour before she caught her first sight of the glistening, yet still painful to look at, sand.

She didn't have any more time to wait and figured she'd tough it out. Pulling the cloak around her head shaded her eyes a good bit and helped with the blinding sun. Stepping foot out into the dunes was both relieving and tense at the same time. She could barely see the kingdom as it was so far away, and every step closer was a step closer to another three or four lectures a day for at least the next month.

Ana did decide on the way out that it was slightly, *slightly* better than living out among the scorpions and trying to learn their venomous ways. Though it was a long haul back to town, she took her moment outside as a moment of relief. Being able to walk through the natural landscape was a rarity, and the night before she did nothing but run into that dry cave. Though she could barely see the mountain beside her through the sun, she enjoyed the walk nonetheless.

It took a couple hours to make it anywhere near town again, and the steps only took longer the closer she got. Those hours quickly turned a nice nature hike into an intense endurance test. The moment she was in sight of any guards, she gave a sigh and enjoyed one more moment of her toes in the hot sand before pulling her cloak tight around to try and sneak her way back in. At least if she wasn't caught by any soldiers, she'd come in with some dignity.

The walk in felt different, as everything had that day. Luckily the cloak she had gotten was too big for her and covered up her features well. The hood on it felt tighter than usual, but other than that, it was fine. The two sentinels standing at the doorway had nothing to say to her as she sauntered in. It was almost too easy, and Ana suspected that someone would be waiting for her back at her castle. If she was lucky, it would be Kasibel. If not, it would be the governess, and if there was any thought that could send chills down the spine of one burning in a desert, it was that.

Making her way through the street, she loosened her cloak a bit.

The worst thing that could happen now is a guard escorting her back where she needed to go. It wouldn't be devastating, but it would make her walk through the market street shorter, which is something she had always looked forward to. Luckily she wasn't far away from it.

The stalls were far busier in the daytime. The crowd was much easier to blend into, and an array of fresh spices and dried food filled the dry air. Of course it was nothing compared to the palace's food, but that's not what she was looking around for. A sword quickly caught the corner of her eye at a much less busy stall. She instinctively made her way over to it.

Ana paid no attention to the stall owner as she picked the blade up to inspect. It was marked from tip to hilt with gashes and looked like it was made at least a hundred years ago, maybe more.

"Do you know what era this one is from?" She asked, scanning the hilt for any engravings that would give away the maker or the year.

"Well of course, miss-" The stall owner started, but something had stopped him. As if he had seen the ghost of a dead relative. Ana knew he must know her identity and was likely warned that she had left the night before.

"GUARDS!" Yup, he definitely knew. Ana's head darted around and saw them coming from the direction of the palace. Something in her, perhaps the idea of a chase making this day out last a bit longer, or be more interesting, made her run. She wanted to go back to the castle on her own terms. Not at the whim of some cheap hired hand.

She began running down the market street straight through the crowd. They were giving way to her, which was strange until she realized she still held the sword in her hand, beat up as it was. She decided it would be easier just to make the treasury pay for it when she got back home, and keeping such a relic would mean this wasn't all for nothing.

In her haste turning a corner off into a residential area, her hood fell down. She didn't understand how so many people could be out today in this blinding sun, as it was immediately harder to even see the buildings in front of her. Looking back, the crowd was behind her, and the guards kept a decently quick pace. This would be easier if the hot desert allowed for plate armour, but the fighters around here had to wear silks to keep themselves cool, which just made them all faster.

The echoes of every footstep rang in her ears as sandals and boots slammed down onto the cobblestone streets. Ana could swear she could tell right where they were by the steps, and it was much less dangerous trusting that than looking behind her, so she kept running. It wasn't long until the houses to either side of her became less and less luscious as they moved further and further away from the market. It was hard to make a living anywhere besides at a stall, or a nice tavern, so the residents here held almost no chance of making ends meet. Ana knew this, and it weighed heavily on her as she kept her pace.

The footsteps following her became more and more distant the further she went into the lower quarter. It was both a relief and a shame. A relief, of course, as Ana could finally slow down, and a shame as the royal guards aren't even willing to walk into this district. She let out a sigh of both feelings and decided to take a walk around.

She immediately noticed a different feeling, as most residents around here kept to themselves and didn't crowd together. Of course, there was a lack of expensive silks and buildings made of anything but sandstone, but she expected that. She didn't expect the looks that she was getting. Sure, everyone there knew the princess in the higher quarter, but she never made her way down here. As a matter of fact, she was forbidden to do so. She could understand if it was an outfit she was wearing, but even some of the clothes around here made her worker's cloak look nice.

It was only then she started to process how differently she felt. Sure, waking up in the mouth of a mountain doesn't make for the best morning stretches, but this was more than that. As she rubbed her hand through her hair to think, things started getting weird. Her hair felt more… resistant than usual. And thick. She could hear her hand running over the top of her head, and it was nearly deafening. It was then her vision came into question. It still wasn't adjusted, even after being outside for hours.

Ana began searching for the first piece of shiny metal she could get her hands on. Something was wrong, and it was something people could see. Unfortunately, cleaned surfaces weren't exactly easy to find around here, especially ones that would show a reflection. Until she remembered she had just stolen a sword.

She lifted it up to take a look, but it was initially too dull to see anything through. It was given a quick spit shine with a clean off from the cloak, but it still took a moment to tell. She lowered the blade so the sun was behind her and bounced off the steel right into her eyes. It hurt at first, but eventually, the image came into view.

The reflection staring back put Ana in shock. Her hair wasn't any taller and instead featured two large, pointy, furry animal ears. The once brown eyes were replaced by two larger, black orbs meant for seeing in dark spaces. Finally, the face, the thing that everyone was staring at. Covered in black hair, a small snout peeking out and letting a single snaggletooth past her much smaller lips. If she didn't know any better, Ana would think she was staring at...

"A bat." She said out loud, not knowing what to think. She was paralyzed, the thought sinking into her that the creature she saw the night before somehow did this. Was it still out there? Or did she fuse with it? Staring off in the distance a thousand questions rattled around in her head. The only thing able to break her trance was that she dropped her sword on the ground. It made a loud metal clang as it bounced off the stones. Even then, she just stared at the blade, hoping that another angle would give a different reflection.

It didn't.

She picked up the blade, not once taking her eyes off of it. There was a hope that she was still dreaming, but waiting for the waking hour wasn't an option if this was real. None of this made sense. There wasn't a single book Ana had read that eluded to this... thing that she had become. After a while, she gained the courage to rub a hand along her face. Any idea that this could have been an optical illusion was gone.

Ana could have stared at herself in that street for hours if it wasn't for the feeling of her hood being pulled back up over her head.

"What are you doing?" A low voice asked, sounding absolutely furious.

"Wha..." Was all Ana could get out. She turned to see a cloaked figure, only much more covered than she was. The garb he wore dragged along the ground. The hood covered his face near entirely in shadow, and the final give that he was hiding something was the gloves. The big, thick gloves someone walking around in a desert would never wear by choice.

"You'll get caught like this, come on." He grabbed her arm and started dragging her along. Ana was in no place to argue, and even if she was, the shock had kept her from fighting back. Sorting her thoughts was a nigh-impossible task, but she eventually got to one. Answers, she knew she wanted answers.

"Who…?" Ana asked. She realized she should probably do more thinking before her next question.

"A friend." The answer came as the man turned down an alley. They started moving in erratic patterns through the quarter, which concerned her even more.

"Where are we going?" She was almost proud she got a real question out. There was hope for a better answer than the first once she received.

"A safe place." The man answered. They started to slow down a bit as he came to a realization. "Are you new?" He asked.

Ana was not prepared to answer a question right now. She knew she wanted answers but giving them out was another story. The question rattled around in her brain for a bit as she stared blankly at the man who claimed he was a friend. After feeling like she was taking too long, Ana finally answered, "Yes?"

"Right, right, good." The man began, clearly not in a positive way. He let go of her arm and started pacing while rubbing his chin. "Of course, I had to pull a new one, of course."

"What do you mean?" She was feeling like she was getting really good at questions now. She almost felt like she was prepared to respond to one but didn't have to regardless.

"Well, you only just transformed recently. So I'm guessing no one has found you yet." The man started, confusing Ana even further. "As you know, our kind are not popular. Especially around here."

"What do you mean our kind?" Ana tilted her head to the side, trying to take everything in.

"This is going to be worse than I thought."

Chapter 3

After confirming the nearby alleys were clear and with no sight of anyone chasing them, the stranger practically pulled Ana out of sight. Before she could protest he sat her down on the pavement and introduced himself.

"My name is Drake, and you're likely very confused right now." Ana nodded in response. One more look over his shoulder was all Drake needed before he began taking off his glove. Ana looked on in intrigue as it slid off to reveal not a hand, but a claw. Covered in pristine white scales that shone a prismatic light even in the shade of buildings pushed too close together. "You've become a hybrid, like me." He slid his glove back on, happy that she didn't recoil at the sight.

"What does that mean?" Ana asked, suddenly more interested than afraid.

"It means you've become one with an animal. A bat, it looks like." When Ana had left her room the night before, this might have been the last thing she expected.

"How does something like this happen?" Years of study in the castle and this phenomenon wasn't familiar to her. "I feel like I would have heard of this before."

"Depends on where you live. I'm guessing, despite your current garb, your highborn of some sort? Or at least from the upper district." Drake looked her up and down, pretending he saw some clue. In reality, it was easy enough to tell as long as someone had never heard of hybrids.

"Yeah, the type that lives under a rock."

"Clearly." Drake remarked snidely. "As to your other question, it comes down to heritage. There was a tribe that was eradicated hundreds or thousands of years ago that had the same ability, or so I've heard. We're all their descendants, and there are many of us."

"But I still don't understand how."

"Neither do I. Or any of us, for that matter."

"How many more are there?"

"Can't say for sure, but there's a group in the city. I can take you to them, but you should keep your hood up until we get there." Drake made sure to emphasize the importance of his advice.

"Why does that matter?" Ana asked. It was clear these hybrids weren't exactly high society. They were also being ostracized for an unknown reason. She still needed an answer.

"I'm guessing you've only been out for a day or so, and you've already felt the eyes on you from every corner. That's why. No one wants us around."

"And why don't they?"

"Same reason highborn don't want the lower district mixing with theirs. We're viewed as a threat and nothing more. The difference is they're afraid someone both poor and part animal will go rabid. Bite them or something."

"That's ridiculous." Ana remarked, not realizing she slipped into her high society voice.

"Welcome to your new life." He responded as he offered a gloved hand to help her back up. "We should get moving. If we stay in one place, someone might find us." She took his hand and instinctively wiped any dirt off her legs. Ana was prepared to run but was surprised when Drake walked instead.

"This is insane." Ana thought, accidentally speaking out loud. She realized she was shaking more and more with every step. This was feeling more real by the second. The dream was turning into a waking nightmare. How could there be a whole race of people she had never heard of? Every moment was getting less believable and exponentially more terrifying. That face her eyes met in the metal can't be hers. It can't be forever. This wasn't possible. "How can I live like this?"

"You might not," Drake replied coldly. "This isn't going to be easy."

"Well, you're just a breath of fresh air." Ana rolled her eyes as she began to take her frustration out on anything that would listen.

"That makes two of us."

Ana was taken aback. Even as someone who wanted to escape the castle daily, the idea of a commoner talking back to her like this was absurd. She took a deep breath and remembered her position wasn't exactly the best. That's when she began to think about the castle. Going back would be much more difficult now than it was before. What would her father think? That brought up a whole other slew of questions. Do they even know about this race? Hybrids were never brought up in any of her lessons or any books she had access to. Someone was lying to her, and she was determined to find out who.

The movements Drake made were hard to follow, even at their slow speed. It wasn't just walking from alley to alley. There was a lot of squeezing through places that didn't look fit for a human. The kinds of nooks you could barely get rats out of, let alone maneuver through. Every now and again they'd even have to climb over a low wall. Ana tried to follow and think simultaneously, but her trains of thought were often broken up with having to focus on not tripping.

"So, what are you fused with then?" She asked bluntly. Anything to fill the dead air.

"An albino lizard," Drake answered quickly as if the response was pre-prepared. Ana was satisfied with it but hoped it would have gone further.

With her feet landing on stone in a particularly close quarters alley, she started realizing one other issue with her newfound ears. The echo from her landing bounced off every wall. She could hear it as if someone was screaming right next to her. It didn't make any sense before, but Ana realized she must have some kind of echolocation, or at the very least the sensitive ears meant for it. She couldn't currently tell what was where, but maybe with some practice...

No. There was no way she was going to entertain the thought of training to be a better bat. The idea of the castle came back to her. Maybe her father had some kind of cure for this. She could be back to normal. Skin and long hair and all. Less beady eyes. The ability to walk around without being hooded.

"Is there a known cure?" Ana decided to ask. It was the wrong question, as Drake stopped dead in his tracks for a second before continuing on and not glorifying it with an answer. She figured it was an innocent enough inquiry but didn't push any further. She'd likely have to look elsewhere for a proper response.

Ana began telling herself this would be a learning experience about her subjects. This would be a matter of fitting in with them for a bit and getting an idea of what they want and if they can be integrated into regular society with some work. She had no plan on staying this way and was already determined to go back to her father and find a healer or magician of some sort who could reverse the process.

Before too long, Drake and Ana came to a brick wall. It looked like any other stone slab unless you paid attention. It was nestled away in a dark alley, and it was hard to tell the difference, but there was a thin outline of a door shape. Drake knocked on it with the back of his hand three times and waited.

"Well, this is hidden." Ana remarked.

"Has to be." Drake replied.

"What happens if someone finds this place?"

"I don't even want to think about it." The response was followed by a long silence. Way longer than anyone could ever expect to wait for a door to open.

"Does it usually take this long?" Ana asked, genuinely concerned.

"Depends on how many he's serving."

"How many who's serving?" Ana's question was greeted with the hidden door swinging open inward. In the doorway stood a well-built man with a face that made him look years younger than his body gave away. It was also evident he was another of these hybrids. This was given away by his right arm being two to three times the size of the other, covered in fur up to the shoulder, and clawed at the end. If Ana had to guess, it looked like a bear arm, which was strange considering the environment.

"Drake!" He shouted enthusiastically. "How are you? Come on in boyo, grab a seat." Drake tried to respond but didn't have a chance before the man's head darted back and forth, looking around the alleyway. "Oh, I see." He said, calming down from his excitement for only a minute before going back full force. "This is why his scowl is worse than usual!"

"Excuse me?" Ana was the first to finally get a word in. She thought becoming part bat would be the most confusing thing she would see today. Something told her it was only the beginning.

"New blood, eh?" The man ignored Ana completely and addressed Drake. He got a nod in response. "Where'd you find her?"

"Middle of the street. Completely exposed. Chased by guards." Drake responded.

"How did you know I was being chased?" Ana asked.

"How could I not know? The whole market district was up in arms."

"And there's the excuse for the scowl." The man rolled his eyes. Ana was unsure if it was at Drake or at her. "Name's Henry. Nice to meet you!" He held out his bear arm for her to shake. Ana took a step back for obvious reasons. "Right, always do that, here." He held out his left hand instead, and it was much less threatening. It was given away by Henry's tone that he does this on purpose. She tentatively took his hand and gave away more than she wanted to with a limp, high society handshake. She assumed he wouldn't notice, but he did.

"How fresh?" Henry asked Drake.

"Doesn't even know."

"Did you prepare her?" He questioned, but Drake just shrugged in response.

"What are you talking about?" Ana spoke up, annoyed she was being ignored.

"You might want to brace yourself. This will be a bit of a culture shock." Henry took a step back, bringing the door to a wide-open state behind him. Ana looked in and thought she knew what to expect, but it still hit her hard.

Not only was this a fully loaded hidden tavern larger than the likes even she had seen, but it was full of the most colourful patrons she could imagine. Ana didn't know whether to run in or run away as the sight of at least fifty hybrids spread out before her, drinking and eating at beautifully furnished wooden tables. At a glance, a few features stuck out to her, including claws, fur, tails, and a few pairs of wings. She could even swear she saw someone with the lower half of a snake.

There were a variety of combinations, from some who could easily pass as human to those who wouldn't even have a way to cover themselves up in public. It was a wonder how she had never heard of them before. How could this secret have been kept for so long? Again the question came back to why they hid like this, but that got pushed to the back of Ana's mind pretty quickly.

"Yeah, I figured he wouldn't tell you much." Henry mentioned.

"What makes you say that?" Ana asked.

"You've been staring in for five minutes." Henry walked past her and motioned to follow with his bear arm. "Comeon in, first drink is free."

She decided to follow, curiosity in her heart, wanting to learn more about these people. She found a want to talk to every single one she passed but couldn't bring a word of greeting to her lips. Ana was uncomfortable, but most didn't even give her a second glance. The few who did wore a look of concern on their faces, which was a strange feeling for her. She thought she would feel like the most threatened thing in the room, not the most threatening.

The bar was long and took up the lower level of a larger building. There seemed to be no other entries or exits aside from the one they came in. The exterior wasn't completely flat sandstone, otherwise it would be too clear that there was a concealed door. The flat walls were broken up by windows into empty rooms and a main door that was barred shut with an eviction notice with the king's seal on it. None would think to look at it twice, as the guards would never come to check this district, and to the residents this was just another building abandoned by the royalty. It was perfectly hidden away, and there was at least one staircase leading down, meaning this place was more vast than it looked at first glance. With all of the actual space being utilized below ground, there was no way to see in. Ana took a seat at the long bar at the back of the main room that Henry had recently vaulted over. Though he could have just walked around.

"What's your poison?" He asked.

"The cas..." Ana stopped herself. "Wine, white." She got a raised eyebrow followed by the hasty serving of a drink from one human hand and a paw that had no right being that dexterous. Drake took a seat next to her.

"You may want to calm down." He said plainly.

"What do you mean?" Ana asked, her voice nearly shaking. All Drake had to do in response was nod his head toward her hand. Ana looked down and saw the sword, which she had forgotten about. She brought it up to lay it on the counter and noticed her knuckles were pure white. There was her explanation of the stares.

"There's nothing." Drake paused. "And no one, to be afraid of here." Not a moment later did the two of them have drinks in front of them. Ana took a sip of her wine, hoping it would calm her nerves, and noticed her new acquaintance drank something a bit harder. And a bit faster. Perhaps, she considered, a new face in a hidden away community is more of a concern than she first gave it credit for.

"So, what do you do here?" She asked.

"Drink, duh." Henry responded while mixing what looked like a complicated cocktail.

"No, I mean-"

"He knows what you mean. Don't humor him." Drake turned in his seat to her. "We do what we can. Most of us work as sellswords for the poorer or cheaper merchants that want to cross the desert. Some find modest work among the lower quarter. Keeping everything quiet is the hardest part, of course."

"Why keep things so secret?" Ana was hoping to get an actual answer this time. Drake kept silent, but Henry spoke up.

"For fear of getting run out." He said in his lowest energy voice yet. "Or worse."

"But if no one even knows you're here, couldn't you give coming out a chance?"

"Do you forget what just happened to you?" Drake asked, his tone unwelcoming and condescending. "You were just run out yourself. Chased down by guards for looking like you do. It would be all-out war if they knew about all of us."

Ana took another sip of wine and gave it some thought. She first believed she was being chased due to her royalty, but he was right. No one would have recognized her like this, or at least she hoped not. It was a small taste of hybrid life, but she both understood more and less of it from the thought.

She decided to give herself a good look over in the blade once more. Yep, still part bat. She kept glancing at it a few seconds after putting it down. Even being in the middle of all the others, it was still hard to believe.

"We have a few spare rooms, in case you need them." Henry offered, noticing her disposition.

"You have rooms here?" She asked, breaking her out of her trance for a short second.

"Of course, where else are we going to stay?"

Ana gave one last look at the blade, starting to come to terms that this was real. There may be no cure. There may be no way of going back home. Upon the first tear coming to her eye, she looked up to Henry and said through quivering lips, "I think I might take you up on that."

Chapter 4

The room Ana was given was quaint in comparison to what she was used to. Just like the rest of the building there were no windows to allow for complete secrecy. She had concerns about this being a good place to build up an army. Though considering the lack of exits, it was terrible strategically. As far as she could tell, there was no threat here. Or at least not a major one.

The room itself consisted of a bed and a desk with a couple of drawers. There was nothing in the way of reading material, but there were ink and quills available for writing. The only light in the room were a few candles, and the door locked from the inside to give way for privacy. All things considered, it wasn't too bad, especially for an express cost of nothing.

This was the thing that confused her the most. The tavern went deeper than it initially looked and consisted of many rooms like this one. Henry had explained to her that almost every hybrid in the city lived here. There weren't many in the whole scheme of things. Maybe 60 or 70 total, with many more that had left a long time ago due to discrimination. When she asked him why anyone stayed behind if that was the case, Henry explained that some just don't want to leave their home. It was a difficult concept for someone left locked in a room her whole life to grasp that someone would actively want to live like this.

Ana laid her stolen sword down on the desk and took a seat on her bed, which was far less luscious than her one in the castle, but still better than a cave floor. It was all she could do to keep her emotions in before closing the door, but they began to flood out all at once the moment she sat down. That's not to say she showed any one feeling, as so many came out in one burst. There was anger, first for why everyone here would be forced to hide, flowing into why this was happening to her. After a short time, that led her into worry, unknowing if she would ever be 'normal' again. This turned into grief pretty quickly, and the tears started flowing at the thought of never being accepted by her family.

Even in the best-case scenario, her family would hide her more than they already do. She might even be hunted and killed for tarnishing the royal name. She had no idea how or what her father thought of hybrids, or if he even knew about them. She worried more about her brother. The two of them fought, but they were close. He agreed that she shouldn't have been locked up like she was but had no power over it. She respected him and believed he respected her. Would that change? Would he suddenly hate her?

It was all so much to process. It was a nightmare too strange to be real. Her life got thrown into insanity in the matter of one night. She tried to keep her sobs quiet, as the walls weren’t the thickest, but every now and again one came out louder than she wanted. The worst part was not knowing what was going to happen next. Does she go back to the castle like she originally planned? That would make the most sense. Get a solid reaction from the people that knew her best, which would pretty quickly make her next decision clear. She could also never go back and just live a new life where she could see the world like she had dreamed. Ana knew she was coddled, though, and didn't know how the world would treat her and how she'd survive in it. Especially since socializing becomes much more difficult with a fur-covered face.

Ana decided her best bet was to sleep on it. It was still the first day, and she was far too emotional. She blew out the candles surrounding the room one by one, hoping that as the room got darker she would get closer to waking up from this dream. Eventually, the room was pitch black, and her wish went unanswered. She crawled into the frankly uncomfortable wooden frame that felt as if it had nothing more than a thick pillow over it and attempted to go to sleep.

Even just keeping her eyes closed was a chore. Her mind racing at a million miles a minute, and her unfamiliar environment attributed to keeping them wide open. The amount of complaining she did at home suddenly felt moot. What life had she walked into? Would she take up her newly found weapon and become a sellsword like the rest of them, hiding away like some kind of scared animal?

Scared animal. The thought repeated in Ana's head. That's exactly what she was. An animal. A creature. Something to be afraid of.

Something to run out of town. It wasn't fair. Not to her, not to anyone who lived here. A reminder chimed in her head soon after.

Ana was a princess. Anachorita Vespertillo Rexharne. The second heir to the throne. She had power, and could use it. She could be a change for these people. These hybrids that she found, in their corner with their tails between their legs, literally. With that, her decision was made. She would march into that castle, confront her father, and use every ounce of pull she had to bring these creatures out of their hole and into society, like proper citizens.

There would be an adjustment period, of course, but she was prepared for them. It wasn't going to be tomorrow that she'd go to the castle, maybe not even this week or this month. She needed to learn more from the people on the ground. These people were her subjects, and she was going to learn everything she could about them. It was her responsibility as royalty.

It was an easy plan to think of, but Ana knew executing it would be much more difficult. She couldn't even bring herself to look some of these hybrids in the eye, let alone talk to them enough and live amongst them in a meaningful way. There was always Drake and Henry. Though Henry seemed busy, and Drake seemed... standoffish was a diplomatic way to put it. Perhaps he could introduce her to someone else. Someone with a better disposition.

Though her decision was made, sleeping still didn't come easy. The anxiety about her new form was replaced by a completely different kind. One of having to socialize. Ana was never good with groups or even individuals she didn't know. Being locked away in a tower does a terrible number on your interpersonal skills. No matter. Exposure therapy would be the best way to get over it. Even with the rationalization, her stomach twisted and turned throughout the night. Nothing more than an hour of sleep was gained at one time without waking up in some kind of cold sweat, worried about the future, the present, and everything in between. The nightmares about every possibility were running through her head. Every choice she could have made found itself in its worst light.

Having no concept of time, considering the lack of windows and sleep, Ana decided to get up after what felt like long enough to by laying in bed. She dusted off her clothes and gave a long glance at her sword. After a moment of thought, she decided to take it with her. It likely wouldn't be needed, but fear is a powerful motivator.

Opening her door made it clear she hadn't slept for nearly as long as she thought. The hall's lights were dim, and there didn't seem to be a soul stirring. The strange setting made the walls feel like they were warping. Every corner could have a hidden enemy that would unveil some kind of plot to take over the throne. The ones who had told her this was a safe place were strangers, so it was plausible that this was a trap. Ana ran her hand along her cheek and was brought back down to reality, at least for the most part. There was no way anyone could fake the fur she felt through her fingers. She thought about going back to bed but knew ahead of time it would be useless. Gripping her sword tighter, she closed the door behind her and walked towards what she thought was the bar. Upon hitting a dead end, upon which she almost ran into and promptly attacked, she turned the other way and found her way out.

To her surprise, the bar still had some patrons, though many of them were unconscious. It wasn't much different from the guard's quarters back home. Thankfully, this meant Henry was still up, and not that she had anything against any of the other hybrids, it would be nice to talk to someone who already broke the ice.

She took a seat at the bar and laid her sword down across it. The blade's ancient design went almost perfectly with the worn down countertop it now sat upon. Without skipping a beat, she was quickly asked by the bear-armed man, "Another wine?". Ana said yes and downed the first drink before the glass had hit the table twice.

"Trouble sleeping?" Henry asked, pouring her another glass. She nodded and took a sip of the newly filled drink. "Don't blame you. It's a lot to take in." He sounded much more serious than before.

"How did it happen for you?" Ana asked, mainly to make conversation. Henry sighed and poured himself a glass.

"It's not a long story if that's what you're looking for."

"Anything is fine to distract me right now." Ana swirled her wine glass awkwardly, watching as the liquid stuck to the side before it sunk itself back down. It was higher quality than she had expected.

"Well, I at least knew about hybrids beforehand. For some, it helps. For me, it didn't." The pain on his face was evident the moment he spoke a word of it.

"You don't have to tell me if you don't want to." Ana didn't want to put him in an uncomfortable position.

"It's alright. My problems are past. It's better you hear this so you know you're not the only one." Henry's words spoke to Ana. He had clearly done this before. "I wasn't part of a family of full on nobles or anything, but my family was well off enough to care about status." If she wasn't paying attention at the start, Ana's new bat ears immediately perked up. "We were told about hybrids as children and told how to treat them if we ever found them."

"We?" Ana interrupted.

"Ah, yes, me and my brother." Henry took another sip of wine. "So, me and him did what we were told, and one day found a part wolf-man in the woods." He finished his drink quickly and poured himself another, leaving a long pause. "We threw rocks and told the freak to get out."

Ana was taken aback. Why would anyone treat anyone else that way? So she had to ask. "Why?" Her tone betrayed her as she talked down to him. Henry was a calm man and didn't snap back but replied harshly.

"Same reason you can't let that sword leave your side. Or why your knuckles go white when you bring it in here." He had no intention of starting an argument but instead wanted to put things into perspective. "Fear. Everyone in this world fears what they do not understand, even if it's only a little."

"Well, I can tell you I'm absolutely terrified." Ana admitted, the wine perhaps getting to her.

"And you have every right to be." Henry leaned back against a wall of spirits that almost tipped over to his weight. He readjusted so as to not cause an even bigger mess of his own bar and granted Ana a reassuring smile. "Everyone has a right to be afraid. It's what you do with that fear that makes you. You can either choose to understand what you're afraid of or stay in ignorance. So, what's your choice?"

The question threw Ana off. She didn't respond immediately and wondered why she didn't. It should be pretty obvious, as she likely doesn't have a life to go back to, that she'd want to understand more. Even if she did go back, she still wanted to know more, right? Or perhaps something in her held her back, and somewhere deep inside, she wanted to stay in her room in that sandstone tower, reading and biding time.

"I want to understand." She finally replied. The sheer thought of going back to seeing nothing but the castle courtyard threw her right to one side.

"Good. You don't have much of a choice, considering your face, but good."

"Hey!"

"I know, too far. I get that a lot." Henry came around the counter and sat next to her, more or less because he could barely stand. "So, I bet you're asking yourself what your next move is?"

"Yeah, I haven't had much of a life yet." Ana quickly stumbled over her next words. "You know, because of how young I am, haven't had a job or anything. Just studying and stuff."

"I figured as much." Henry put his back to the bar to lean against it from his wooden barstool and proceeded to use his oversized bear arm as a makeshift pillow. Where he laid his head put his eye directly in line with the tip of Ana's sword. It wasn't clear if he just forgot it was there, or was trying to challenge her sense of protection. "Well, you don't have to choose now, but you can either help out here at the bar or go out and do sellsword work. Rent isn't free, you know."

"I know." She didn't. "I'll have to think about it."

"I suggest thinking before the sun comes up. Drake will drag you into the mercenary life the moment he can. Something about 'having to see the world and interact with other people to get our story out there' or some crap." It was clear Henry had moved on to drunken rambling. "Just be careful with him. Do what you want, not what you're dragged around to do. You're free now, just… like a bird…" Henry yawned loudly. "Fly, little birdy… fly." And promptly passed out on his own arm.

Henry had shared a lot with Ana that night. A bit of his past, though not all of it. Good insight into why the hybrids hide, and most of all, how to fall asleep on a bar.

Chapter 5

Ana woke up the following morning forgetting where she was, how she got there, and why there was a man with a big fuzzy arm next to her. Nor did she wake up naturally. She could feel someone's hand on her shoulder nudging her up. The first thing that was clear to her was the pain in her back. It felt like she'd slept up against a bar all night long. That's when it all came back to her.

If something had to change about this new life, it was where she was going to sleep. Between the cave and the floor, her muscles were screaming. She didn't even want to bother acknowledging the one who woke her up. Whoever it was, they eventually gave up.

"I bring her here for one night, and you manage to make her pass out on the floor." The voice that came was angry yet quiet.

"I'd say that makes me a pretty good bartender, all things considered." And the reply was aloof yet confident.

"I'm fine," Ana chimed in with a yawn. She tried to get up, but her legs wouldn't let her, so she tried playing it off as just adjusting position. "Just tired, that's all."

"I swear Henry, you'll be the death of me." Drake walked back over to Ana with purpose in his step. He hoisted her up as if she was made of paper and ensured her legs didn't give out on her. Though they considered it for a second, both limbs decided to stay upright instead of bringing her face back to the floor.

"With any luck I will be." Henry had no intention of making it up from his spot on the ground.

"You two have problems." Ana said bluntly. She tried to make it look casual as she leaned up against the counter for support. As a half drunk glass clinked to the floor after her arm bumped into it, she knew she had failed.

"Well you're observant." Drake rolled his eyes as he picked the glass up off the ground and handed it to Henry. "Now, get your bearings and eat something. I assume you want to stick around here for a while?" Ana nodded and took a seat at the bar, lacking any grace. "Then, once you're done, you'll come with me and earn your keep."

"But Henry said I could help at the bar for that." Ana had no idea how she remembered that.

"You really don't want to, trust me." Drake assured her.

"Oh, come on, it's not that bad." Came the slurred voice from behind the counter. Soon after, the sound of vomiting at a nearby table took over the room. Drake crossed his arms and gave Ana a smug look.

"Alright, you have a point." She admitted.

Henry grumbled and groaned as he made his way to a backroom with a lack of any enthusiasm in his step. "Why does no one ever choose the bar?" Henry moaned, pretending to talk under his breath. Whatever facade he had was quickly shattered after he left sight. With the door closed behind him, he yelled loud enough for everyone to hear. "Henry, clean this! Henry, mix that! Henry, where's my eggs? We're in a god damn desert, you simpleton! Where am I gonna get eggs? Snakes? I swear to god, these people." Ana let out a chuckle, the first one since she had left home.

"You ever fight before?" Drake asked, taking a seat next to her.

"No, never had the need to." She responded, running her hand along the hilt of her sword. The thought that she'd have to use such an old relic in actual combat saddened the history buff in her.

"We usually don't have to, so no worries there." Drake assured her, taking a lean back against the bar. Not to actually take a load off, but to make sure Henry saw him relaxing as he came out with a bucket to clean up last night's dinner. "If we do get attacked, just point the sharp bit at whatever shows up, and they tend to go away."

"How are you so sure I'll go with you?" She asked again.

"You don't seem like the freeloading type. Besides, you want to sit here with your thoughts all day or go out and see the desert?"

Somehow Drake knew the exact words to say. Ana wanted nothing more in her life than to go out and explore the world outside of nobility. "Desert it is. After breakfast, anyways." She turned an assuming look towards Henry.

"How can you even be hungry?" He groaned while he took care of the mess on the floor with a rag and water bucket.

“How do you go about getting work, anyways? With having to hide, and all.” Ana asked.

“We put on our cloaks. Go to the edge of town, any of the merchants’ entrances, and they come to us.” Drake answered.

“And we’re sure they won’t out us to the guards or anything?”

“Our clients care more about their coin than anything. We’re both cheaper and more effective than normal sellswords. So we’re looked at as a good investment. No one asks questions, and they turn away if we have to fight. Plausible deniability and all.”

“Sounds like a lot of work to save a couple of coins.”

“Not from a merchant family, are you?” Ana shook her head. Before she could even think of being hungry, there was a plate of bread and freshly cooked eggs dropped down next to her aggressively.

“Breakfast.” Henry said, somehow managing to fill a mundane word with animosity. Ana didn’t know whether to eat hers or leave it out of fear of them being poisoned, or worse, that they were actually snake eggs.

“Ignore him. Not much of a morning person.”

“Makes sense, especially considering last night.”

“You mean every night.” Drake corrected. Henry groaned and hid behind the bar for a nap.

It wasn’t long until their stomachs were filled and Drake and Ana were on their way out the door. Seeing Drake’s full getup of thick, overlapping leather armour made Ana wonder how he could ever survive the desert. Even her thin tattered cloak felt like it was too much for the scorching heat. She wondered how it would fare in an actual fight. It would be nothing for protection, but at least it gave her a full range of movement. Ana started playing around with the weight of her blade, making sure she’d actually be able to swing it if the time came. Hopefully it wouldn’t. The closer they got to the edge of town, the more nervous she became.

Her brother had far more chances to spar than she ever did. Ana had tried to get in on the lessons at a young age but was told it wasn’t appropriate for a young lady. She had to play with sticks as she watched the guards train. Trying to match their movement was surprisingly difficult without a teacher, and she never had much time to study. It was far too often she’d get caught and get a talking to, or worse. Now she had cursed her family even more, as those lessons could come in handy right about now.

As if she wasn't already worried enough, Ana noticed she was following Drake to the upper-class district. "Where are we headed?" She asked, unable to hide the uneasiness from her voice.

"To the market, of course." Drake answered, thinking the question benign.

"But I figured we'd be working with someone in the lower quarter."

"They don't pay nearly enough to keep the bar running." Drake noticed something was off. Not about Ana, he expected that, but as they got nearer to the castle gates, patrols were up substantially. Guards seemed to be barreling through the streets on a mission, like the king himself put the fear of god into them. As long as they weren't looking for hybrids, though, it didn't matter to him. Ana, on the other hand, was far, *far* more concerned.

"I feel like there's more security than usual. Maybe we should go back." Ana said nervously. Wanting to find any way to get out.

"It's not like they're looking for us." Drake responded confidently. "One of them would have stopped us by now. We don't exactly blend in."

He had a point. Though they were surrounded by a small army, none of them paid any mind to the two sellswords walking through the street. It was almost refreshing. Even though she had to cover herself up for a different reason than usual, at least there wasn't anyone fawning over her everywhere she went. You'd think it would be nice, but having every guard, citizen, and noble you walk by asking you if you need a glass of water and worshiping the ground you stand on gets tiring after a year or seventeen.

As they made their way into the market street, Ana made sure to cover up her sword. She hadn't forgotten that it was a stolen item and was willing to pay for it later when she had the chance. Right now was neither the time nor place for chivalry, though. Now was the time to make it through to the next day. It didn't make it any less awkward walking by the same merchant she had stolen it from. Nor did it make her want to go over and browse any less.

"How long do you think until we get a client?" She asked, trying to keep herself distracted.

"Could be immediately, could take all day, could be not at all. The important thing is that they pay well."

"You seem to care about money, like, a lot." The princess in her voice snuck out again.

"It's not like you can hide a whole tribe in a city for cheap." Drake's answer made sense to Ana, and it was nice to not get chided for sounding so sassy. It was a minor luxury, but the ability to speak her mind felt like a much-needed vacation.

It wasn't much longer before they walked through the opening in the kingdom walls, and the beauty of the desert spanned out before them. The yellow sands glimmered with nary a track in them. They spanned out like a shimmering lake of molten gold. The only thing breaking the perfect horizon was a camel stand with creatures ready to be rented or bought. Ana wanted to appreciate it as much as she always did, but her new eyes made the sands much brighter. It was all she could do to keep from staring at her own shadow to keep her retinas from burning. She was just hoping no one would notice her new weakness, whether it be the other cloaked figures looking for coin, or worse, one of the merchants looking to hire them.

"Not going to be much use fighting in the daytime, are you?" Drake noticed, which was to be expected. Ana shook her head.

"I'm not sure I'd be too helpful at night, either." She admitted. After a moment of thinking, a worry came to her. "What do you mean daytime? Is this going to take more than a day?"

Drake almost keeled over laughing. It was the first time she saw him react like this, and honestly thought it was quite rude. "Do you really think we'd be able to cross over the desert and into Ingress in less than a day?"

"TO INGRESS!?" She unintentionally exclaimed. It made sense, as Ingress was the closest kingdom, but it was so far away. At least two days march out through the sands. That much work sounded insane to the princess, but she had to admit the idea of sleeping in the sand under the stars didn't seem the worst.

Once an awkward enough silence had passed from the princess's outburst, Drake confirmed. "Yes, Ingress. We'll be out for a fortnight or so, assuming we get hired."

Ana let herself slide down the exterior stone wall and into the soft sand down below. Her hood covered her features as it needed to, but anyone could tell she was pouting like a spoiled brat. "How will anyone even know we're mercenaries?"

"What else would you call two cloaked figures outside a city wall?"

"Bandits?"

"This close to guards? You're insane." Drake took a look out over the desert, and speaking of guards, saw movement off on one of the dunes. They weren't too far away from the city and were bearing the Rexharne royal flag. And he thought the patrols inside the walls were strange. It was noted but of no concern just yet.

The sun made its path through the sky as the two sellswords made it nowhere closer to any kind of work. Most of the merchants had already been set up by the time they got there and likely wouldn't be leaving until they shook every single coin they could out of the locals. Usually, one of them would be out of stock by now, but the traffic was low. Ana figured it had something to do with the extra patrols that were almost definitely looking for her. Making it in or out of the city was tricky under current circumstances. Still, something about it made her feel cared about, that there was such a heavy emphasis on her return. There was still a question as to whether or not that care would remain once they laid eyes upon her face. She questioned if she knew what would happen if she would have still decided to leave the castle two nights ago.

Though the day felt long, Ana killed some time listening to the conversations happening inside the walls. Though her sight was worse in the daytime, she couldn't deny that the hearing was amazing. It was hard to get used to, as every conversation and footstep rang in her ears like a scream. If she paid close enough attention, she could pick up on individual things she wanted to hear, such as the seller she stole from going on about how his items were exceptional and how many wars they survived. It kept her busy.

Good thing it did, too. Drake was as dull as a lesson on how dry sand is. He did nothing but dart his eyes over the horizon for hours. Ana decided it was more effort than it was worth to strike up a conversation with him. Honestly, she figured he used this time to get away from Henry's chatter. That relationship is the other reason she didn't want to talk, as that's a whole other can of worms she was afraid to open.

The sun had turned the sky a burnt orange before Ana heard the first stall closing up for the day. She could hear the remaining wares being shoved away and the jingle of metal coins being counted. Pushing herself up off the stand, she stood up, preparing in case one of them planned on travelling through the night.

"What, done already?" Drake spoke up for the first time in hours.

“No, just getting ready in case someone comes this way.” Ana answered.

“Why now of all times?” He asked mildly but audibly intrigued.

“I can hear someone packing up in there. They might be on their way out.” She almost stuck her chest out in pride that she did something, for once, but was quickly shut down.

“Huh. Good ears, rodent.” Drake wasn’t much for letting someone have their moment.

“What. Did. You. Call. Me.” Ana took in a heavy breath between each word, and though not suited for combat, was ready to tear this man-beast down.

“Relax, it was a joke.”

“I didn’t know you were capable of those.” Bam. Two for two. Useful and sassy today. The rough sound of wooden wheels against flagstone soon came to Ana’s ears, and shortly after, everyone else who was waiting in the wings as well.

About a dozen or so sellswords dotted the outside wall, and not a single one approached the cart as it came out. It was a small thing, being pulled along by a portly little man in some far from perfect silks. It didn’t look like much, and even Drake didn’t move to try and offer his services, but Ana noticed something. Heard something. The clink clink of silver and gold in the man’s pocket. This guy was loaded. She took the initiative and moved forward. Not enough to get in the man’s way, but enough to be noticed. Drake followed and quickly grabbed her shoulder as if to pull Ana back, but she turned and gave him a look. She mouthed the words “Trust me” as she pointed to her bat ear under her cloak. Drake smirked, both happy she was getting it and that she was on his side.

As they were the only ones even close to looking like they wanted to help, the short man asked the two of them. “Do you offer protection?” Drake nodded, and Ana mimicked his nod. “How much?”

“Where to?” Drake quickly asked, keeping his head down so his face was covered.

“Parvus.” The man answered. The closest border city that straddled the line between Ingress and Rexharne. It was the most common destination, but it didn’t lower the price any. Drake pulled Ana to the side, looking away from the man.

“Pretend like we’re talking.” He whispered in her ear. “Also, good job."

"Sure thing." Ana answered, "And thank you!" She was too enthusiastic for his liking. Drake noted he might have to reel back the compliments or he might never hear the end of it.

The two of them turned around, somehow in sync. "Four hundred silvers." Drake answered. Ana immediately thought he was starting way too low. She was proven incorrect as the small man almost jumped back at the proposal.

"And how is that fair for two days' work?" He asked in a huff.

"Four. Two to bring you there, and we both have to make it back after." Drake's replies were cold and unwavering.

"Two hundred. Fifty per day is plenty fair. Besides, you could find work on the way back." The merchant countered.

"Meet in the middle." Drake came back quickly. "Three hundred. Take it or leave it."

The man puttered about for a minute, pacing back and forth in the sand. He was threatening to bring attention to them by making a scene. "How do I even know you'll offer me enough protection?" He asked.

Ana took the cue pretty quickly and pulled her sword out. Initially, it was pointed towards the man until she noticed her mistake and put it to her side, the tip buried ever so slightly in the sand. It didn't seem to impress their potential client as he made a dismissive grunt. Drake had another tool up his sleeve, literally.

He pulled his glove off just enough for his scales to glisten off of the setting sun. The merchant could hardly contain his interest. It was as if he had struck the goldmine of mercenaries. He did pull back to keep his bargaining face on and pretended to think for a few awkward minutes longer.

"Very well." He answered. "I've decided three hundred is fair. You're lucky I made a decent pull today." Ana had to hold her tongue. Luck had nothing to do with it.

"We'll come up from behind after you get your camel." Drake stated. The man nodded and wandered off.

"I'm guessing that's to keep a low profile?" Ana asked.

"Exactly," Drake answered. "You know, depending on how you do over the next couple of days, we might actually have a good thing going here."

"That was the last thing I expected out of you today." Ana claimed, and it was true. There was one thing itching at the edge of her thoughts. “Question.”

“You have a lot of those.” Drake stated.

“I know, but when we met, you said you were fused with an albino lizard. What kind of lizard was it?” She asked. The reaction from the merchant wasn’t exactly normal, even for one looking for a hybrid guard.

“You’ll find out when you’re older.”

“Why now?” She asked in disbelief. “Why now do you decide to joke?”

“He’s heading out. We should be on our way.” Drake very obviously dodged the question, making his way out into the desert quickly.

“I will get it out of you!” Ana yelled, running after him. For the first time in her life, she left the city without guilt and was able to enjoy the red sky of the sunset as she began her journey out into the desert night.

Chapter 6

Ana found the first night of marching through the desert exhausting. Even though she had sat against a wall all day, just trying to stay awake became difficult. She could attribute a good part of that to her drunken night with Henry. The other part came from never having to do even the slightest bit of labour in her life. She questioned how this merchant, Drake, and even how the camel managed to get by. On the bright side, their journey was taken in the dark, so her eyes weren't burning.

"Honestly, why does he even need us?" Ana asked quietly. They were trailing far enough behind their client she had no fear of him hearing.

"We haven't been out that long. Did you think bandits attack every hour?" Drake asked, guessing the answer was yes.

"At least it would break up the night."

"What, do you want to fight all of a sudden?"

"No." She answered though unsure if she believed herself.

"Well then be glad. If we can get through both days without incident, we get paid for walking." Drake was reminded why he usually worked with someone he didn't know. The silence was so much better than this whining.

Ana had been briefed about how a fight with bandits might go. Drake explained that they usually run off at the first sign of protection, so all she'd have to do is raise her sword and they'd be scared off. If they did get into a battle, he explained that they'd have to be ruthless. This wasn't some sparring match in a castle courtyard. It would be a battle to the death, and all she had at her side was a stranger, an old rusty sword, and no skill.

"How many fights have you gotten into?" She asked, trying to fill the air.

"Not many." Drake admitted. Great, she also had a partner without much experience.

"I haven't seen a weapon on you." She stated as she started walking backwards to look at his cloak. "I assume you have some hidden?" Ana got far too close for Drake's comfort, so he nudged her away.

"I'm a hybrid. I use what was gifted to me."

Somehow Ana didn't even consider the fact that the man she was travelling with had claws. It didn't change that he was apparently both unskilled *and* unarmed. She promptly decided a journey without conflict would be much better.

For the first night, it remained that way. Just more sand, rocks, and the odd snake their merchant friend would get scared of and call one of them over to kill. Drake and Ana took turns fulfilling the request, but every time Ana had to shove her relic into another poor creature's head, she cringed at what she was using such an artifact for. Drake, on the other hand, seemed to complete the task with extreme prejudice. He was quick, but brutal as he crushed the creature's head before it could feel anything. Since Drake was on her side, Ana felt the only thing daunting was the mountain range on their left, and that wasn't going to jump out and attack anytime soon.

The fact remained, they were getting paid for this. It was as simple as that. The client asks for something, you oblige. Ana had never seen the other side of the coin before. If this trip had done anything for her, it made her want to apologize to her family's servants for the mundane tasks they had to go through. Everyone *besides* her governess. For lack of a better term, she could shove it.

When enough hours had passed for the sky to turn a dark blue, the three of them started looking for an alcove in the mountains to hide out in until the next day. It didn't take long until they found one big enough to fit the cart, but not so big they didn't know what was going to come out of the other end of it.

By the time they had settled, the merchant on one side of the short cave, Drake and Ana on the other, the sands began to turn their golden yellow from the sun's reflection. Ana quickly averted her gaze towards the inner wall of the cave. The last thing she needed now was a headache. Drake had brought rations that Ana complained tasted like, well, rations, and she promptly attempted to sleep.

"So you're taking second watch then?" Drake asked.

"Mmmm... what." Ana asked, as more of a verbal reaction than an actual question.

"Second watch. You sleep halfway through the day, I wake you up, and I sleep the second half." Drake could swear he was dealing with a child. Ana took a moment to process the information and jolted up, turning to him with bags under her eyes, her pupils filled with death.

"What do you mean wake up?" Ana questioned through gritted teeth. 'Why can't we just both sleep through the day?"

"And get attacked while we're sleeping? What do you think we're here to do?" This girl was just simply unbelievable.

"Fine!" Ana exclaimed, pulling her cloak over her head completely while laying down on the stone floor. Much the same as an annoyed child would. Drake questioned what decisions he made that brought his life here.

Ana fell asleep with no issue but was soon woken up by something shaking her back. She looked up to see the boot of her companion on her arm.

"How dare you!" She exclaimed, still half asleep and moving away from under his foot. "I have half a mind to call the guar-" She stopped herself when she remembered where she was.

"Your turn." He explained while taking up his own spot on the floor. "Wake me when our merchant friend gets up. Or when we get attacked. Whichever one comes first."

"Don't even joke about that." Ana replied as she stood up, grabbing her sword along the way. "Battle wouldn't last long if I'm the only one awake."

"You'll be fine." Drake reassured, shooing her off with one hand. "There's a comfy rock over there to sit on. Enjoy."

Ana grunted, and on her way over to said rock, dragged her blade behind her for a few steps. At least until she realized what she was doing and picked up the historic artifact so it wouldn't get any more scrapes. The thing was still heavy to her, and swinging it, even if necessary, might be out of the question. She just wished it was a new weapon, so it would actually be intimidating.

Even if someone did try and get the jump on them, it wouldn't exactly be effortless for her to see them. Especially right after waking up, the desert was hard to look at. Though Ana did know the importance of her task. She stared into the white-yellow blinding light, soon with tears in her eyes. Mostly, they were from the pain, but they were mixed in with sorrow. Having time to look out over the beauty of her land and not being able to enjoy it hurt her more than anything else. Her heart sank as she could barely see it, and what she could see fought back. If there truly was no way to reverse this… she didn't even want to think about it.

It began to feel like she was doing damage to her eyes. Damage that may be irreversible, but she wouldn't stop. She wanted to see the glory of those golden sands no matter how much it hurt her. This was a fight that Ana had no intention of losing. She could feel her own tears hitting her feet which only made things worse. She covered her mouth but couldn't stop the sobbing. The thing she had cherished the most, the place she wanted to escape to, had been tarnished permanently.

It took Ana a long time to fight back through it, but the thought that the lives behind her could be on the line kept her going. She began justifying her situation. Her life had been lived out with too much ease. Ease that she took for granted. The world was throwing itself at her, and it was deserved. Even if her life went to complete hell from this point forward, her experience would still be easier than those who had to live this life from the start.

Much to her help, as the sun fell below the horizon, the desert became easier to look at. Its beauty not just in the glimmering jewels that were the grains of sand in the daytime but also in the cool air and calm dunes that gave in to the flow of nature around them. Ana had to be like the sand and let the wind take her where it would.

As if her day alone wasn't hard enough, Ana saw a group of figures off in the distance. At first, she didn't think much of them. Even though they were the first humans that she had seen all day, the likelihood of them being bandits was slim. Between other merchant caravans and the plethora of guards that were undoubtedly looking for her, it was nigh impossible.

Or at least that's what she hoped. Upon further inspection, they didn't carry the flag of Rexharne with them, so that ruled out guards. If they were a caravan, they'd be heading either towards Arid Retreat or Parvus. They were doing neither. They were making their way closer to the alcove, or at least she thought they were. It was hard to tell. Though the day was beginning to get darker, it didn't make it much easier to see. It was only when she heard the crunching of sand from a few hundred feet away that she had an idea.

Ana closed her eyes and paid close attention to the direction of the patrol. She could hear their feet patter along the desert floor. She tried to gauge how many, but it was hard to tell for someone with nearly no experience tracking. The critical pieces of information came when they started talking. All she needed to hear was "The tracks go this way." in a broken, lower-class tongue to know she was dealing with bandits.

Immediately she stood from her spot and went to kick Drake, similar to how he woke her. He grunted but sat up quickly.

"Bandits." She spoke.

"Really?" Drake looked off into the sands to see the same group she did. "Are you sure?" He asked, standing and making his way to the mouth of the cave.

"I could hear them. I'm sure." She stated with certainty.

"Are you ready?" Drake asked. Ana nodded. "Then stop shaking."

Ana didn't even notice until he pointed it out, but she had a full grip on her sword. She held it in front of her, and tightly enough that it was wavering back and forth. Taking a deep breath of the dry air she was so familiar with, she relaxed her grip. The tip of her blade lowered and rested on the ground. Her knuckles still gave her away as they were white as snow, but it would have to do.

Drake was the real threat for those who weren't prepared. He got ready by taking off his oversized gloves and letting them fall to the cavern floor. This was the first time Ana could fully appreciate the prismatic scales that covered his skin and the razor-sharp claws that protruded from the end of his long, talon-like hands. Ana noted she really needed to bother him about what kind of lizard he had fused with but now was not the time.

The following minutes felt like an eternity. Ana had to focus entirely on keeping herself calm. The two of them stared off in silence, and she hoped that the very sight of a couple of mercenaries would be enough to ward off the bandits. Her ears quickly dashed her hopes, as what little bit of conversation that she could overhear, they were talking about how they could "Easily outnumber these sellswords."

"They're not going to back off." Ana stated. She managed to keep confidence behind her words.

"Remember, to the death if it comes to it."

"I know." Ana replied. "Though don't remind me next time." The minor amount of humour she could pull helped. Especially since the bandits were close enough to make out their group. Five, all armed with a variety of scimitars and axes. Ana quickly wondered if this would be how she would die but put the thought aside for later.

Every one of the thieves had their weapons drawn yards before reaching the cave. Ana stayed in silence but pulled her sword back up in a ready stance. Her practice with sticks might get her one hit in, but she was really hoping Drake would take care of the rest. Hell, she was hoping Drake would be able to talk them down, sit them down for a cup of tea, and the whole group would have an enjoyable afternoon. Some things were too much to ask.

Ana expected them to charge but was pleasantly surprised when their apparent leader stopped a good ten feet out. He was the shortest of the group, and like the rest of them, had an unwashed appearance about him. Nothing but a tattered cloak and some leathers, which Ana no longer had the right to look down upon. He had a shortsword out but didn't appear ready to use it, at least not immediately. Perhaps this wasn't going to go as poorly as she thought.

"Aight, you know what we're here for." Said the short man in front, his accent as rough as if he had eaten a mouthful of sand before approaching. Any vague hopes Ana had of not using her weapon were out the window. "Now out the way before 'nyone gets hurt."

"It's alright, I get it." Said Drake, in a strange reassuring tone. Ana had no idea what there was to get. "I'm after the same thing you are." If this was some tactic to confuse them, it at least worked on his partner.

"You are?" The leader bandit asked, rapidly blinking in stupefied response. The rest of the group murmured about themselves. Ana picked up that they were wondering if Drake was another thief or just plain crazy. She didn't know herself.

"Yeah, I don't want anyone to get hurt." He clarified. This angered nearly the entire group, except for one in the back who still didn't quite know where this was going. "Now, move along."

Ana knew what was coming next but could never prepare for it. She attempted to lift her blade before the first attack, it didn't work. The steel felt as heavy as lead. Not only was she unfamiliar with wielding the weapon, but pointing it at another living thing was harder than she ever thought it would be. Even with her own life on the line, it was hard to justify. That was until she heard one of them shifting their feet in the sand. Something gave way, and her human brain gave way to her animal instincts. The sword came up in front of her, though she felt she wasn't the one controlling it. She was ready.

"Get 'em." Came the simple command of what Ana considered a disgusting man. She could have sworn she heard Drake growl as he stepped forward faster than she could ever have seen. Even before the group of bandits had the time to react, he was upon their flank. Once she realized what was happening, she ran forward too.

Before Ana even hit the front lines, Drake had one down. They didn't expect his speed. Whatever he did was quick. He took out one of the group standing right behind the leader who was wielding a worn-out axe. All he was able to do was let out a short yelp of pain after a couple of claws quickly tore into his flesh. One of them thrust forward to pierce the man's chest, causing him to nearly fall back in reaction. This gave an opening to his bare neck, where the second claw lethally made its way across. If you could say nothing else about the hybrid, you could say he was brutally efficient.

The battle was overwhelming for Ana. The moment she got in there, it was like a sandstorm. Disorienting, painful, and felt like it was going on way longer than it actually was. She came up against the tallest of the group, and the only one that didn't immediately focus on Drake after the first move. Ana considered the bandit as nothing but a disgusting thief, which helped in what came next. She didn't know if that was the insect hunter in her or the princess. Either way, she surprised herself by attacking first.

Her sword came down, but it was too far outside. She wasn't even sure the tall man moved, but she knew she missed as the blade buried itself a few inches into the sand. Her opponent took the opening and immediately went in with his own sword to her left side, but Ana moved out of the way. She reacted without knowing what she was doing, but she heard his move as he made it. Something in her was so focused she could listen to the tensing in his muscles and knew where he was going to hit. This was to great advantage, but a power like this only works well when you're experienced in battle. Ana was not, and though she knew to move earlier than she should have, his blade didn't get lost in the desert. Luckily, because she knew when to move, it didn't get lodged in her arm where it was aiming, either. Instead, it found her ankle.

There was a quick jolt of pain and then nothing. The adrenaline took over. Ana knew she couldn't focus on it, so she pulled her blade out of the dunes and prepared to strike again. This time, she knew what she was capable of and listened for his movements *before* she struck. She couldn't say her first opponent was clever, as he immediately made the same attack as before. Ana held up her sword and barely had the strength in her arms to keep him at bay, but managed to angle the blade down so it got stuck in the sand.

Though not practically trained, she had watched enough of her brother's combat sessions to know that the best thing to do is disarm the opponent. She was only halfway there, as the thief still had a hold of his sword. She could have struck back again to try and harm his hands but knew her weapon was dull and couldn't rely on it. Instead, the moment her opponent's weapon hit the ground, she kicked the flat side with her undamaged foot, leaving the edge of the weapon flat on the sand. Then, she did something even she thought was insane and jumped on the thief's sword.

It was insane, but it worked. The additional weight pulled the hilt from the scoundrel's hands and put it firmly in the control of Ana's feet. It took him a moment to realize what had happened, and at that moment, Ana hesitated. The threat was gone, and she knew the kill was right there, but this was a human. This was another conscious person, and even though he devoted his life to these misdeeds, was it in her right to judge him?

He rushed at her, ready to grapple, and in that split second, her arms made the decision for her. She thrust out the tip of her blade directly into the man's stomach. She didn't have to do all of the work, as he practically skewered himself on it. It was far from feeling like a knife through butter, as Ana could tell when the notches of the blade got caught on his shirt, skin, and eventually insides. She had to look away as his white-ish shirt began turning red, and the arms he had raised to grab her fell to his sides lifeless.

Her animalistic instinct came back as she was reminded there was still a fight going on. Or, at least she thought there was. After tilting her blade down and kicking the body off of it, she turned over to the rest of the group to see only two left standing. The ground under Drake's feet would have been a good enough excuse to call this place "The Scarlet Sands" even if it didn't already have that name. The last combatant he had was another axe wielder, and Ana saw him come in for a strike that was sure to hit Drake in the side.

And it did. Yet, it did no damage. From the rest of his cloak, it looked like this wasn't the first one either. The blade of the axe simply... stopped. Right where it hit him, it cut through his cloak, and you could practically see the attacker's arms shake with the impact as if he had hit a brick wall. Ana figured he must be wearing some kind of armour under his cloak. Knowing Drake and the line of work he was in, it would only make sense.

Her initial fears of having an unarmed companion were put at ease that day, as she got a clear show of what that hybrid could do in a fight. After the bandit's strike failed, the lizard-man wasted no time going straight for the kill. It was painful to watch, but Ana told herself what he was doing was necessary. She had, after all, had just done the same. It was hard not to admit there was something more brutal about a hand-to-hand method, though, as Drake's claw passed over the attacker's throat and brought a trail of blood with it.

The last threat fell to the ground as Ana and Drake inspected the battlefield around them, making sure no one else was moving. The moment Ana felt safe, her body let itself collapse to the ground as the searing pain of her ankle started catching up with her. Drake ran over immediately.

"Injured?" He asked. It was the shortest question he could get out as to handle the situation more efficiently. Ana nodded and awkwardly held her ankle to stem the bleeding. Drake took up part of his heavily damaged cloak and used the tip of one of his claws to cut off a substantial strip. Ana wondered how he managed to keep them as sharp as he did.

Almost as effectively as a seasoned soldier, Drake had Ana's ankle wrapped up in a couple layers of cloth. "We'll have to change that every couple of hours." He informed her as he handed her another strip that she could use later.

"Thanks." She said, shifting herself in the sand to get more comfortable and keep the cut off the ground. There was a wince of pain on the way, but the adrenaline was still running hot enough to keep her from noticing.

She did get to take a look at how much of a hybrid Drake really was. Of course, everyone else she had seen in the bar had some major transformation, but none of them quite as far as his. It was clear why he wore as many layers as he did. Not only were his arms covered in scales, but they went from his legs up to his neck. On that note, there was one more thing Ana realized. He wasn't wearing any metal armour. It was just his cloak, a thin bit of leather, and those white prismatic scales keeping the blades bouncing off of him.

"Question." She stated, almost demanded.

"What?" Drake asked. Ana expected some kind of animosity in his voice, but he almost sounded concerned. That would quickly go away once she asked her inquiry.

"What kind of lizard are you fused with again?"

"An albino one." He answered, same as he did before.

"You've said that. Give me something new." Ana challenged.

"Fine. A big one." He replied, slightly more annoyed. Ana figured she wouldn't push her luck any further. At least not just yet.

She left him alone as he went back to the cave to check on their client. Mostly because moving with her ankle was painful, as the sight she was left with wasn't pretty. Five lives were ended in front of her that day, one of them by her own hand. She couldn't help but question if he really deserved it. If maybe an opportunity was given to him if he would have taken it. Ana knew it would weigh heavily on her mind for a long time, likely forever. She would hate herself if it didn't.

It was then she realized that she hadn't given up on being a princess. If she could even help one other person avoid a life like this, she would.

Chapter 7

"I don't understand how, but he's still asleep." Drake said before sitting down next to Ana in front of the day's carnage.

"The longer it is before I have to walk, the better." She reminded him. It was questionable how long she'd be able to stand, let alone walk for another day. "I'm not sure I should keep going forward."

"Well, we're dead centre between Arid Retreat and the border of Ingress. One direction we get paid, the other your cut ankle was for nothing." Drake stated. He was always thinking about the pay. Ana could have smacked him for that. Though she hated to admit it, he was right. There was no difference in the amount of rest between back home or the border city. If she was going to have to fight it, might as well get paid. She couldn't help the thought that if her father saw her as an injured child, she might be able to go back to the castle.

"Fine." She finally whined. "Might as well try getting up." Ana was just trying to spite him now. She dug the tip of her sword in the sand to try and use as a crutch. If it was any sharper, it might not be effective, but it managed to hold up. She pulled herself up by the hilt and winced as she felt the pain of being sliced open yet again. Ana could still feel the cold steel in her exposed flesh. She was unsure if that feeling would ever stop.

Managing to get fully to her feet, Ana nearly fell over when she tried to put any weight on them. She remained standing, though, knowing Drake wasn't exactly going to help her out. It was strange. He was almost like the kind of teacher she asked for. One that would let her do what she needed to and only guide when necessary. The old idiom of being careful what you wish for rang clear in her head.

It took a few minutes of shifting her weight around to find out where she could stand without wobbling. Then came the problem of walking. Her good foot went forward first, and it left her in an awkward spot where she had to plunge the sword into the ground while standing on one foot before bringing her other one ahead. The first attempt left her with both hands on the hilt of the weapon, it being the only thing keeping her face from diving into the blood-soaked desert.

Quickly adjusting, her good foot came forward again, and she pulled herself up. Ana felt like a wounded animal before realizing that's exactly what she was. A flightless bat with a cut foot. There weren't many more useless creatures out there than that. Regardless, she was doing way more now than she ever did before. As much as she would hate to admit it while standing amongst a sea of corpses, this journey was oddly refreshing.

"Eh? What happened here?" Came the high and mighty voice from a tiny man that had just awoken. He hadn't spoken to either of the hybrids since the start of the expedition. Still, it would be more worrying if he said nothing to the aftermath of the previous day.

"Bandits," Drake said, trying to keep the conversation short. "None left. We're ready when you are."

"Speak for yourself." Ana commented under her breath. She didn't stop trying to walk no matter how many times she had nearly failed. It was going to be a long night, but at the very least, her eyes wouldn't burn once they were on the road. Not from the sun in the sky or the blood on the sand.

"I'll eat hastily, and we'll be on our way." The merchant replied, his voice breaking just enough for Ana to be reminded that he was human. "I can't stand looking at... this anymore." He motioned to the bodies. Yet somehow he didn't have a problem eating in front of them. Ana guessed this wasn't his first time, and it wouldn't be his last, waking up to something like this. Her vision of the perfect desert landscape was getting slowly corrupted. No wonder she wasn't allowed out of her room.

Drake gave a nod in response to their client and continued looking out over the horizon. Ever the sentinel standing guard for his charge. Ana wondered if he really was looking out for threats or just trying to look more professional so he would get return business. It was likely a mix of both.

It didn't take long for the camel to be hitched back up to the wagon and for everyone's feet to hit the sandy road. Like the previous night, they let the merchant go first and kept a far distance behind him. At his request, they kept the separation between them longer, as Drake no longer had full coverings from what he really was. The battle did a number on his cloak and armour. This reinforced to Ana how much people must hate hybrids. This man nearly lost his life, and he was more concerned about being seen with the pair of them. Perhaps it was just one man with his priorities out of whack, but from what she had seen, it fit the narrative.

Even if he did want them closer, Ana wasn't entirely sure she could oblige. The first half an hour or so, she was able to keep full speed out of pure spite. Being stubborn has its perks when trying to ignore pain or get your way. It doesn't help forever, though. Between remembering her ankle was cut in two and realizing she was sanding down a many-years old relic, it wasn't long before she had something to say about it.

"Couldn't he at least carry me on his cart or something?" She asked, tripping up in her step and debating dramatically falling over to prove her point.

"His life would be ruined just as much if someone found a hybrid in his cart as if he died." Drake reminded her.

"I still don't get why everyone hates us so much." Ana continued. Drake was noticeably impressed that she used the term 'us'.

"A variety of reasons. Fear, because some of us are stronger, or just because we're different. Regardless of their reasons, convincing a horde to accept us would be difficult, to say the least." Ana could have sworn that he read her mind. How does he know that she couldn't be the one to bring the two sides together? If only he knew the power she really had, not just the bat ears and potential echolocation.

"Can't we take a break?" Ana asked, stopping dead in her tracks and leaning on her sword.

"Nope." Drake said as he kept walking. It was like an unstoppable force had finally hit an immovable object. The sheer amount of stubbornness in this group would make a mountain say "Fine." and proceed to move out of the way.

The thought of being left alone in the desert kept the immovable object from staying that way, and Ana hobbled her way forward as fast as she could. Honestly, the more she walked, the less she felt the pain. It was hard to tell if she was getting used to it or her foot finally fell off. Ana liked to believe the latter.

Conveniently the night's travel remained uneventful. Aside from the howl of coyotes, that is. Oh, and the complaining of a short merchantman that there was yet another snake near him. Luckily Drake took up snake duty all night so Ana could continue at her slow pace. It wasn't a major win, but she'd take it.

The main event of the night was seeing the border of Ingress come into view. Not many kingdoms had such apparent separation, but the treaty was clear that where the sand stops, so does the jurisdiction of Rexharne. And the sand stopped alright.

It was like looking at paintings of two completely separate landscapes. One side, a flowing sea of sand. On the other side, the greenest fields and forests this side of the globe. It was one of the most shocking sights of nature. It was to the point where not everyone believed it was natural, especially the emperor of Ingress.

There had been trade and land wars for years, and the treaty was the first point of peace between the two kingdoms. Even so, tensions were high. It was why Ana was always confined to her room when a representative from Ingress visited. She had always thought the disputes were ridiculous. Where the sand stopped, Ingress started. This was the biggest cause of conflict. There were fights over whether Rexharne added more sand to the edge of the border or if Ingress was taking it away. Honestly, it was likely both. That's what's kept the line in check for so long.

From the way it was explained to Ana when she was a child, the emperor would jump at the chance to take her for ransom. She wasn't sure how much she believed it, though she still pulled her hood tighter the moment they could see the edge. It wouldn't have made a difference as the king's daughter wasn't often described as having a short snout and fluffy black ears.

The trade and land disputes set aside, Ingress was a beautiful kingdom. The green field was broken only by the city of Parvus. It was the only blemish to the eyes, as its grey stone buildings stood drab and lifeless. Even so, it was exactly what Ana, and her foot, needed to see. It meant the end of their journey in one direction. In a few hours, she could finally sit down again. In the meantime, the landscape wasn't that bad either. Ana had never seen such lush greens out in the wild. Especially ones that were so clear in the dark, though that might just be the contribution of her new eyes. Back at the castle, some fantastic gardeners made their own little forests and shrubberies that used far too much water to keep plants alive in the desert. Their results were unquestionable, though, as they had matched the greenery of a far less harsh climate.

"It really is a sight, isn't it?" Ana spoke up.

"Ah, so you've lived under not just a rock your whole life, but a desert rock." Drake pointed out. She really wished he wasn't as right as often as he was.

"Shut up." was the only response she had. Two words that meant you were defeated but weren't willing to go down without a fight. "Where can we stay when we get there?" She asked, trying to get away from his verbal victory.

"It's slightly more free in Parvus than in Arid Retreat, but not by much. We should be able to find a cheap tavern and spend the night." Drake answered. It concerned Ana.

"Wait." She said, stopping in her path. "Is Arid Retreat really that much worse for hybrids?"

"The whole kingdom of Rexharne is." His response made Ana's heart sink. How could her father let it get so bad? Did he even care?

"Well, what are the king's thoughts on it?" She asked, knowing that she was giving away too much. Even more so that she was giving it away to someone who clearly needed the coin. Drake raised an eyebrow before answering, but only for a second.

"Aside from the fact we're completely outlawed? He doesn't speak about it often."

"OUTLAWED?" She exclaimed. There were clearly tensions between the government and hybrids, but she didn't think it was that bad. Was she now an illegal citizen simply because of something she had no control over? This couldn't be right.

Ana knew she had overstepped her bounds just a bit too far when their client, his fifty or so feet in front of them, stopped for a second and turned. It luckily wasn't a long stop, and she let out a sigh of relief.

"How couldn't you have figured that out? You were chased down by guards the moment someone saw you." Drake spoke purposely quieter to try and bring her back down.

"I just thought it was for another reason." She answered. This piqued Drake's interest, and Ana *really* didn't want it to.

"Oh yeah? What kind of reason would they be after you?" He asked, a coy smile revealing itself at the corner of his mouth.

"I'll tell you when you tell me what kind of lizard you are." It was her turn to be quick today. To her credit, Drake thought about telling for a moment but shrugged it off.

"You wouldn't believe me if I told you."

"And neither would you." She stuck her tongue out at him, which was far longer than she expected it to be, reaching almost a foot out of her face without trying. Ana decided she didn't like finding more parts of herself that were no longer human and hoped that was the last one.

"So I guess we're even." was thankfully the response she got from him. If he had pointed out her tongue, Ana would have given herself the legal right to kill him. She didn't care if that was in her power or not. Even if it was, she'd have to wait until they got back to the castle, and that was too far away.

"I guess we are." She said smugly, thinking she won some kind of victory when no one made any progress anywhere. If anything, Drake knew she had something to hide now. That was if he didn't already.

"Regardless, Ingress still isn't fully accepting, so keep your hood up." Drake went back to the previous topic. Ana noted this, as he was clearly too close to getting uncomfortable with information with the latest conversation. She still didn't know if this was a cue for her to let it go or push further later. "Most importantly, it means we likely won't be getting work on the way back."

"Because of your cloak, I'm guessing?" Ana asked.

"Exactly." Drake commended for picking up on at least a little bit of their oppressed nature.

"Can't you buy a new one once we get paid?" She asked, immediately removing any respect she had just gained.

"As I said, the most likely thing we're getting is a seedy tavern. Nowhere that actually sells clothing to the public is going to let us in. Don't even think about doing it yourself, either. The citizens aren't dumb. They'll know why you're covering yourself up in the best-case scenario. In the worst, they'll think you're stealing."

Well, at least thieves were looked upon worse than hybrids. Ana was definitely getting tired of him reading her thoughts, though. Was she really that easy to get through to? As someone raised to be a political leader, Ana figured she could lie much better than this.

As they got closer to the edge of the kingdom, the tensions on the border showed themselves. Guards patrolled back and forth at the sand line from both sides, and not a small amount of them either. It was as if they were trying to keep the desert itself contained. Ana supposed that was one of the main disputes to begin with.

It was about an hour before they were to reach the border town of Parvus. It was a small thing, but enough to have to clearly separate districts that you could even see from an hour out at night. Or at least Ana could. It was strange seeing a city without walls on all four sides. Though remembering her history books, Parvus was quite often the first town taken in any given war. Not because of a huge strategic advantage, but more because it had buildings, and it was there. It did once have military protection long ago, with towers and bunkers. They were deemed too costly to rebuild after being taken down more than once. Parvus was the pinnacle of a town that had given up, as it had been occupied one too many times.

It made Ana uncomfortable to look at. It was her ancestors, her own *family*, that had run these people there out of their homes. She understood the same goes for the other side but having that direct link gave her a feeling of guilt the more she thought about it. As if she wasn't already uncomfortable enough stepping into enemy territory, the fact that it was Parvus made it so much worse. It wasn't like she could speak about her problems with it either.

The hour passed as she got more and more worried. Not just at the town but the guards patrolling the border. She knew the men that took this job because they were Kasibel's men. Her brother's men. If anyone was going to see through the bat snout, it would be them. She just had to pull her cloak tight and keep to herself.

The caravan was about to cross, but just as it hit the border, he stopped. Drake stopped as well, and Ana wanted to yell at them to keep going.

"Why aren't we moving?" She asked, clear worry in her voice.

"He has to get his cart checked before going through. If you carry supplies like this through without waiting for a guard, it's immediately considered smuggling."

"Well, that's pretty strict of Ingress." She said snottily.

"It would be if it wasn't a Rexharne law to keep borders closed." Drake replied, taking away her moment and making her wonder how little she knew about her own kingdom. How could she be taught by the king's staff and not even know their laws? A thought came to her mind.

"If everyone has to be checked, what about us?" Ana asked. It was strange to her that hybrids could be outlawed yet still be allowed to pass the border.

"We'll be fine. The guards at the border are different than the ones in the retreat." You could say that again, Ana thought. "They don't care as much about hybrids, especially when it comes to letting them out of the kingdom. Getting in is a slight bit more difficult, but no more than stating that you aren't making your way to town and are just passing through."

Well, at the very least, this proved someone in her family had a good head on their shoulders. It was hard to believe Kasibel would ever be part of this, and Ana was glad he wasn't. Of course, he had to follow father's orders to an extent, but at least rebelled the rest of the way. This did bring her to a confirmation she didn't want to admit. Her family knew, both her brother and father, and neither of them told her.

"So, what do we do when we cross?" She asked, trying to get the thought out of her mind as the cart started making its way through.

"Stay quiet and pretend we don't exist. It's not like this is the first trip a merchant has made with someone like us. He would have already cleared us."

Ana wasn't sure how much she believed him but had no other choice. It's not like she was willing to do a two days march back on her own on a messed up foot, so as Drake started stepping forward, she did too.

Her heart pounded in her chest as they got closer to crossing the sands. She started going through every law she knew she could possibly be breaking, including a major one about royalty stepping foot from kingdom to kingdom without paperwork. She couldn't remember if it was considered espionage, treason, or smuggling. Hell, it might be all three. She was so worried about it that she didn't even notice when they finally did cross over, but once she felt grass on her feet, she let out a sigh of relief.

The feeling didn't last long, as the first thing she heard upon arriving in a new kingdom were the words of a guard shouting, "Hey, you!"

Crap.

Ana looked over, and she didn't know if it was better or worse that an Ingress guard was the one making his way over. She took a deep breath and tried to remain calm, but her grip on her sword gave her away.

The guard stopped a decent stretch away from them, which again was questionable as either comforting or concerning. He was wielding a spear, so distance would be to his advantage if he was looking for combat. Not that Ana would have had any chance anyway, as the glimmering steel armour of the Ingress soldiers covered their whole body near perfectly. Her rusted old blade would have no chance and would likely snap in half upon the first strike. She wondered for a moment if Drake's claws could pierce steel.

"Please remain calm." The guard said in an oddly peaceful manner. Ana loosened the grip on her blade and let her shoulders relax. It appeared to be enough. "Thank you." He responded. This was odd to her, as her teachings mentioned the ruthlessness of the Ingress guard. She supposed they were looking at it from the other side, though.

"What do you need from us?" Drake asked impatiently, exactly what they needed in this situation.

"I would just like to ask you to keep your weapon hidden." The guard explained to Ana, motioning to her sword. Unfortunately, she didn't have a scabbard or anything for it, so she just threw her cloak over it. This seemed to appease him. "And sir, if I can ask you to remain in the lower district. At least until you can acquire new garb." He addressed Drake directly.

"That was our plan." Drake informed him. Both of them knew full well it would be impossible for him to find anything, but the positive gesture was noted.

"Thank you for your cooperation. Do enjoy your, what I assume to be short," There was emphasis on short. "stay in Parvus." And the gesture was stricken from the record.

"Thank you?" Ana said questioningly. Drake had already started walking into town. Ana hobbled after him with the loss of her makeshift cane. It wasn't the worst, though, as the grass was much nicer to walk on than the sand. Breathing a sigh of relief, the princess took her first step into another kingdom, and she couldn't have been more elated.

Chapter 8

The two of them took no time finding a tavern. It was clear Drake had done this before. The problem was this place didn't look any better than the cave they just slept in. If you asked Ana, she would say the cave was better as it had a clear view of the most beautiful desert in the world. Or at least the most beautiful one that she had seen.

Parvus surprised Ana for the worse. She had read about how war-torn it was but wasn't ready for sights that were worse than Arid Retreat's own lower district. Most of the grey brick buildings and cobblestone streets were in at least some amount of disrepair. It ranged anywhere from torn-up stones in the walls to full-sized holes in rooves and anywhere in between. The citizens lazily pushed around carts of produce and other basic goods. Both the items they pushed around and the people themselves seemed to only be here out of necessity.

One of the most surprising things were the hastily placed flags hung with as much care as a wife would give to her husband's mistress. It seemed every time this place was invaded, the kingdom who took it over raised yet another banner and burned the previous ones. The current banners adorned a silver owl in flight over a royal blue cloth, the mark of Ingress. A mark Ana was told she should hate but never really took to it. Aside from the new ones, there were various strips of cloth, both red and blue, for the warring kingdoms that still stuck to the side of buildings. In some cases, the only thing left was a strip of black soot where one had been burned off. In others, there were still full-sized banners from Rexharne, the gold roaring lion on its red background representing the desert, hanging in full glory. The town square, in particular, was the only place they made it clear who owned this town. Even the inhabitants didn't seem interested in what side of the border they currently belonged to.

It was a sad sight, to say the least, and not what Ana expected her introduction to the world to be. She also didn't expect that same introduction to come with blood on her hands and a cut on her foot, but it was par for the course. Two nights before, she had never had enough wine to lose balance. Now she was craving the feeling of inebriation.

She sat at the bar with Drake after he had paid for their rooms. Ana didn't even want to go take a look at hers. She thought if it was anything like the rest of this place, she'd be sleeping on wood so soaked you'd think it was made out of wet bread. It wouldn't be long until she found out she was right. For now, wine, in both liquid and verbal form.

"How do you do this all the time?" She asked Drake, taking the first sip of her wine. It was substantially cheaper than she thought wine could be, and quickly found out why. She almost spat it on the first take, but the idea of getting drunk enough to forget about this city and her foot pushed her through the taste.

"Usually with less chatter." He responded coldly.

"Are you always such a sour apple? Henry says you're always such a sour apple." Didn't matter how cheap the drink was, her slurred words proved that it was doing its job.

"We don't exactly live a glorious life. Why should I be happy about it?" Clearly, whatever he was drinking opened him up more than Drake wanted it to.

"Well, why don't you go and do something about it?" Ana asked, poking a finger at his chest as if it was a dare.

"I'm doing what I can. Hybrids don't exactly have the power to change laws and perceptions." Drake admitted.

"So the laws are the problem?" Ana asked, remembering shortly that she was a princess before another taste of wine reminded her she might have lost that position.

"They're one of them."

"Overthrow the kingdom." Ana said quietly, though she thought she had only said it in her head.

"What was that?" Drake asked, thinking he just heard her wrong.

"OVERTHROW THE KINGDOM!" She doubled down happily, spilling the last half of her drink on the floor. No wonder this place smelled of mouldy wood. Drake could have tackled her then and there for the outburst. It might have happened if the bartender didn't open her mouth first.

"I think she's had enough." The gruff human behind the counter said, more as a fact than a thought.

"You think?" Drake answered sarcastically. Ana tried looking around for this 'she' who had had enough but couldn't find her. So she tried to drink out of her empty glass, getting nothing but a drop of wine in her eye.

"Can you take her out, so I don't have to?" The grit in their server's voice got more defined. Drake took one look at her muscles and decided that if someone was going to drag Ana along, he would likely do less damage along the way. Not no damage, but less.

"Alright, come on." Drake said to Ana, hoping he wouldn't have to literally drag her.

"Where to?" She asked excitedly.

"Bed. We need to look for more work in the morning."

"But I'm not done with my wine!" She exclaimed, holding up her completely empty glass.

"Wouldn't you rather have it in your room? They deliver." The muscular lady behind the counter tried to explain that they didn't, but Drake shot her a look pretty quickly that let her know what he was doing.

"Ohhhh, bed wine? I never thought of that. I didn't get any wine in bed in the castle." Ana didn't realize what she had just said. She would know in the morning upon her line of questioning, but it didn't occur to her that night. Drake took a heavy note of the slip-up.

The trip to bed wasn't quite a drag as Ana was happily willing to go along. She wasn't going entirely of her own power, either. The trip up the stairs would have been enough to kill her. First time fighting a bandit? Fine, no issues. First time tackling stairs while drunk? That's a whole other question.

He brought her to their room. The door was barely held on by its rusted hinges and made a loud squeak on its opening. The wood felt like it was going to fall apart in Drake's claw when he pushed it. Upon entering, he closed the door behind them and latched it shut. He had no confidence in the worn metal lock actually keeping the door, well, locked. But at least it would be an extra point for the door to be held closed. It certainly wasn't doing that on its own. You get what you pay for, he guessed.

"Where's the wine?" Ana asked, nearly falling onto the floor as she let go of Drake's shoulder. He helped her fall into one of the two 'beds' in the room instead. It was really more of a bedroll on raised flooring.

"Lay down, and they'll bring it to you. I've already ordered it." Drake answered, getting as comfortable as he could in his makeshift bed. He always hated this place for trying to sleep, but if she somehow stayed awake, Drake figured he was about to hate this place a whole lot more. Luckily, the sounds of snoring quickly followed.

The next morning, Drake got an earful from a hungover Ana. Apparently, sharing a room was a mistake, even though this tavern only had rooms with two beds. Not to mention if you don't have someone else with you, they'll rent out the second bed to a stranger. Nope, this wasn't a good enough excuse, and he got to hear about it over their gruel of a breakfast.

"On top of all of this. You take me into a room. Drunk, mind you. I don't remember anything about last night, and you won't even do me the favour of going somewhere nice for breakfast? Come on." It was starting to get unbearable, and he had to fire back.

"It was instead of sharing a room drunk with a stranger. You're the one that wouldn't stop drinking, and we're not even allowed in the upper-class district." he answered coldly. He didn't raise his voice, but his frustration was evident.

"This stuff tastes like pig slop." Ana complained as she ate another mouthful. Being hungry from the road will really help you down anything.

"That's because it is." The bartender responded. Ana almost spit out her meal then and there. "I'm joking." She gave in, "But I had to get you back for what you did to my patrons last night. The whole group of them were yelling 'Overthrow the kingdom!' because of you."

Ana blinked in disbelief. She turned to Drake to confirm she wasn't joking, and he just nodded in response. Upon taking one more bite of her slop, she asked. "What the hell happened?" in a whisper.

"I'll fill you in on the way back." Drake assured her. She wasn't sure she wanted to know.

"Speaking of, are we going to look for another job?" Ana asked. Drake motioned to his cloak again. "Oh, right. So just a boring walk in the desert with nothing to make out of it?"

"We did make three hundred silver." Drake said quietly, not wanting anyone to try and mug them. "That's plenty, and to be honest, it's thanks to your hearing."

"I mean, that's barely anything." Ana had no concept of what the commoners thought of money. She figured the same amount in gold *might* be fair, but it was pushing it.

"Speaking of, I've got some questions for you." Drake suddenly remembered her line about a 'castle' from the previous night. He stood up, not bothering to clear up his plate as no one else in this place did. "Let's hit the road. The sooner, the better."

"Fine." Ana said her favourite word while rolling her eyes. Honestly, she would just be happy to get the smell of this place out of her nose. She picked up her sword that was leaning against the table. Drake had told her to put it there even though she was told to keep it away. Said it deterred anyone trying to fight you. He also said it didn't matter this time since his scales were showing, but it was a good habit to have for seedy bars in the future. Just always keep an eye on it in case someone tries to take it. She then followed him out, but not before a "Thank you!" to the bartender that wasn't used to being thanked.

The moment they hit the broken up cobblestone street, Drake almost immediately asked her, "So, no wine in bed at the castle?"

Ana raised an eyebrow in confusion and could mutter nothing other than "Huh?"

"You spoke about 'The Castle' last night. Once while awake and a few times while asleep. What castle?"

Ana froze in the middle of the street. She clearly misjudged her ability to keep a secret while drinking. Sure, she had fought side by side with Drake in a fight to the death, but she still didn't trust him with that information. This man was money-driven, and a stolen princess was worth a lot. Maybe not in her current state, but he wouldn't know that for sure until he tried. Even she didn't know if she was worth anything anymore.

"Drunken ramblings, I'm sure." She tried to pass it off and began to walk again.

"You think I'm going to believe that? Who are you?" He asked directly, this time being the anchor that refused to walk.

"And what kind of lizard are you again?"

"That won't help you. I told you, you wouldn't believe me."

"Then I thought we were even."

"Until you're the reason that the guards were going crazy back in Arid Retreat." Drake sounded accusatory. Madder that she might be the princess than happy, and boy did Ana like to make him mad.

"Very well." She gave in. "Can we at least wait until we hit the desert so no one can overhear me?"

"I think that's a fair tradeoff. As long as you don't get me stuck at the border." Drake picked up substantial speed. He was practically excited.

Ana was filled with nothing but dread. What was he going to do? Would there be a kidnapping for ransom? Would he just kill her on the spot for being a part of the problem that hybrids face? She started to regret saying she'd tell him in the desert. If she was going to die, she wanted to get it out of the way now.

If nothing else, her foot was feeling better. It seemed her makeshift bandages got changed overnight. Ana was hoping if he was willing to do that, he wouldn't be so quick to attack her. On the other hand, it could have been so she didn't spill blood on the floor, and he'd have to pay the tavern owner for it. She knew that latter was more likely to be correct.

She was worrying so much about Drake she forgot about her problem at the border. Right before they reached the sand line, she caught up with him and grabbed his shoulder. He turned and asked her, "What?"

"If the Rexharne guard tries to talk to me, explain to them that I'm mute." She answered. Sure, her facial features had changed, but she still had the same stature and, more importantly, the same voice. That's the last thing she wanted to risk right now.

"Why?" He asked.

"When I tell you in the desert, you'll find out. Simple as that."

"Very well." He kept moving forward and stood without a foot touching the sand but close enough to let them know he was looking to pass. Ana followed suit. It took less than five minutes for a guard to notice them. It was either luck that they got one so fast, or the border security had just become this tight.

"Business?" The armourless guard asked indifferently.

"Passing through. No business in town." Drake answered.

"I would hope not." he said, looking the hybrid up and down. "Any way you can go around?"

"No." He answered simply. "Don't have enough rations to survive taking the long way. This will be a one-time passing, and we will prepare better next time."

"Acceptable." The guard answered, standing aside. "Stay away from the town. Your kind are hunted there."

"I couldn't be more than aware." Drake answered. Ana thought about the warning for a moment. Hunted? Really? That's the word he used? She knew it was bad enough to be outlawed, but hunted? Was there a bounty on the head of every hybrid all of a sudden? This was far from acceptable.

At the very least, they made it through without issue. Drake wasn't entirely lying, either. They didn't have nearly enough food to last them a round trip. They also didn't have enough food to make it past the town, but the guard luckily didn't bother to check for that. Drake waited until they were a good hour into their journey to ask the question again.

"So, what castle were you talking about?"

"If I tell you, will you at least tell me what kind of a lizard you are?" Ana asked. She wanted something out of this.

"You wouldn't believe me." He repeated.

"Don't care." She stated. "I want whatever unbelievable answer you have. I don't like giving away personal secrets for free."

"Neither do I." He reminded her.

"This isn't free."

"It practically is."

"Yeah, but you won't get your solid confession." She felt like she was being interrogated. She was.

"Alright. I'll let you in." Drake gave in. "But, you can't go and tell me to give you a real answer because I swear to you it is."

"Fine." Ana said. She put her hood down in some kind of dramatic fashion to reveal who she really was. Not that anyone would ever be able to tell. "You're in the company of Anachorita Vespertillo Rexharne. Princess and second heir to the Rexharne throne, behind the leader of the guard, Kasibel Rexharne. Daughter to King Rolfe and shut-in princess since she was born."

"That's what I thought." Drake said. "You're the reason the guards went crazy and are still going crazy. At least it takes the heat off of us for a while. Unless they think we kidnapped you."

Ana took a moment to process his response. She was prepared for an attack. She was prepared for him being furious. But this? Indifference? To finding out she was a princess? How dare he.

"How dare you!" She blurted out.

"Excuse me?" He asked.

"I tell you you've been walking with one of, if not the most esteemed royal woman in the entirety of Arid Retreat, and you just say it makes sense? Be in awe or something."

"I'd rather not." He said, crossing his arms. "If anything, I'm slightly peeved you didn't tell me earlier. If the king finds out I have his daughter, they'd have all of our heads for sure. Not that they don't already want them."

Slightly peeved. It was something. It was a reaction, and she was satiated with it. "Fine, so what's your big secret, lizard boy?"

"Dragon."

"What?"

Drake sighed. "That's 'Dragon boy' to you."

"You're trying to tell me you fused with a *mythical* creature? As is, does not exist. Is part of children's fairy tales?"

"Told you you wouldn't believe me."

"Of course I wouldn't when you lie to me."

"What was part of the deal? Oh yeah, you can't tell me I'm lying."

"That's because I didn't think you'd so blatantly lie!" Ana threw her arms to her sides in frustration.

"You didn't even know hybrids existed four days ago. How is this so hard to believe?" He tried to reason with her.

"Because it's a lie." There was no reasoning with her.

"Fine, believe me or don't, we have to make it back to town." Drake continued walking.

"Well, I don't, and we're not going anywhere until I get a real answer." She stayed where she was.

"Good, so we're going then." He kept walking. She ran to catch up with him. Stood her ground. Argued some more and repeated the process.

This was going to be a long night. Drake really wished he could make this walk back alone.

Chapter 9

Ana decided she needed a new dream. She had always wanted to go out and walk the sands but never imagined it could be this boring. Somehow it was even worse without a merchant to follow. Her travelling companion wasn't exactly entertaining either. She could only push him so far to try and get his secrets, but he wouldn't budge. Eventually, she figured she might as well use the time to learn more about the world.

"So, how good is three hundred silvers anyway?" Ana asked. She recently realized her view of the economy was skewed. Now that Drake knew she was a princess, she didn't have to try and hide her ignorance.

"Enough to last a family for a week comfortably." He answered.

"Really? I figured they couldn't last a day on that amount." Ana was a bit more than taken back. She pondered for a moment. "Though, doing two days' travel and risking your life being barely worth three days off is something else. I just don't get it."

"What's there not to get?" He asked.

"With the amount of money I've seen royalty throw around, it's hard to believe people are struggling out there. I knew they existed. I just thought trade was more expensive."

"In other words, you didn't know how good you had it?"

"Pretty much." She admitted, much to Drake's surprise. Her behaviour made sense when he found out what she was, but he didn't expect her to come to terms so quickly. Even most nobles he worked with would rather be back in their gilded rooms than play in the mud for more than a minute. "You know, some perspective in the castle might help."

"You're right there." She struck a chord with Drake.

"Perhaps I should talk to my father. If he'd take me back."

"About what?"

"The situation hybrids face the struggle of the lower classes to earn a silver. You know, that kind of thing." Ana didn't know it yet, but she had just found her new daydream.

"I wouldn't tell him about us." Drake said grimly. "The last thing we need is the king with some of the best military knowing that his enemy is hiding within his walls."

"He's different than that, I swear." Ana didn't know if she believed herself but defended her father nonetheless. It was a question of her pride to do otherwise, and besides, who could possibly understand their dad better than his own daughter?

"Do you really think that?"

"Of course I do! How could I think otherwise?" Ana felt insulted by the question.

"Then why haven't you gone back to him yet?"

That question, on the other hand, was near impossible to answer and threw Ana's entire point into contention. Why hadn't she gone back yet? She was afraid, of course, but she knew now that hybrids were a known quantity. It wasn't *completely* unprecedented for a daughter to come back home with a bat face. The laws against them made her think for a second, but those must have been from their ancestors. There's no way her father would uphold the outlaw of a whole group of people unless it was already in place and there was a political reason for it.

"If the people hate us, it would throw the royalty into question." Ana answered.

"What?" Drake asked. Her pause was long enough he nearly forgot about his question.

"It wouldn't be right for me to go back. He could lose his throne over me if he decides to take me back. If his people decide that hybrids are some kind of sub-race." Drake was clearly uncomfortable with that term. "Then going back could end our family's rule. It is a lot harsher for me out here, sure, but in the worst-case scenario, everyone I care about could be beheaded."

Drake narrowed his eyes at Ana, stopping in his tracks. "Good excuse." He said, quickly continuing on his way. This girl would not back down from an argument, clearly.

"Excuse? We're talking about me losing everything I had." Ana was clearly hurt.

"You already did the moment you met that bat. Keep going, forget about the past." Drake's words were colder than the desert night's wind.

"How dare you." Ana said, stopping in her tracks. "I say that a lot, but this time I mean it. How can you be so callous? You don't even understand what I lost."

"Like you're the only one who lost something becoming a hybrid!?" It was the first time Ana ever heard him yell. She definitely hit somewhere she shouldn't have. "Every last person in that bar you saw doesn't have a place to go home. That tavern is where they live because their families won't take them back. They can't take them back. Their mothers and fathers, sisters and brothers would lose their heads the same as yours would. The only difference between you and them is a throne. Don't you ever forget that."

Ana had never thought of it. Since turning, she had never thought of why everyone was in hiding. She knew they were oppressed but didn't think of the people they had left behind. It was so much more dire than she originally conceived. She had to find a way to fix it.

A coyote howled in the distance, and not being in the mood, Ana yelled out and told it to shut up. She and Drake continued on their path in silence, mostly because she had some thinking to do. There had to be a way to fix everyone's problem somewhere. It was just a matter of finding it.

The howls got closer. Ana instinctively gripped her sword tighter, but instead of fear, turned it into more anger as she yelled out for them to shove it. There was something she was missing. Some piece of the puzzle. Why would everyone go and hate the way they do? In history, humans usually hated other humans from different kingdoms. Be it for war, or religion, or other reasons such as trade disputes. Regardless there was always a deep-seated reason. It wasn't for nothing.

The howls were now uncomfortably close. Ana, getting tired of it, yelled out into the distance. "Shut your traps, or I'll have your head!" Drake thought to himself it was some princess he was travelling with.

"Why don't you come and take them, then?" Came the response from over the nearest dune. Ana froze in her tracks and was even more worried when Drake took off his gloves.

"Who was that?" She asked him quietly.

"Something I'd hoped to explain to you before you got to meet one." Drake answered as cryptically as ever.

"Can you explain now?"

"No time to. Treat these things as bandits when they show up."

"Oh…?" Came the response from over the hill. "You… think we're… like bandits? Human… bandits? No… No no no no no." The voice was strange. It was broken up like it didn't fully understand the language. There were often small growls and barks in between the words. Ana couldn't even begin to think what she was up against. "Bandits… Thieves… useless. They… go for useless… shiny things. We… hunt." They howled. There was more than one of them.

Before long, the pair found themselves surrounded by three creatures. They walked on all fours and were covered in fur, just like a coyote. They were different, though. They had human parts, the same as how Ana had her bat parts. One of them had an arm instead of a paw, another had a mix of both human and coyote features on its face. Ana almost considered it disgusting until she realized there was virtually no difference between him and her. The last one had a fully human lower half, and to intimidate them stood up on its legs. This left a dangling coyote body in the air, and a naked lower human half, with bulging muscles able to hunt and balance.

"Go look for something else to eat." Drake said, brandishing his claws. "You'll have an easier time with a merchant."

"No…" The one who stood up was the one able to talk. It was strange to hear a human language come out of a coyote's mouth. "The hunt is fun. That's one thing you humans gave us… The feeling of fun… I like fun… It's fun!" It then divulged into a mix of cackling and barking. Ana gripped her sword tighter and pointed it at him.

"Watch the others." Drake said to her. She obliged as they were being paced around. The other two were clearly circling to mark off a boundary. If they crossed that boundary, the chase would start. "I hope you know she was serious about you losing your heads." He addressed the apparent lead coyote.

"If you think… you can… try!" This creature was having too much fun. Ana took a step forward, but Drake held her back.

"This isn't a normal fight." Drake told her quietly. "These creatures will tear you limb from limb. Don't attack unless they attack first." Unfortunately, he wasn't quiet enough.

"Attack… first?" The leader questioned. "Sounds… like… plan…" The intermittent barks and yelps were getting closer together until they began to blend into a frenzy of strange noises that kept rising in volume. At its peak, the creature yelled out "HUNT!" and they knew they were in for a world of hurt as the leader joined with the other two in their circle formation.

Ana didn't even notice the first one coming at her. She was looking straight at one of the two circling as it ran off in a strange direction. At that moment, the other one on all fours leaped up and took a gash out of her shoulder before running off. She let out a yelp of pain.

She knew this was another fight for her life, but this one was much more terrifying. It likely had to do with Drake not moving in for an attack. Instead, his eyes darted the battlefield and seemed to wait for one to strike. Unfortunately, the second strike came and again, it wasn't at him. Ana felt a gash in her leg but didn't even see the creature that created it. Her body wanted to collapse, but she knew it would mean death, so she stayed standing. Why did it have to go and be the one with the damaged foot, though?

Ana decided to completely give up on her eyes. There was no way she could see one coming. She already missed them twice. She didn't think it would be possible to tell them apart from the pitter-patter in the sand of all three, but there was no other way. She closed her eyes so she could focus. It was just a matter of waiting for the next strike.

The attack came shortly after but hit the wrong target. It's like they could tell Ana got smarter and went for Drake instead. It was either that or just random chance or whoever was closer. That was the most dangerous thing. Their strategy was impossible to decipher. There was a good chance they didn't have one at all. Luckily the one that attacked Drake tried to claw his leg, but similar to the weapons of the bandits, made no mark.

Ana could finally hear one coming at her. Left side, but without enough time to raise her weapon at it. All she could do was try and move out of the way by dodging forward or backward. She chose backward and instinctively opened her eyes to see teeth that barely missed her throat, followed by the amalgamation of human legs that lept the animal into her. She noted that his steps sounded different and that he was able to jump higher.

The next attack came even faster, but she was ready this time. The moment she heard the pitter-patter start in front of her, she swung her blade. It was just in time, and it caught something. She didn't know what, but it screamed out in pain. Not yelped, screamed. She must have hit the one with the humanoid face. It ran back to the others, the damage not severe enough to stop it.

"You get one?" Drake asked hastily.

"Grazed it."

"How?"

"Hearing." Ana said as she heard another one go for Drake. This time he barely dodged, and the animal got naught but a strip of cloth.

"Let me know when one is coming."

She didn't even think about him not being able to see them either. From that point forward, she called out what she heard. Starting with her next attacker.

"My right." She said, already moving her blade to catch the assailant. Her swing was too early, but it didn't matter as the drawn blade kept the creature off.

"You, straight ahead." She gave the instruction upon hearing the footsteps behind her. Drake listened, and his claws at the ready, caught the one with the human arm by said arm. He kept it grappled until it could find its way out but took chunks of flesh with it. The whimpering could be heard in the tornado of footsteps.

"My right." It was the first time they had attacked her in the same direction twice in a row. Something was off, so Ana kept listening as she prepared her swing. Once she heard it, she could tell right away. "And left!"

She had caught the human-faced one again. This time her sword dug itself deep into the creature's front leg. It was enough that it had to pull itself out, screaming the whole time while running back to a safe distance. She turned to see what she had already heard. Drake was locked claw to claw with their leader, but the power struggle didn't last long. The lizard threw the coyote into the sand and immediately leapt on top of him. Drake managed to get a deep cut into its face before it struggled free by flailing its legs like a newborn deer and returned to the other two.

The time before the next attack was worrying. They were still running in circles but taking much longer. Eventually, they stopped running, and though they were damaged, started stalking their way in as if they had finally pinned down their prey. Ana found Drake back to back with her soon after, so neither of them would be caught off. She also noticed he turned just enough, so she only dealt with one while he dealt with two.

"Ready to run!?" Drake challenged the group of them. Ana was unsure if it was advisable considering their current position.

"We... Don't run... We hunt..." The leader was not as excited as he once was. It wasn't enough to dissuade him, though, as the pack kept getting closer and closer. It was as if they were hoping for Drake and Ana to give up then and there and not bother fighting back. That wasn't going to happen.

Instincts kicked in. Something was different. Ana didn't know how she did it but found herself performing a few quick movements to end the life of the one stalking her. It was the human-faced one that she had damaged before. It dodged the first couple of strikes, but she managed to get a stab that went straight through its skull. Or, at least as straight through as a dull blade crunching through thick bone could be. It was clear by the lack of any vocalized pain, there was no coming back from that attack.

She turned to see Drake in a similar situation. The human-armed one had its throat removed with the same brutality the bandits had done to them. The leader had managed to get his mouth around Drake's exposed neck, but it didn't last long enough to kill. By the time it had made its way there, a claw was already wrapped around its throat tight enough to crush its windpipe. With his prey immobilized with one hand, the rest of it was hard to watch, as strike after strike came though. The sand was soon covered in blood and fur as the final assailant fell before them. Ana let her sword hand fall limp as she looked around to make sure none of the bodies were moving. It wasn't the right order to do things, but she was tired.

"Were they just like us?" Ana took no time asking the question, as Drake was still wiping the remaining blood off of his hands.

"No. Not the same, just similar." Drake answered.

"What do you mean?"

"They were feral. More animal than human."

"How does that make them so bloodthirsty?" Ana was genuinely concerned. Were other hybrids in the bar like this? Was this something she had to worry about turning into? It was certainly on her mind, considering how easily she took out the last one.

Drake answered with another question, "I mean, what makes a coyote bloodthirsty in the first place? As I said, more animal than human. Their instincts had more control over them than their brain did."

"Is there any chance I could wind up like that?" She asked, genuine concern in her voice.

"It's unlikely." Not exactly what Ana wanted to hear, but she'd take it. "If you're going to be feral, it's *usually* right upon fusing. There's only rare cases where one has switched from one side to the other. We should get moving in case they were part of a larger pack." Ana couldn't do more than agree as they kept marching forward. The sun was starting to rise, but they would rather be as far away from the bodies as possible when sleeping.

"What makes them like that?" Ana asked along the way.

"They lost their fight for control when they met their counterparts, simple as that."

"There's a fight for control?" Ana didn't remember anything like that. She remembered a blue light and passing out. That was it.

"Yes, though in your case, a bat is so small it had almost no chance to take you over even without a fight back. Honestly, I'm surprised it took over as much of you as it did."

"Are you calling me weak?" Suddenly she found a reason to be offended.

"That or you found a strong bat." Drake found out that was not the correct response as he got torn into verbally as they went to look for a cave to sleep in. It seemed like it was never going to stop between the "How dare you"s and "Do you remember who you're talking to?". He really wished he never found out she was a princess. Now she threw her weight around like it was nothing. It was annoying.

"And another thing!" She was still going. "Whose hearing saved you back there? You know you couldn't see them coming fast enough. I had you covered."

"They would have broken their teeth off on my leg eventually." Drake denied that she was helpful. He really didn't want to give her an inch. Once again, the wrong response.

"I save your life, and this is the thanks I get. I swear." Ana went on, even knowing she was exaggerating as she would have been mauled to death without him too. Somehow through the back and forth bickering, they found a place to sleep for the night. It was a smaller cave than the last one they had made home in, but this time there wasn't a caravan and a camel to shove in there.

Eventually, there was a length of silence between eating and resting for the night. Ana took second watch. Being more damaged than Drake, she needed her rest first. Using her cloak as her only form of bedroll, she laid down on the harsh mountain rock that she had come to resent more than love. It was then that one more question came to her head.

"Something happened back there. I don't know how I killed it." She stated. Though it wasn't a question, Drake knew he had to answer.

"Bats are predators. You don't just have human instinct anymore. You, yourself, have become a predator."

Ana slept through her half of the day uneasily, the thought of battle weighing heavily on her mind. She was a predator now, with an instinct to kill at a moment's notice. If she couldn't control this, she'd be no different than the beasts she slaughtered.

Chapter 10

The next night was thankfully uneventful. The trip went as quickly as it could, considering the damage to Ana's leg. It felt like no time before they could see the city on the horizon. Ana always liked the look of Arid Retreat from the exterior. To most, it wasn't nearly as beautiful as the inside. Since it was made to be an impenetrable fortress, the walls weren't exactly ornate. Something about the wear in the exterior stone, showing the true power of the desert, as well as the sheer size of the buildings, made it something to behold. It both represented humanity's fight against nature and its inevitable loss if they don't keep it up.

Regardless of how nice it was from the outside, she couldn't deny wanting to get back in so she could sleep in an actual bed. There was more than a minor issue, though. The town was guarded more heavily than usual due to the whole missing princess thing, but each exit had at least one guard on a good day. Also, neither of them were fully covered. Each of their cloaks had at least one tear that revealed fur or scales. In the case of Drake, a lot of scales.

"We might have to climb the walls." Drake informed Ana, ready for a protest.

"Sounds fine to me." She sounded almost excited about it.

"Really?" He was genuinely concerned.

"Wouldn't be the first time I've done it."

Drake wondered, once again, what kind of princess he had found himself with. At least the last argument he expected to have was resolved quickly.

"Admittedly, you'll need to help me up first." Ana noted, motioning to her leg. Something about this journey *really* didn't like that one particular limb. Drake nodded in response, and the two of them decided to take a wide berth around the walls. Far enough away that the guards couldn't see them well, but still close enough for Ana to find the best place to enter. Drake had to admit that, if nothing else, those eyes and ears were beyond useful.

They took about an hour scouting and finding the best place to enter. All of the arches were an immediate no. Sentinels stood guard at each one. They were also exterior guards on patrol, which made it difficult to find a spot in the first place. Ana had guessed she had made enough of a name for herself climbing out the castle walls that it was warranted. It was a valuable skill to have but a double-edged sword considering the tightened security.

Eventually, they settled on one spot in the lower-class district. It was right where the wall intersected with the mountain. The closest entrance was far enough away, and Ana noted the guards were the least on watch out of any of the ones they had seen. Made sense since it was considered a low-priority area, at least in times of peace. The whole reason the lower district got its status was due to being the easiest flank to break. The uneven surface of the wall gave away the repairs that had been done over the years, mostly covering damage from siege weapons. Even now, Ana and Drake found it to be the easiest point of attack, as that previous damage would make the wall easier to scale. Being right up against the mountain helped with the patrols as well. Once the guards got to the edge, they had to turn around, and it left it as one of the most open spots to climb up. It was almost too easy.

The pair hugged the mountain as they snuck their way up to the town. Once they started approaching, they used any jutting out rocks they could for cover, just in case someone caught them moving. The patrols came around every fifteen minutes or so, and they were further away from the city than that time allowed. They took what distance they could, and Ana would inform Drake the moment she could see the patrol so they could duck behind another rock.

It was arduous, but they eventually found themselves right up against the city walls with less than a quarter of an hour to scale it. Normally not an issue, but with Ana's leg, they knew to be cautious.

She went first. Drake helped her up by her good food, so she had something to stand on. The wall itself was about twenty feet high, with barely any proper footholds. Just what the sand had worn away from some of the weaker repairs. Luckily, with the mountain right there, it left one side covered in crags and one side nearly smooth. It just had to be Ana's damaged leg on the side that held most of her weight, making the usually easy climb a test of pain tolerance.

She felt the pain in her leg anytime she put weight on it but was able to make it up without too much of an issue. There was a close call or two, but Drake was down below, ready to catch if something went terribly wrong. He was actually quite surprised at how quickly she made it up, especially with no claws to help her. It brought up questions on whether or not she was actually a princess or was just messing with him. He'd have to drill into her when they got back to the bar.

Unfortunately for Ana, going down the other side didn't have a failsafe. The wall continued against the mountain, which removed her craggy surface, and unlike the castle's shrubbery, there was nothing but a cobblestone street underneath.

The first move she made was simple. Hold onto the top of the wall, leaving her feet dangling, and worst-case scenario, it subtracts her body height from the fall distance. This left a little over fourteen feet, which was still better than twenty.

The second move wasn't as easy. She didn't think it through enough and left her feet blindly looking for a foothold. Of course her damaged leg found one first, and she tried to put weight on it but almost slipped, so instead, she moved her other foot over to it. This didn't help as much as she'd hoped since it left her body angled strangely. This was no time to think too hard, though, and she took the next bump in the wall she could and started to make her way down.

Well, slide her way down.

The moment the second foot found a spot, she lost almost all grip. All Ana could do was hold onto the wall a little bit to slow her fall. It worked, but not perfectly. She couldn't help but let out a short cry of pain upon hitting the stone. It didn't go unheard.

"Princess?" She heard way too close behind her. Crap, crap, and crap again. That was not the word she wanted to hear. Despite the agony, she lifted herself to her feet and attempted to respond. She almost fell over a few times, and the guard made a motion to come and help her. Ana held out her hand in a stopping motion quickly enough that it startled the worker. The more distance they had between them the better.

"Uhh… No?" She tried to mask her voice by making it gruffer. It didn't work.

"Where have you been all this time? His majesty has been worried. We need to bring you back." The guard gained confidence in his deduction and approached her slowly. It seemed he was on his own.

"I told you I'm not the princess." She didn't even try to hide her voice anymore, but she spoke in a warning tone, holding up her hand and backing up slowly. It was barely two steps until she ran out of space and found her back against the wall.

"You can't fool me. Come on now. I was one of the guards for your door early on." He kept coming closer.

"Ugh, fine." The guard thought she was agreeing to come with him. It was all the more of a shock to him when she lowered her cloak to reveal her new face. This stunned him just long enough for a second surprise. Ana made one quick step forward, followed by performing a swift bash to the guard's temple, courtesy of the pommel of her blade. After taking a moment to question whether or not she did still consider herself a princess, she settled on never liking that title. Ana was too caught up with the guard to notice Drake had already landed behind her.

"Do you think it was the smartest idea showing him your face?" He asked.

"What's he going to say? The princess turned into a bat and knocked him out? I think that's a hard enough story to sell." Ana was proud of her logic, though it remained under question. "Well, get moving. It's not exactly like I remember where it is." Ana deflected the possible line of questioning. Luckily for her, Drake didn't want to bother getting into that argument and did as she said.

No matter how much she tried to follow the path, it was just as winding and confusing as last time. She didn't know if the bar was purposely placed somewhere this hard to get, if the lower class district was just this chaotic, or both. She would have asked Drake, but she could already hear him in her head, going on about how 'Straight paths are a luxury' and 'You should be grateful you're even alive' and yadda yadda yadda. This guy was even starting to get boring in her head. Ana could swear she had to deal with fewer lectures back home. One thought of her governess set her back on paying attention, though.

Even upon reaching the hidden door, Ana almost walked right past it. If she ever had to look for this place without help, she'd take more time than their whole trip to Parvus. It never occurred to her that seeing a seedy bar in the middle of nowhere would be such a beautiful sight. The moment the door opened, she was the first one to greet Henry.

"Spent four days in the desert, and you're the first ray of sunshine I've seen." She said to him immediately, to his surprise followed by quick realization.

"He really does suck the life out of you, eh?" He tried to chummily wrap his bear arm around Drake, but the lizard man slipped through and walked right past into the bar.

"Shut up and get me a drink." Were the words of a man that had given up.

"Right to refuse service to anyone, bud." Henry yelled across the bar as Ana walked in past him.

"I swear to god Henry." Drake sounded ready to kill him. After the past few days, Ana could picture it. She could feel the images burned into her memory.

"Anything for his majesty." The bear-man said, grabbing a couple of bottles from behind the bar. One of questionable liquor, but another of white wine fresh and ready for Ana. This guy was good.

Drake threw their pouch of silvers on the counter from the trip, and Henry traded the bottle for them with glee. Ana was lost at the transaction.

"Wait, all of it?" She asked, surprised that they weren't going to keep any.

"Room and board for upwards of 60 guests is difficult, to say the least." Drake responded. "This pulls our weight and then some, for the ones who can't fight or can't work."

It was strange. At first, Ana could swear the amount Drake just handed over was chump change. Now she was kind of angry that she worked for four days straight and got the same amount as someone who did nothing. Before speaking up, she had enough time to remember that was her whole life before this. Doing nothing as the workers poured in taxes. She was glad she dodged that bullet of a conversation topic, but it really made her think about how good she had it.

"Anything exciting happen?" Drake asked Henry after his first couple sips of booze.

"Not much." He responded, polishing off his own glass of god-knows-what. "Oh, Angui came back. That was exciting."

"Oh god, no." Drake had the sound of dread in his voice. Henry couldn't help but give away his excitement.

"Who's Angui?" Ana was curious as to who could terrify Drake.

"Her." Henry said, motioning his head toward someone coming their way. Drake buried his head in the counter, but Ana turned around to see what he was so afraid of. She was surprised to find someone not walking towards them, but *slithering*.

Angui appeared to be half-snake from the waist down. The size of her snake-like body feathered out perfectly into her human half. She was wearing some of the nicest silks Ana had seen, had hair that was clearly taken care of, thick and black and fell nearly to her waist. Finally, the made-up face of a lady of the night, though there was something off about the whole thing. Likely it was the curved scimitar Ana could barely see the hilt of as it perfectly hid against one side of the snake tail. She slithered the rest of the way over with a giant grin on her face.

"How's my favourite ex-target?" She said, chummily getting right into Drake's face.

"Please leave." He said, muffled as he refused to lift his face from the bar.

"Target?" Ana asked, clearly falling into the snake's conversational trap.

"Oh, he hasn't told you about me?" It was clear this was a question Angui already knew the answer to. She turned to Ana and left her hand out in introduction. "I'm Angui. It's nice to meet you."

"Don't listen to her. She's a snake." Drake shot his head up before Ana could respond.

"I can see that?" Ana was confused as to what the problem was. "I'm Ana." She took Angui's hand and shook it. The grip was incredible, much like her brother's. Which is saying something, considering he's captain of the guard. "What do you mean by target?" She had to know.

"The first time we met, she tried to kill me." Drake complained, shocking Ana in the process.

"Can't you just let bygones be bygones?" Angui said in her charming voice.

"Wait, really?" Ana tried to turn to someone who would give her a straight answer. Realizing the two people in front of her were Drake and Angui, she turned to Henry, who nodded in response. "You tried to kill him?"

"Fiesty little bugger wouldn't fall for my charm or my blade." Ana could swear Angui hissed after she said that. She had no idea whether to hate this woman or be mystified by her. Instead, Ana just stayed to the side to see what would happen.

"Yet you keep trying." Drake moaned.

"Lies." Angui definitely hissed that time.

"Go slither away and eat a rat or something." Drake looked ready to throw a glass at her head.

"I already bothered Earl tonight." Angui shot a look over at another table, where a man with white fur and a rat tail shook his head. "He's gotten boring." Ana could swear she was in some kind of fever dream.

"Why did she want to kill you?" Ana asked Drake, but the snake answered.

"Dragon scales are worth a lot, and I needed the money." Angui said all too quickly, inspecting her hand lavishly to make sure it was up to standard. Or it could have been just to bother Drake. Or both.

Ana couldn't believe what she was hearing. "But... Dragons aren't real." Her voice was deadpan, still denying her colleague's claims. Angui burst out into laughter.

"Another one who doesn't believe you? Must be hard, being all mythical and fake." Angui got way too close to Drake yet again. He whacked her away with the back end of his claw. Angui slithered back a foot and hissed. "Did you forget I bite?" She seemed ready to strike at a moment's notice but soon simmered back down to charming. This woman was insanity incarnate.

"I thought all you did was spit." Drake narrowed his eyes at her.

"Oh, don't you wish." Angui put a hand on the hilt of her sword. Ana moved from the seat next to Drake until she had at least two stools in between them.

"Henry?" Ana asked, concerned.

"Yes?" Henry replied, unconcerned.

"Do something." Ana couldn't take her eyes off of the two deadly combatants getting ready to tear each other's throats out in the middle of a bar. Though, it did surprise her that the thing Henry decided to do was take her drink away and get a fresh glass. He uncorked a new bottle of wine and began to pour it. This one was a deep red and looked to be from an old vintage.

"Fortified." He explained. "It'll help."

"I meant help with these two!" Ana exclaimed.

"What? Do you want me to get in between them? If so, you're insane." After he finished topping up her glass. Right to the rim, as a matter of fact. He chugged down some of the bottle himself before putting it away.

The fight never really started. Both Drake and Angui continued to rant at each other for what felt like hours, requesting drink refills in between. It eventually got to a point Henry found the right beats to top them up without them even asking.

"Are they always like this?" Ana asked, having completely lost her care for the situation an hour ago. Coincidentally, that was after the second glass of wine.

"Oh no, not at all." Henry replied seriously, to Ana's surprise. "They're usually much worse." And there it was.

"How can you stand it?"

"Are you kidding me? I've got the best seat in town. Especially considering I have a bar I can duck under if things go flying."

"Do they usually?" Ana asked. Right on cue, a glass crashed right behind Henry.

"Hey, leave me out of this!" He said, ignoring Ana's shocked expression.

"Then shut up about us!" The drunken lizard and snake replied in unison.

Henry turned back to Ana, "See what I mean? Match made in heaven." Immediately after, he ducked as two more empty glasses came flying over his head. They would have hit him directly too. Ana could swear she got hit by a shard somewhere but didn't know where.

"I think I'm going to turn in for the night." Ana said, keeping one eye on the rising tensions way too close to her head.

Henry poked his head up, a look of absolute terror on his face from what he had done. "Don't blame you." He said quietly before slinking back down. Ana's sensitive hearing could make out the sound of another cork being removed from a bottle behind the bar.

Thank god for Ana, the door to her room was not past the battlezone, so she could slink away easily. Apparently, it was just in time, as a loud crash that could be heard by anyone rang in her ears. It was followed by Henry yelling, "You're going to have to start paying for those!" And Angui returning, "You know I'm good for it." Ana had no idea what she had gotten into but hoped whatever it was cleared itself up by morning.

When Ana opened the door to her new room, she found to her surprise, a lit candle on the desk. Henry really did think well of his patrons, and she would have to thank him in the morning for preparing it for her. She'd also have to thank him for the heavy doses of wine that got her through that night. Ana took off her dusty clothes, blew out the candle, and laid down for the night.

It was then that it hit her. Between the throbbing pain in her cut leg, the lack of reward for her work, and just how uncomfortable she was, this wasn't the life for her. She wanted to see the desert, but not like this. She knew she had to go home, and it would have to be soon. Maybe she would sneak in and see Kasibel first? It was a hard choice. Then there was the question of what she was going to do for the people here. These were citizens. Somehow they were considered outlaws, but they were people of the city who did nothing but try and better it. It was then her mind was made up.

There's only one person she could see about this, only one person who had control over the laws. As of the next night, she would go to the castle and talk to her father.

Chapter 11

Ana expected the night to be long as she had plenty weighing on her mind. Instead it turned out after four straight days of mercenary work, sleeping isn't difficult. Waking up on the other hand was quite the task, let alone getting out of bed. The sheer amount of fortified wine she downed didn't help the matter, either. Thinking of that, she wondered if anything was left of the bar. She decided it was best to take at least an extra half hour before going out there and dealing with it.

Though her sleep was good, she knew this day would be anything but. She would either have to sneak back into the castle or try and get one of the guards to escort her in. The one from the previous night who refused to believe she wasn't the princess was likely an exception. If anything, the rest of them would never consider the thought. There was also going to be the problem of the castle walls since there's no way she'd be bringing Drake along on this one, so scaling them was out of the question.

Ana admitted her ignorance but was smart enough to know telling anyone where she was going wouldn't be good. None of them knew her father like she did. She knew she could talk sense into him, while everyone else would likely be afraid he'd launch a full-scale attack. He wasn't that kind of man, though. Sure, he had his problems with Ingress, but as long as he was willing to take her back in the first place, he'd be willing to help these people out. If there's anything Ana knew he cared about, it was his own people. During her lessons there was no denying that.

The next problem came with keeping a poker face throughout the day. Opening the door to the bar and seeing the state of it, she knew it would be easy for at least the first bit. She would instead be distracted by the sight that greeted her.

"How...?" She asked to the empty air, as most in front of her were still passed out. The bar wasn't in much worse shape than when she left it, but she didn't expect to see Drake and Angui passed out together on the floor with the stupidest smiles plastered on their faces as they snored away. Ana needed answers and knew where to find them.

She made her way behind the bar and gave a swift kick to a big fuzzy bear arm propping up the bartender's head. Henry woke with a jolt.

"Huh?" He asked in a drunken daze, rubbing his eye with his human hand.

"What, in the gods' names, did I miss?" She asked, both concerned and intrigued.

"Oh yeah, those two." Henry shook his head to try and get his thoughts straight. "You see, Drake doesn't really hate her because she tried to kill him. You should have heard the two of them singing. T'was both beautiful and terrifying."

"Singing!?" Ana's face contorted into a twist of surprise, awe, and the tiniest bit of disgust.

"I told you you'd be dead if you told her, Henry." Drake popped his head up from behind the bar, a look of pure hellfire in his eyes.

"Geez, thanks for ratting me out, kid." Henry gave a disapproving look to Ana.

"Don't try and pin this on me." Ana stood her ground. "Also, I need breakfast."

"Oh good, he's rubbing off on you." Henry complained, though he loved the chance to slink away from his soon-to-be murderer. Ana then took a seat next to Drake on the other side of the still passed-out snake.

"Singing?" She asked with a raised eyebrow.

"I'm willing to kill two today if I have to." It appeared to be a sensitive topic, yet Ana wasn't about to let it go forever. For now, she'd rather keep her head, but this would come back later.

"So, really. What's up with her anyway?" Ana asked, trying to change the subject. It didn't calm him down much, but it at least turned his attention away.

"Probably one of the best money makers for this bar, yet one of the dirtiest." He explained, leaning in to speak quietly into Ana's bat ear, keeping his voice so low even he could barely hear it. To Ana, it was loud and clear. "Don't let her know who you are." Ana nodded in understanding and didn't need it to be spelled out for her that she was looking at an assassin. It was sad to see that someone would have to stoop so low to make a living. If anything, Ana noted that if this place was brought up to legality, she should still be tried for what she was. For now, she was in no position to speak, but hated anyone who killed in anything but self defence or for their country.

Henry soon came out with whatever meat he was able to procure this week. Turned out to be lamb, which wasn't the worst. Ana did wonder how hybrids thought when it came to eating livestock they may have fused with. It brought up moral questions she didn't want answered.

"So, how are you planning on spending your day?" Henry asked Ana. "I assume you're not going out on another expedition so soon."

"Absolutely not." She recoiled at the thought but then realized she had to come up with a lie. "I hadn't thought about it yet." Well, a half-lie, at least.

"Don't waste the days you get free. They can be few and far between." He assured her. It wasn't a thought she liked. The idea of going out constantly like this to keep one tavern running and being confined to that same tavern on a daily basis. It was a life she didn't want to lead. It was a life no one should have to lead.

"I might browse the market." She said out loud. It was a genuine thought, as she did enjoy seeing what relics might be up for sale, even if she couldn't buy them.

"Please don't." Drake said, his eyes widening remembering their first meeting.

"Relax, I know what I'm dealing with now." She gave some reassuring laughter, though it was clearly nervous. It was apparent she had to get out as quickly as possible, so her plan wasn't revealed. "I didn't exactly know I was a hybrid that day." Rushing out too fast would also be suspicious, so she figured a short conversation shouldn't hurt.

"You planning on bringing that with you?" Drake motioned to her sword.

"Oh, right." Ana completely forgot the thing was stolen. It didn't really matter if she left it here, though. Her father wouldn't allow her to have such a weapon in her room, and it lost its value the moment it saw modern combat. No one would ever be able to tell the fake wear from real anymore. Even Ana's amateur eyes as a collector could tell many of the scratches were fresh. When it came to protection, it would also be useless, as if she got into a fight with her father's soldiers, that would be it, weapon or not.

"I think I'll join you." Drake said, much to Ana's dismay. How was she ever going to escape if he was with her? Not only was he the last person she wanted to know about her plan, his watch was like a hawk.

"I'll be fine on my own." She said stubbornly, prepared to fight about it. He didn't even state he was going to look after her, but the gamble paid off as that was the route he was taking.

"And how are you going to find your way back here? You yourself told me how much you'd be lost." Drake raised an eyebrow.

"How am I going to learn to find it if I don't try?" She pulled out a good point, and it was hard for him to counter. He found a way to regardless.

"Risking it this early could compromise you completely."

"Aww, you don't want to see me killed." She went in straight for the 'You really DO care.' line.

"It would be inconvenient." Drake was unhappy with where this was going.

"I'll be fine." She said, polishing off the last of her food and standing. "I'll leave the sword behind, and I won't *compromise* you." Ana was becoming a master at pushing Drake's buttons.

"Fine, but if you go and die, I'll hunt you down and kill you again." Strangely enough, that was the most reassuring thing she had heard all morning. It meant he wasn't going to follow her, at least not noticeably. Ana took the victory where she could.

She broke away as soon as possible, leaving less of a chance for any slip-ups. Barely halfway back to her room and she found herself looking over her shoulder, making sure Drake wasn't watching her. Ana already knew it was a habit she'd have to break in the next few minutes, as it made anyone look suspicious. The guards might even come at her with that kind of behaviour.

It was upon laying down the relic on her bed Ana had one quick thought. Maybe there was a reason these people didn't want her to go back home. It could be a good reason. Perhaps her father *would* kill everyone here without even batting an eye. If hybrids were hidden from her perhaps he was hostile towards them. She threw the thought out of her head the moment she had it. She knew him. He would never condone such pointless bloodshed. They might be scared of him, but there was nothing to be scared of. Her mind hit another place that maybe some of them, like Angui, wouldn't want to get found out by the king. It would leave her jobless, considering her set of skills, and likely in the dungeon. But hybrids like that deserved it, right?

Ana shook her head to clear it out. She had already made her decision the night before. This was the only path available. Any other one would leave her wondering for the rest of her life what would have happened if she just went back home. Following in the footsteps of the hybrids here, or even fleeing the country, would leave her missing her own bed. It would leave that chance on the table. It had to be either taken or removed, and the sooner, the better.

As she closed the door behind her, she couldn't help but wonder if she was leaving another life behind. That sword staying on that bed unused. It was another thought she had to get rid of. It's not like she enjoyed the battles in the desert or the sore feet. Somewhere inside her, though, she couldn't help but admit the predator did.

The hall back to the bar was fine, as there were few people around. The few that were she didn't know, so it was easy enough to act natural. Upon opening the door to the bar, it was like she had forgotten how to walk. Every step was taken slightly differently as she either forgot to bend her legs, tried to walk on the tips of her toes, or just plain stalled and looked around the room as if someone was going to attack her. Even if Drake could somehow ignore the strange behaviour due to her damaged leg, the pools of sweat coming from her forehead gave the rest away.

"Heading out now?" He asked, and it practically made her jump.

"Yes, yes, yes, right now, heading out to the market!" Come on, Ana, none of those were the right words or the right order.

"You sure you don't want help?" Drake asked, genuinely concerned for her wellbeing. Something was definitely up, but he didn't want to go digging in it. He'd find something too fast he didn't want to see.

"Yes, sure, of course I don't." That was closer, but still not quite it.

"Alright then." He said, not breaking eye contact for an uncomfortable amount of time. Even when he did let up, the corner of his eye was still lurking on her. "Enjoy your day out, then."

“Thank you.” There we are. Too little too late, though. Ana decided to give up and practically bolted for the door. This brought her to another problem. Even from the inside, she didn’t know exactly where it was or how to open it. She stood at the wall for an awkward amount of time before finally turning around and yelling out, “Henry!”

The bartender rolled his eyes as he made his way over. If anyone out there was a morning person, it wasn’t Henry. He practically dragged his paw behind him on the way, giving Ana a disapproving look the whole time. She wondered if he had figured something out, but it was soon apparent that it was quite the opposite.

Henry looked at Ana, back to the wall, and back to her again. He pushed on the woodwork with his human arm, showing that it took almost no strength to do and showing that the wall was very, *very* clearly marked from the inside. It was only Ana’s overthinking head that kept her from seeing the way out.

“Thank you.” She said meekly and quickly before slowly making her way out. Before pulling her hood down and wandering off into the street, the last thing she saw was Henry burying his face in his bear paw. It was clear he had had enough for the day.

If there was anything Ana overestimated that day, it was her sense of direction. The amount of twists and turns it took to get to and from that bar was insane. At the very least, she could tell where the castle was from her starting point, but that turned out to not help much. As she tried to make her way to it, she found herself turned around more than once. She could even swear she walked past the bar an extra time but still wasn’t entirely sure since the door was so hidden. At this rate, it was going to take all day just to get out of here. It was a shame because she really did want to browse the market before her inevitable meeting.

If nothing else, she at least made it away from Drake. If he ever caught wind of this, she was sure he’d somehow lock her down just as bad as her father did. It was still hard to believe not a single hybrid tried to plead their case with the king. She knew they couldn’t have tried. If they did, they wouldn’t be at such a low point.

As if some kind of miracle occurred, more than an hour of being lost in thought Ana stumbled her way into the main street of the lower quarter. It was lucky she noticed, too, as it wasn’t much wider than the alleys she’d been traversing. The only thing that gave it away was the opening to the desert that she came out next to, which also told her she was as far away from her goal as can possibly be. No matter, since that just meant it was a straight line there.

One thing Ana never had a good look at until now was the lower quarter. Every moment she had spent here, time was an issue. The first instance was running from the guards, then trying to make it out to work, and finally, breaking into the city the night before. The disparity between the two sides of Arid Retreat was shocking. Where the beautiful stonework of the upper classes deteriorated into the barely held together sandstone, wood, and straw huts of those less fortunate was a line that was all too easy to see. It was clear the guards had forsaken this place, too, as the few that were around clearly didn't want to be.

It wasn't something she had to worry about now but knew it would come up in the future. At least if she had a future. Historically it was a divide like this that caused uprisings. Monarchs have been overthrown for less. It seemed even if she did make it back to her royal status, her work wouldn't be done quite yet.

The last thing Ana noticed she couldn't help but sneer at. Upon crossing over into the beautiful marble and other fine stones that houses had been made out of, she started recognizing faces. It was hard to keep herself from staring, but she managed to keep her head down and her hood over. The nobles she had met that lived around here barely did anything. The odd merchant lord did keep his nose to the grindstone and run a successful business, but most were here because of their name. They had land in some kingdom that made it worthwhile for them to be kept close. Many of the houses were even vacant. Vacation homes for nobles from other countries to come and enjoy their stay. Substantial, beautiful buildings that shadowed over the lower class, and they weren't used for anything more than recreation. Ana was almost sick that she came from that life and even considered turning away from her current quest.

She was convinced she couldn't help from the ground nearly as much as she could from the throne, though. Just a couple hours in the market and then somehow make it into the castle. The tricky part would be not getting caught on the way in. That bridge would have to be crossed in the dark. For now, the wares from the world sprawled out before her. The stalls lining the street differentiated themselves by different cloth banners and various curiosities at their tables. For the first time in a week, she felt genuine excitement as she saw some vendors with war relics again and hurried her way over as she was a moth to the flame. After all, she was only one step up the food chain.

She usually would hate viewing a crowded stall, but today it worked to her advantage to blend in. It was strange that so many were crowding around a historical vendor. Normally these guys had a very niche market that included high-paying nobles such as herself. Today everyone was interested. One of the items on display was an old rolled-up sheet of paper that even the odd passerby would know the value of.

Her large black eyes lit up like the sun. The broken seal on that paper was the old crest of Rexharne from a few hundred years back. The tattered edges of papyrus that stood the test of time, clearly made to last but having taken damage along the way. The discolouration that showed off the true age of the piece. What everyone was fawning over was one of the first official declarations of war with Ingress. It was in almost too good condition for what it was, and it took everything Ana had to keep from reaching out and reading those ancient words. Words that caused so much bloodshed, so much violence, but that shaped the very borders of the kingdoms this continent now saw. It was intoxicating. She practically had to have it.

Urges can only be resisted for so long. It started with working her way to the front of the crowd, where the merchant was going on about how amazing his other relics were. He was clearly leading up to the big piece on the table everyone had their eyes on. Eventually, he got to the piece in question, and Ana started listening as he started going on about it.

"...and this, my friends." He said in his charming, chummy voice. "Is the, and I repeat, THE first-ever declaration of war sent from our great nation to our now friends at the borders, Ingress." Ana couldn't help but clear her throat at the misinformation. It was a really early piece, but it was clearly not the first. The first was before the Rexharne name even known the sands of Arid Retreat as this was once Ingress territory. That aside, it wasn't even the first one after they were in. She had to keep quiet, though. The merchant continued.

"It was delivered nearly two hundred years ago." It was much closer to four hundred. Ana was almost twitching with anger. "The original messenger brought it along by way of one of our finest camels." He travelled on foot, not wanting to draw suspicion to himself before he got there. This guy had no idea what he was talking about. "And it was on that fateful day that it was delivered to the Ingress monarch," Emperor "King Nicol the fourth!"

"Third." Ana finally spoke up, and it wasn't as quiet as she wanted to.

"Excuse me?" The merchant stopped and walked his way over to the corner of the stall where she was standing.

"It was Nicol the Third that this piece would have been delivered to." She wasn't about to back down. Misinformation was her enemy. "And while I'm at it, this wasn't the first declaration of war with Ingress; it was the fifth. The messenger travelled on foot to deliver it to keep a low profile, yet was still killed on his way there by an Ingress soldier who was actually the one to deliver it to the emperor. Finally, it was exactly four hundred and seventy-eight years ago that it happened, not nearly two hundred. Even someone with the most simple amount of historical knowledge in their head would know that." Ana was almost out of breath by the end of her corrections. How can someone selling this stuff know so little? His anger soon met hers, though, as salespeople don't like being interrupted in the middle of a pitch.

"So, you think you know *so* much about history, do you!?" He was clearly furious, and his voice raised to the point it carried out over the crowd. "Why don't you show us that face so I can see who could possibly know more than *I* about my own products."

Ana had to take a step back to keep him from pulling down her hood, but she wasn't about to stay silent. "Anyone who studied the history of this kingdom for a *second* would know it better than you would. You're a sad excuse for a merchant, you know that?" She spoke her heart. She knew it would backfire but knew she was already in too deep.

"Not willing to show your face? Know so much about ancient history?" He was speaking loudly but not yelling anymore. It sounded awkward. Just another thing this merchant had wrong with his head, she figured.

"It's not even ancient history. Ancient history denotes at least a thousand years prior to the current date. How can you have such an eye for relics and be so ignorant of them? That piece is wasted in your possession." Ana made a point. His stock was almost perfectly curated. It was then, she realized something was wrong. He had a nearly perfect document that even stated the date it was delivered but didn't know that date. No merchant could be this incompetent.

It was too late for her to notice as she was already held hard by both shoulders. One guard on either side kept her from moving. This was a trap set specifically for her. She hated to admit it, but her father was a genius and probably had this stall running since she left the castle. If she was in town, it was only a matter of time before that document drew her, and the guards were at the ready.

"Princess Anachorita, I presume." The one on her right-hand side said. Her hand was tight on Ana's shoulder with no sign of moving off of it. Ana stayed silent, but it didn't help. "Fine, if you want to stay quiet, I'll check for myself." It was then the guard reached for her hood. Ana struggled to try and get free before they pulled it down to see what was underneath, but to no success. Soon, the whole crowd and even the merchant gasped at the bat face that lay hidden. If nothing else, this would dissuade them from thinking she was the princess.

"Yep, this is definitely her." The same guard nodded to the other. Ana was confused as if it was some strange joke, but it didn't seem that way. "Come with us, princess. Your father's been worried sick."

Oh, this was getting all too weird. The two of them started walking her along, and she had no choice but to follow. Not only did they not deny she was their target, but the female guard referred to the king simply as 'Your father'. No one was that casual with the king except his own personal guard that stayed posted in the throne room at all times. He really did pull out all the stops to find her, which she supposed she shouldn't be surprised at, but then not recoiling at the fact she was a hybrid now? How could they know? How could they ever expect such a thing? Did her father know something she didn't?

Well, if nothing else, her way into the castle just got much easier, but her game plan became thrown into whack. The last thing she expected was her father to already know she was a hybrid. There were a lot of questions, and Ana started preparing the moment she was found out. Now, it was only a matter of if she was being taken to the throne room for a meeting or the dungeon for execution.

Chapter 12

Ana couldn't be more relieved to be escorted to the throne room. It wasn't the way she wanted to have this meeting, but at the very least she wasn't being thrown in the dungeon. Though depending on how this went, that was still a possibility.

It had been a while since she had entered the throne room. Usually it was to be avoided, since it was where all the important meetings were held with other kingdoms and nobles. The rich and powerful do value their privacy, after all. Generally a throne room would be a place for hospitality in a castle. Lush carpets, beautiful seating, a place for ceremony. This was not the case for Arid Retreat. This was an intimidation chamber. The throne itself was the only thing that had any semblance of beauty. It was large and covered in red velvet, with ornate and detailed carving done throughout the dark wood that made up most of its composition. This particular chair was commissioned in the image of Ana's father's takeover of the throne. A bloody affair that involved rallying his own regimen of soldiers and countrymen after they had been sent out on a suicide mission by Ana's grandfather. The King sat upon it proudly, being illuminated by the three large windows that faced his back. Someone could easily lose themself in his spot and consider themself a god.

As for the rest of the room's design, it was as if it was meant to turn off anyone who entered. The castle itself did have nice spots to eat and take a break. Not here. You weren't even given so much as a chair. You were to do your business and leave. That was that. The walls were the roughest in the stronghold, nothing but bare sandstone, and there was no carpet save for a small spot under the throne for the King's feet.

The last feature of the room was the real intimidation. Typically, the King's guard would be stationed here, but it appeared they were all out looking for Ana. The King wouldn't leave this place unguarded, though, and today the room was staffed by the Red Guard. Even Ana didn't know much about them, aside from they were known for getting things done when none of the other soldiers could. Because of this, much of the army resented them or wanted to work their way up to join their ranks. Though it had been rumoured that the ranks of the Red Guard hadn't changed in over thirty years. It was unclear how accurate the rumour was.

The elite soldiers themselves wore facial coverings so they wouldn't get noticed outside of their line of work. Their oversized vibrant red cloaks kept any other features from being seen as well. The only thing they gave away was their country as the proud emblem of the Rexharne kingdom was embroidered on their backs, a roaring gold lion. Every one of them looked exactly the same, with the exception of the leader's mask having a large horn jutting out the front of it. This made him all the more intimidating compared to the rest of the crew.

Even if they weren't here, the King was, and he was all too intimidating in his own right. King Rolfe was not a small man, and the Rexharne throne was always taken from the previous owner by combat, so he had seen his share of battle. Of course, since it was in the family, the fight wasn't *usually* to the death, though there were rare cases. The battle between Ana's father and grandfather was one of the exceptions. The man sitting in front of Ana that day looked initially unimpressed, his finger tapping on the armrest of the throne. He adorned his ceremonial crown and red cloak, which covered all except his face and quite frankly magnificent golden beard.

Ana's heart pounded in her chest as the guards that brought her in did the favour of pulling her hood back up. This made her more worried than she otherwise would have been since her father piqued with interest upon them making it halfway through the room. What was he going to say?

"What is the meaning of this?" The King asked. His voice boomed through the room like the roar of the very lion his flag had upon it.

"We... Believe we have your daughter, sir." The female guard let go of Ana's shoulder and saluted her king.

"Ana?" His voice immediately changed. It was much softer. There was a look in his eyes that broke through the exterior presence he let off. It was that of a man's broken heart who had been fixed in an instant. He leapt up from his throne and started slowly making his way to the centre of the room like he couldn't believe his eyes. "Is that you, Ana?"

It was difficult for her to speak. The hood over her head covered her until now, but her words would start giving her away. For a moment she even thought of denying that she was his daughter, but the look in his eyes was too much to take. Through tears of homesickness that Ana didn't even know she had, her lips quivered as she answered. "Yes."

The fear elevated as the man before her almost jumped with joy. The warrior king of a war-torn sandy kingdom had made a noise you may expect from a small child with delight. "Are you hurt? Where have you been?" He got closer to her, but Ana recoiled, much to the king's surprise. "Ana? Something must have happened." He shooed his guards off, all of them. The two that came with Ana and the Red Guard as well. Initially, the Red Guard didn't move. "Off with you then! Leave me and my girl in private." The leader of the guard went to protest before the king gave him a look that told him it was a very, very bad idea to do so. In unison, the elite soldiers made their way out of the room, their cloaks dragging behind them as if they were all some sort of phantoms.

"Father I..." Ana started before cracking up again. What had she done? She didn't even think about how her family truly felt. Hopefully, he'd understand why she was so afraid to come home.

"What happened, Ana? Why won't you let me see your face?" He asked with the most genuine concern.

"Because..." She started to pull herself together. "I'm not sure I'm ready." She paused for a moment. "I'm not sure you're ready."

"Whatever could you mean, child?" He asked. Ana decided she would be leading on a broken man if she kept going. She couldn't tell him before pulling down the hood. That was too hard. Getting regular words out was hard enough right now. One physical motion was all it would take. Her hands still trembled as they made their way up to the hood of her cloak. Initially, she had pulled it tighter by instinct.

"It's... difficult." She said in the calmest voice she could.

"Take your time." He said in the most reassuring tone. A tone she had missed for far too long. She made the decision quickly to pull down her hood. She made it so fast that her hands weren't allowed to protest the response. In one swift motion, it was out in the open, her face for her father to see. The fur, the ears, the black beady eyes. All of them were out in the open now. Her hands tried to reel themselves back, regretting the decision, but Ana wouldn't let them until she saw his reaction.

The first part was expected. Shock, it seemed. He reeled back at the sight. He even brought his hand up in a guarding position, which wasn't exactly the reassuring feeling she was looking for, but the moment passed. The king regained his composure and pretended to dust off his already spotless robe awkwardly, looking for the words to say. The room was silent for all too long. And it stayed silent as King Rolfe ran up and hugged his daughter tightly.

Now it was Ana's turn to be surprised. It was an embrace she had felt before, but it never felt better than it did right now. No words had to be said. The father wanted nothing more than to have his daughter back. It didn't matter what had happened to her, in that moment, he accepted her. That was what she wanted. That was what she needed. It would still remain a question whether her life would go back to normal, but right now, it didn't matter. Right now, a family was reunited.

"Dad I…" She tried to speak. Tried to explain what happened, but her father just held her tighter. The time for talking was soon, but he didn't want to let go just yet. After a few minutes, he finally did and took a step back to give his daughter some space.

King Rolfe cleared his throat and looked around awkwardly like any dad would who had shown too much emotion. He then finally spoke. "This was my fault. I'm sorry."

"What do you mean?" She asked with worry in her heart.

"I never told you about them. Hybrids. I never told you something like this could happen to you, but here you are before me." He still sounded shocked. At least he knew about them, but why hadn't he told her? "Quite honestly, I didn't believe it myself, that I could lose that precious face that had grown up in this castle for so long."

The tears came back to Ana's eyes as she clenched her fists. "I'm sorry." She spoke. She didn't know what she was apologizing for but felt she needed to do it. Perhaps it was her fault for killing the image he had of his daughter.

"Dear, there's nothing to be sorry for. Perhaps my grip was too tight on you here. It was only natural that you'd take a chance to explore when the chance presented itself." The king forced out a chuckle, "Now, of course, I'm not ready to let you go roaming the city streets after I had just got you back. I think that's at least fair."

Ana forced out an awkward laugh, but a question came to her mind. One she wanted to ask since she first found out what she was. "Why?" She asked. He only responded with a questioning "Hm?" as her voice was too low. She repeated herself. "Why didn't you tell me about them? Why keep me in the dark about a whole race of people?" Her tone went from worried to outright accusatory.

"Oh yes, of course. I figured you'd ask that." He almost seemed to stall for time, as if he wasn't ready to answer. "It was for... political reasons."

"Political?" Ana reeled back the accusation in her voice. Even if she was his daughter, stepping out of line in front of the King was never the best idea. She felt even pushing the topic might have been going too far.

"Yes, political, well, for two reasons, to be exact." Thankfully, he didn't seem angry. "The first is I knew the moment you heard about an oppressed group, you would be the type to want to integrate them immediately. The civilians aren't ready for that just yet, but I knew you'd push."

"And the other reason?" Ana almost asked impatiently, but she managed to be as elegant as her teachings would allow her.

"I didn't want to worry you with that burden." He said, hanging his head low. "You're my daughter. A princess. In a time of peace like this, you shouldn't have to worry about the struggles around you. You should enjoy your life while you have the time to."

"But isn't it my job to worry about things like that? Sure, I'm not in positions like you and Kasibel are, with actual control over the kingdom, but I am a figurehead. I'm someone that should be able to connect with her people. *All* her people. Didn't you think of that?"

"I suppose I didn't." The King responded, becoming much more short with his tone. He awkwardly paced his throne room, hands behind his back, with a lot to think about. "For now, my mistakes aside, I'm just glad to have you back."

Ana took a moment to take in those words. They felt warm and calming. She still knew it wasn't going to be easy from here. A hybrid princess isn't exactly something the people wanted to see, but for now, she needed to relax. But really though, there was only one chair in this room, and she had been too uncomfortable for far too long. "Dad?" She asked.

"Yes, dear?"

"Mind if I sit on the throne? My legs hurt." She said in the most honest voice.

The king's laughter boomed through the room as she asked the question. Initially, she worried it was crossing a line. She hadn't even gone near the throne since she was a small child, but as with many other moments today, her worries faded away as her father said, "Yes, yes, of course! I can only imagine the accommodations that you had to settle in for the past few days."

Ana didn't say another word but instead quickly made her way over to the plush chair to have a seat. She had sunk right into it. If no one else could be comfortable in this room, at the very least, royalty could be. Ana was reminded that she was royalty that day, half-bat or not. What mattered was that she was accepted by the royal family. She knew she would have to enjoy her time, though, as there would be much to discuss in the very near future.

Chapter 13

Ana never thought she'd be looking at her room with so much joy. Just a week ago, she hated this place and wanted to leave, but between the books, the open space, and most importantly, the bed, it took her no time to get in and lay down.

It didn't feel normal at first. She thought it was because it had been too long but soon figured out that one of her bat ears had flopped over on itself. That was still something she'd have to get used to. Not everything was quite the same as before. It was similar enough, though. Admittedly, falling asleep was a bit more difficult as her mind wasn't as clear as it could be.

Ana wanted to get back into everything around her. She wanted to sleep in her nice bed, wanted to read history until the sun came up, and wanted to devour absolutely everything in the kitchen. The last task would be the most difficult one since she was understandably confined to that room of hers again. Not that it mattered. This time it was where she wanted to be.

She had worked out an agreement with her father before coming up here. Wandering the castle at all was completely forbidden. If any staff saw their new princess, it might cause an uprising, which Ana understood. Instead, she was given one guard from the king's staff to be on top of her at all times. He would bring her food and whatever else she needed. Ana did feel a bit guilty pulling aside one of the staff like this, but it was necessary considering the circumstances.

There was one thing she couldn't help but wonder. Would Drake and Henry be looking for her? They likely wouldn't. She was just some new face that disappeared after a few nights. It wasn't like she was a regular that had been going there for years. Though there was a good chance Drake would figure out what she did, by the time they spoke again she would be able to tell him she was right. That Princess Ana had brought hybrids back into society where they should be. The thought was quickly pushed out of her head as a knock on her door snapped her back to the real world.

"Yes?" She asked, her royal demeanour coming through now that she was back in her chambers.

"The tea you ordered, your highness." Came the very straight answer from the other side of the door. It was Calvin, her appointed guard. She liked him enough, but he followed demands a bit inorganically, as her father would say all good soldiers should.

"Come in." She said, trying to mock his wooden tone. The door creaked open to an array of ornate silver trays filled with tea and tiny scones. Ana had already begun to miss the sheer amount of food Henry offered her and the ability to not eat it like royalty. Her manners needed work even before she had left, and it was a good thing no one could see her eat. Seventeen years of etiquette was completely undone by a week in the slums.

The guard placed the tray on her desk off to the side of the room. "Thank you, Calvin." She said as she made her way over. He backed away immediately to give her some space, which meant it was time to have a bit of fun. "What? Does my new face scare you?"

"N-no." He answered, stuttering through his words. That was win number one, as she broke his wooden demeanour. "I, of course, am just giving the lady space." He bowed as low as he could. "You are just as beautiful as you were before you left."

Oh, now it was time to have a field day. Ana started up in the sassiest voice she could muster. "Oh? So you think I, the fairest princess of Rexharne, nay, the *world*, had features that were no better than that of a flying rodent?" Calvin was sweating now. You could swear he was starting to fear for his life.

His brain was locked in a paradox. He couldn't say she looked more beautiful before, as it would insult her now. He also couldn't not agree with the royalty he was charged with. It looked like he was about to pop a blood vessel before Ana decided to lighten the mood.

"Calvin, Calvin, Calvin..." She started, breaking back into a more comfortable commoner's tone. "If you're just going to let me mess with you like that, you'll have a heart attack by the end of the week."

"If you excuse me, I think I'm about to have one now, princess." Calvin took a deep breath and let out a sigh of relief. It wasn't every day you had to have your whole existence questioned and then given back in the course of a minute.

Ana couldn't help but laugh at him and had to calm down before dismissing him with a "Very well." It was difficult hearing the title princess again, even though it had only been a week. She figured since this was the only person she'd be interacting with, she gave him one last instruction before he walked away. "And Calvin?"

"Yes, my lady?"

"Please just refer to me as Ana. I'm finding it hard to get used to the title again." She stayed completely open with him. Something about him allowed Ana to let her guard down, but the attempt at honesty didn't completely go as planned. You could tell by the look on his face that he thought this was another trick.

"But your highness...." He was worried, to say the least.

"It's fine. Do it only if you can. I understand your position." Ana was as genuine as genuine could be.

"It's an honour serving you as always, your...." He paused for a moment and considered the request. "Ana." You could tell it was hard to get out and had a weird taste on his tongue. Ana smiled in response.

"Thank you, Calvin. You're dismissed and feel free to sit down by the door. Standing all day has to be hell on your legs." She knew that more than anyone after her week. Calvin closed the door behind him, and she was entirely sure he would stay standing for the next eight or so hours. It was hard watching them be so loyal and beat themselves up over the slightest slip up in words. That was the one thing she hated about the castle. The tea, on the other hand, was absolutely delicious. Almost worth the questionable servitude around her.

She couldn't help but stare at herself from time to time in her full-length mirror. Everything had gone by so fast she didn't even know the extent of her transformation until she was back in the kingdom. Not only did she barely have a human feature left on her head, but it spread down her body quite a bit as well. It was mostly down her shoulders and her back. There were even tiny nubs that looked like the beginning of wings. Ana questioned if she would have wanted them or not. They probably wouldn't be big enough to fly with, but she'd be lying if she said she didn't want to try.

She had no idea if she had been blessed with her abilities and new knowledge or cursed as an outcast of society. The only thing she knew for sure was that warm honey tea is a good thing to have to help you rest. She laid down in the softest linen sheets she had ever felt while making sure her ears didn't fold over, and for the first time in a week, shut off her mind and went to sleep.

The princess in Ana had found herself rudely awoken to a knock at her door. The bat in her found the same. So she grunted and yelled out, "Give me a minute."

It took her much longer than a minute to get ready. Not just because she was spiting whoever was behind the door, but because royal clothing was much more challenging to get into than she remembered. All of her clothes were as she left them, and she put on the most basic dress she could find. It was an elegant white number with gold fabric lining its edges. The silks it were made from were fine and helpful with the desert heat, though it was tight and hard to do up on her own. As always, it felt uncomfortable and far too gaudy, but it would have to work. She couldn't spend her time in the castle covered under the cloak she had stolen. Even then, it was questionable whether a hybrid or a thief would be more welcome around here.

"Alright, come in." She yelled out, expecting Calvin. To her surprise, the door opened to reveal a much larger man than Calvin and one who was willing to wear steel armour in the middle of the desert. He was tall, blonde, and had a face that had seen battle. The only thing comforting about him was his eyes. Two blue orbs that had a way of calming even the most raging of citizens. It was her brother, Kasibel. Ana took a step back and tried to hide her face, as she was unsure how the new look would come off on her sibling. It didn't seem to bother him as much as intrigue him.

"So, the rumours are true." He said, taking a confident step in and closing the door behind him.

"I don't remember inviting you in." Ana snarled. She gave up on covering her face since that was obviously what he was here to see.

"I mean, you just did." He had a point. She didn't miss his sass. "Welcome back, Ana."

"Thanks." She said dishonestly. She wasn't expecting to be thrown into this minefield of an interaction this early in the morning.

"Hey, I don't plan on staying for long. I'm not even supposed to be here." He lowered his voice.

"I go missing for a week, and you're barely going to say hi?" She was mad that he showed up and was suddenly also mad he was leaving. Even Ana knew it was a logical fallacy, but her brother had gotten good at ignoring those over the years.

"I just want you to know two things, ok?" He asked, hoping she would take him seriously.

"Shoot." That was about as close as he was going to get.

"One, I was genuinely worried about you. If you believe it or not, that's up to you, but more than anything, I'm glad you're back." It was clear Kasibel was setting up for something. He sounded honest but it felt like he was laying it on a bit too thick.

"Alright, sap, what's the second one then?" She did appreciate the comment but didn't want to show it.

"Don't trust anyone if you know the whereabouts of the hybrids in the city." He was dead serious and said it as a command. It surprised Ana that he even brought it up.

"Why do you think you'd need to tell me that?" Now it was Ana's turn to be intrigued. What did he know about hybrids? How did he know they were in the city? They were supposedly outlawed, so it was the job of his men to take them down. He should want to hunt them down more than anyone else in the city.

"Because it's important. I may follow the law as best I can, but the last thing I need is to be ordered to send my men to slaughter innocents."

"Who would even willingly give that order?" She raised her voice. He was clearly insinuating something about their father. The same man who lovingly embraced his hybrid daughter as she reentered the castle.

"Look, that's not important. Keep it close to your chest, I beg of you." Her brother got down on one knee with his hand over his heart in a salute of respect. His head was bowed low in a position one would rarely see him give to anyone but the King himself.

Ana let out a sigh. It was clear this meant a lot to him. "Very well." She said, in her royal voice, as if accepting the request of a lowly commoner. If he was going to go this far for the plea, she was going to rub it in when she could. Kasibel stood soon after, not wanting her to savour the moment any longer than she needed to.

"Thank you, Ana. I mean it." He said through the clanking of his armour. "And if you need anything, if something goes wrong, come and find me." He walked out without another word, making sure to slowly close the door behind him.

What was the meaning of that, Ana wondered. It was clear there was something else she didn't know about, which wasn't a surprise. New knowledge was kind of the theme lately. She would have to do some snooping later. It wasn't like she was already planning an escape. It was practically second nature. There would just be some convincing for Calvin to let her out of her room at night, but he seemed easy enough to manipulate. From there, it was just a matter of where to find what.

She could always just ask her father directly about it, and she didn't throw out the option. They had planned daily meetings for the next little while in private. A handful of trusted guards would escort her to the throne room. That way, no one could see her transformed face, and there wouldn't be widespread panic. This would also give her time to catch up on what little tutelage he wanted to give to her and give her time to ask questions about what her life was going to be like moving forward.

There was still one thing that didn't add up, though. When Ana sat down and thought for a minute, she couldn't get it out of her mind that the guard who escorted her back from the market already knew she might be a hybrid. Her father was surprised when she came back in as well, leading her to believe he didn't actually think she would be one. Yet, how could he have instructed his guards so that they knew? Ana knew she'd have him in an empty room later with the perfect opportunity to back him into a corner, but for now, it was time for breakfast.

As good as Henry's cooking was, it couldn't come close to the spread Ana was brought that morning. Now, of course, Henry was one person, and the castle had a team of chefs. That still didn't change how delicious the meal Calvin brought her was. Not only was it extravagant to royal standards, but this was also her first meal back. Her father clearly wanted her to feel welcome as the number of rare ingredients used were off the charts. Eggs from at least three different birds, herbs from all over the world, and even some mushrooms harvested from the forests of Ingress. You know it's a good meal when Rolfe Rexharne swallows his pride and cooks food from their main competitor of a nation.

Ana didn't realize how much she missed the cooking. It was far better than surviving on four days of rations and alcohol. The alcohol, of course, is there to make you forget about the taste of the rations. If Ana knew any better, she would call the King suspiciously kind, as he never gave her this kind of a meal before. There was so much food she even had to share some with Calvin, who was hesitant at first but eventually joined in.

It was then she got back to her next joy, reading. Her meeting with her father wasn't until far later in the day, so she got to enjoy flipping through old history textbooks. Though there was something missing. Everything she had gone over the wars that had long passed and kingdoms that had risen and fallen since ancient times. Not a single one of them mentioned hybrids anywhere in their text. Didn't matter the kingdom nor era. She wondered if it was just because these were catered to her or if there was something more significant going on.

It wouldn't be the first time something was attempted to be written out of history, that was for sure, but this one seemed so successful. She knew almost everything about every fight Arid Retreat and its neighbouring nations ever had, so why was there such a significant missing piece? She even had old law books that explained the creation of rules and regulations for centuries. It had nothing about outlawing hybrids, yet it seemed everyone was on the same page about it. Everyone except her.

Ana would have to add to the demands and questions she had for her father that night. Of course, he could come up with some generic answer as to why these books have no mention of them, but she would have a request ready. She wanted a book on the history of hybrids. There had to be one out there somewhere. If not in this kingdom, then in a kingdom they had trade with. She was a princess, and she would pull rank and demand such a thing. There was a need to know about what happened. Something had to have sparked all this hatred. War was never fought without reason. Those that seemed that way were rewritten by the victors.

Reading wasn't distracting enough, and eventually, Ana got down to planning. She played scenario after scenario in her head. Sometimes if she had a good one, she'd talk out loud into the mirror. It was going to be a battle, that was for sure, but she was going to get answers whether her father liked it or not. The problem was she knew her opponent, and he wasn't one to back down or break easily. Thus is the case when you rule a kingdom built on the bodies buried underneath it.

Though she had all day, it was all too soon that the knock on her door came, and she followed Calvin and three other guards out to make it to the throne room. She put on her battered cloak again to cover her face but was still stuck with the gaudy royal attire underneath it. Sure, it was terrible and uncomfortable, but it would help in her fight. Anything to show him that she was his princess right now would tip the scales in her favour. For the second time in the past day, Ana's heart was racing outside the throne room doors.

And there it was. The battlefield laid before her. Only two chess pieces in the room, one of them the king sitting before her. It was just a matter of backing it into a corner.

"Good afternoon, your highness." Ana started with a deep bow. She wanted to play up the charm as much as she could. Show that she was getting back into her old life quickly, though it couldn't be farther from the truth.

"Ana!" He said excitedly, a smile widening to the two corners of his beard. "I'm sorry it took me so long to see you today."

"It's fine." She said, although it didn't feel like it was. "I know you're still a king, so there's still plenty of work to do."

"So, tell me, child." He started to sound more serious very quickly. "How is your transformation treating you?" The question came too fast. The king had made a move before the pawn had even hit the board.

"Uhh... fine." The answer didn't come easily, so she had to think of something. She wasn't expecting him to even bring up her face. "I mean, it's strange to get used to, for sure. The heightened hearing is both a blessing and a burden."

"Heightened hearing you say?" The king had gotten something he wanted. Hopefully, this would open him up to more answers. "Does the noise around the castle bother you?"

"No, not at all." She answered truthfully. The tower was pretty far away from everyone save Calvin, who barely even snored when he fell asleep. "Tell me something, father."

"Yes?" He asked. She had him on her hook pretty quickly.

"Why do none of the history texts explain anything about hybrids?"

Her first move was made. It was just a matter of if he would fall for the bait.

"Oh, yes, of course." The words of a liar trying to think. Ana had spoken them all too often herself. "As I said before, I didn't want to burden you with the information of a repressed race. I knew you would hang onto it for too long, so I only procured biased books that kept such information out."

Perfect. That was just what she wanted to hear.

"Then, now that I know, and, well..." She flicked one of her ears, and it bounced back into place. "Am one. Could you get me some texts that include the history of hybrids?" She pretended to jump with joy at her next idea, a play which hoped would earn her an extra point. "Oh, or even a book specifically about them?"

"Uhh.." The king was stunned. The piece moved back on the board as he got closer to being cornered. It was rare for someone to even surprise King Rolfe and Ana savoured the moment while she could. "I suppose I could, but it might take some time. What, with the problem of them being outlawed and all."

"Oh, silly." She was playing up the charm harder than she was even comfortable with. "You're the king. You can get anything done. Please?" She begged with puppy dog eyes. Er, baby bat eyes? Either way, it worked.

"I'll… see what I can do." She knew that was the best she was getting out of him for that. This was only the beginning, though, and it opened her up to so much more. Before she had a chance, he made another move. "So, where did you spend your time away from the castle? It must have been terrifying."

He was right. It was. But answering something like that might be a problem. What was he getting at? There shouldn't be any harm in telling the truth, but Kasibel's words from the morning rang in her ears. He just meant sharing the information in general, right? Her father should be fine. He was so understanding. She could at least let him have a little slack. "I spent most of it with a group of hybrids in the city. They took me in when I didn't know what to do." She was hoping to not have to give away any more than that.

"Why didn't you come straight home?" Another move, and an easy one to give in to.

"I was afraid of what you'd think." Again, truthful.

"So instead, you'd worry your poor old man for so long? Please, next time, just come home to me." It was a genuine plea, at least by the look in his eyes.

"Yes, of course father. I apologize for worrying you." She gave a quick bow of respect. Something she had picked up anytime she was given a lecture, it seemed to get him to lighten up a bit.

"Where are the ones that took you in?" The question hit Ana like a rampaging camel. This is precisely what Kasibel warned her about. Now, again, she didn't think he'd do anything wrong with the information, but she also didn't know who might be listening in. It didn't matter regardless, as she didn't know the exact location. Giving away any information could be a problem, though. Every nugget he didn't know was like another bargaining ship.

"They're all over the city, of course hiding." She gave a half-truth. They were all in one spot, and somehow the king knew something was off. He raised an eyebrow.

"How about the ones you were with?" He asked. This put Ana on the backfoot.

"A hidden tavern, they gave me room and board there." Honest, but not enough to work with. She didn't even know why she was trusting Kasibel on his word from earlier. Why shouldn't she tell her father?

"Where was this tavern?"

"Quite honestly, I couldn't tell you. The lower quarter somewhere? I've been there a few times now but still lose track of it." Once again, entirely truthful, and she hoped she didn't give too much away. She may have, because the king seemed pleased with the answer.

"I do have one question that's been bothering me." She started, almost puffing out her chest to try and assert dominance. "How did you know?"

"Know what, dear?" He asked, sounding genuinely surprised.

"That I might already be a hybrid."

"I had no idea." Now it was the king's turn to lie, and she caught him in it. He didn't suspect his own soldier would have already given away his position.

"Then the guard who brought me here came to that conclusion herself?" Ana began to think she might be stepping too far out of line, mostly because she could see a vein in her father's forehead pop out at that one.

"Can we leave that story for another time?" He asked, almost sounding angry. Ana knew it was time to back off on the topic, but not completely.

“Very well, but could you at least confirm that you thought it would be a possibility?” She already knew the answer but wanted to hear it right from him.

“I had no doubt it had already happened to you.” The answer she thought she had was wrong. This news hit her even harder as she unknowingly put a hand on her chest, almost looking offended at the information. “To be honest, it’s one of the reasons I kept you under lock and key for so long.” Ana could feel her heart pumping with something. Was it possible to get adrenaline from confusion? Was she just that angry? “I didn’t want to miss my little girl’s face, though I know how wrong it was to do that to you.”

The half-apology at the end made it a bit better, but he knew? How could he know? There was something so much more than what she had expected. It put her in a position that lacked any angle. She had no more questions ready to ask and wasn’t even happy with the answers she did get. She had been beaten at her own game.

“I suppose we should leave this for next time?” Ana said after regaining her composure. It would have to be all niceties from here on.

“Yes, yes, we shall. There’s going to be much to discuss over the coming days.” He turned his back to her and looked out one of the large windows behind the throne itself. “For now, enjoy your carefree time while you’re still young.”

“Thank you, your highness.” The princess said with a large bow. That night, she left her first meeting with her father more confused and angry than when she went in.

Chapter 14

Something was off, that much was obvious. But what was it? Ana pondered her evening away. How could her father have already known she was a hybrid before she came back? She wanted answers, but they were all out of her grasp. Why did this feel like a battle? Where was the man that welcomed her back with open arms? On top of all of this, there was Kasibel's warning. Everything was far more convoluted than she expected it to be.

Ana figured sleeping after getting home would be easier, not more difficult. She could only think of sneaking out and demanding her father tell her everything from beginning to end. Unfortunately, he didn't break easily and would likely leave her in the same state. After having a few hours to mull over the conversation, Ana noticed a pattern.

He was using war tactics against her. It was all he knew, sure, but why would he go so far? Every time she thought she had the upper hand, another major revelation came up that threw her for a loop. It was as if he was verbally attacking her supply lines. She had just got home, and now all she could think about was escaping. There was no easy way out, though. Calvin was blocking the door, and her window was far too high up. If only those wings had grown all the way, she might have a chance.

One thought kept poking at the back of her mind, but she wanted to ignore it. The possibility was there that her father did hate hybrids. That he wanted them out of the city, or worse. The evidence was there. Hybrids were still outlawed under his rule, he was keeping information from her, and what Kasibel warned her about could only point to the King. Ana shook the thought out of her head. She couldn't believe it. It was an impossibility, and she made sure not to go down that line of thinking again. Without it, though, the pieces didn't come together. There was only one place left to go.

Kasibel. He should be easy enough to get contact with. It would just be a matter of sending Calvin to go get him. He might have some answers. She had no idea what he might know, but at the very least, he was let in on way more than she was, especially when it came to army movements. For now, though, it was time to sleep.

Of course, the night was far from smooth. Ana's brain tended to work on overdrive. Especially when she was stuck in one place. Between the tossing and turning, the strategizing and analyzing, she may have gotten a grand total of one hour of shut eye. The nights had been much more difficult after she had transformed. One of these days she would realize it was because bats are nocturnal, but for now, it was chalked up to her tense situation.

While still lying with eyes open, the sun made its way into the room. As it had every morning this week, it burned like no tomorrow. She knew she would have to adjust her eyes, but she covered her head with her sheets for now. It may have been hot as hell, but at least it kept her retinas from burning. It was too soon when the knock came at her door for breakfast, and she couldn't do more but grunt. Eventually, the thought of Calvin standing outside with a tray full of food not moving for hours bothered her, so she spoke up.

"Just leave it on the table." She yelled out. She could hear him come in, clank everything down, pour her tea, and leave. Hell, she could even hear him bow before he closed the door.

Ana was frankly tired. Tired of the confusion. Tired from the travel. Tired of being treated like a princess. It was hard to enjoy anything anymore, making it difficult to even get out of bed. It was the only comfort she had left. The only thing in the world that wasn't against her.

Aside from getting up to eat a few bites, this was how she spent most of her day. It was all becoming too much for one person to handle. How do you even handle something like this? Being thrust into a position you didn't know existed and suddenly be hated for it. There was a life ahead of her before. She could have either stayed here as a figurehead or be married off to some nobility. Because of one decision, what she now considered a mistake, of leaving the castle for one night, her life was destroyed.

She couldn't see things ever going back to normal. If anything, she was stuck in this room more than she was before. There was no way around the idea of never being able to leave, the idea of this being it.

If she wanted to play nice and not go against everything the kingdom wished. Everything her father wished. This was her life. No decisions, just eating, reading, and sleeping. It was nothing short of a prison with good room service. Perhaps escaping again wouldn't be the worst idea.

Though if she escaped again, she'd be on the run. She couldn't show her face anywhere. She didn't know of any kingdoms that accepted her if she ran from her home. Ana didn't even want to run from her home. The desert was what she knew. These sands were what she read about in ancient stories. This was the landscape that upheld the lives of her ancestors and eventually came down to her existence. Leaving this place would be like forsaking her entire family, living and passed.

Upon her meeting with her father that night, there were more questions she wanted to ask, but she couldn't find the nerve to bring them up anymore. He tried to get more information out of her, but all she could give were generic responses, not knowing what was right anymore. He was clearly dissatisfied as she was released back to her room. That made her even worse.

She was doing what he wanted, but apparently, it wasn't enough. Being back. Being his daughter. It didn't mean anything after just a couple of days. No one cared for her. No one was going to care for her. This was it. The days started feeling like chores. Rinsing and repeating the same motions over and over again. Every meeting with her father, she talked less and less. A week passed and she barely noticed. She couldn't find a solution. No matter how many times she went over the problems in her head, she just felt more and more trapped. Trapped in her own life. This wasn't something she had ever wanted to deal with.

Ana even kept talking herself out of meeting with Kasibel. At first, she thought it was a good idea, but she played the conversation over and over again in her head. Every time he had a response that would make her feel stupid for asking the question. Every time she played it over, the answers from him got worse and worse. All of this was too much to take, and she had no one to talk to. No one would listen to her, not now, not ever. Not even being allowed to speak to anyone else in the castle wasn't helping either.

Another week went by. Another week in bed. The stress piling on more and more. Ana frankly felt useless. All she did was eat. For her people, all she did was take their money and live lavishly off of it. This place would be better without her. This was when she found a solution. Ana knew it wasn't a good solution, but it would work. It was the only answer she had.

There was a lot of analyzing to do, but in every scenario she could think up, no negative would happen. Everything would only wind up better for everyone. Right now, this included her. There was fear behind the decision because that was only natural, but it only took a few more days of monotony to overcome that fear. She kept playing out the new solution in her head, and it was the only one that always turned out the same. Day by day, it only felt like a better and better option.

By this point, her father was practically shunning her. Some days went by where she didn't even get a meeting with him. Those days got more and more frequent. It was clear he wouldn't miss her. She couldn't even see her brother, and he never really cared for her anyway. The people would never see their princess again, so they wouldn't miss her. The only person she felt she would be affecting was Calvin, as he'd probably lose his job over this, but there was no avoiding that. It wasn't going to be his fault, but unfortunately, the world is cruel.

It was cruel enough to have her born into this family. It was cruel enough to keep that door locked when all she wanted was the beauty of the outdoors. It was cruel enough that when she finally got to see that beauty, it took away the rest of her life and worse, made the desert harder to look at. Made it feel like it was fighting her back. Not even the landscape wanted her around anymore.

Every day she looked at the open window. Every day she got closer to it. Every day she had looked in the mirror, and the person looking back, and she was more and more of a mess. It was building up, and any decision she had made so far only put more and more on. The only solution was to tear it down. Take it down from the base.

She had looked out the window and down below, many times over. The ground was far from soft, as there was a rocky outcropping and a castle wall, making it much easier to finish the job. Every night that she lay awake, she stared at that window, considering her option carefully. All it would take is one move.

That move was made when she had the first meeting with her

father in days. He demanded she act more like she did before, and she blindly agreed. His fury was shown. He wanted what he had before back. A nice, obedient girl who looked like a human. It was clear he was never going to get that, and he was coming to that realization. Ana had already reached that point.

That night was going to be it. She felt the anger in her heart and the sorrow in her head. It was time. There was no holding back anymore. She had stood on the ledge before, just to see, but it wasn't time yet. There was still hope before, no matter how little it was. Now, there was no hope left. The time for the solution had finally come. It was time to make the world a better place.

Ana looked over the ledge to the rocky outcropping below, and with no hesitation, jumped.

Chapter 15

Something kicked in the moment Ana walked off that ledge. It happened so fast. She took a look down to see the rocky outcropping below her, but she was still what felt like a hundred feet above it. On top of that, her arm hurt. A lot. She looked up and noticed she was hanging on the ledge by one hand. It must have stopped her fall completely, but why?

She wanted to go down just a moment ago. She wanted to end it all. The monotony, the lack of feeling, she wanted it gone but had saved herself. Why? One thing was for sure, it was hard to think while in such a life-ending situation, so Ana swung her other arm up and tried to climb back to safety. The problem was she couldn't. Her strength wasn't enough to pull the rest of her body, and it felt like she had dislocated her shoulder. It hurt so much. She had hoped it would be painless and instant. No time to regret, no time to feel.

Turns out a split second was all she needed to regret. Normally she would have realized her mistake far too late, hit the ground, and that would be it. She assumed it was the predator's self preservation that kicked in so fast. The animal in her didn't want to die, and now the human in her didn't either.

There were other ways to fix this. There were other things to try. It was just that she couldn't bring herself to try them and left herself with one easy solution. That's the thing with solutions, though. The hard ones are usually the right ones. The hard ones are the ones that get you the farthest. She wished she had realized that before making one hasty move and dangling for her life. That was the cruellest thing the world had done yet, making her feel the weight of her decision with no way out of it.

Calvin came to mind. She had ignored his situation almost entirely. She had convinced herself he would get fired for this. Ana knew deep down he would get beheaded, and his family would be run out of town if they were lucky. It was selfish to think she wouldn't affect anyone. Even if she was right and her family didn't care, it wasn't worth tearing another family apart, but now it was too late.

Or was it? It was time for Ana to make the first hard decision of her new life.

"CALVIN!" She yelled at the top of her lungs. It was a guttural scream she hoped he would hear from the other side of the door. There was no movement. She could hear nothing coming from above her. She yelled again. "CALVIN, HELP!" This time something. Faint, but there. She had rested her fate that night in the man whose life she was about to destroy. She needed him immediately.

And he came. Calvin reached over without even thinking and pulled her up, at first by the painful arm. Ana had to yell out for him to grab the other one, he did without hesitation. Her hands scrambled to lock onto his arms. The moment he had full hold, Calvin put his foot against the stone wall for leverage and pulled as hard as he could.

Calvin wasn't a particularly strong guard, but Ana didn't bring much weight with her, so the pull was easy. Ana found herself dazed, in the middle of her room, with a guard next to her that had fallen over in his hoist. The thought that she may have sentenced this man to death over her actions fell heavy on her at that moment. Even though he wasn't family, and sure, he was paid to do it, he saved her life without hesitation, without asking questions. It was clear to her now that some people cared about more than themselves. It was clear that some people cared.

"Thank you." She said, terrified as if she was a small child. Her eyes watered, but she held back the tears.

"Are you alright pri-." Calvin stopped himself. "I mean Ana. Are you alright, Ana?" He asked, the most genuine concern in his voice. It hurt just that much more.

"Yes, of course." Ana lied. "I must have been sleepwalking." Might as well continue.

"What matters is that you're safe." He replied with a sigh of relief. "Are you hurt?"

"It seems so." Ana tried moving her right arm, but all she felt was pain. Her shoulder wasn't where it was supposed to be. She winced as she tried to move it again.

"I've practiced field medicine, may I?" He asked, cautiously motioning closer to her. Ana nodded. “This will hurt.” He warned her before taking any action.

“Do your worst.” Ana closed her eyes and prepared for it. Though it turned out to be difficult to get ready for a shoulder relocation. Calvin grabbed her arm before she could even think and made one quick movement. There was an uncomfortable popping sound and a wave of agony that ran from the base of her spine to the tips of her fingers. She let out a short scream but settled quickly.

“I'm so sorry!” Calvin apologized as quickly as he could.

“Nothing to be sorry for. You just saved my life.” Ana could barely get out the words without weeping. What had she done? Her thought process was off. All she wanted to do now was go for a long walk, far away from that window.

“Any of us would have done it for you.” He replied proudly.

“Yes, but the important thing is you're the one that did it for me.” Ana wanted to make sure this didn't get lost on him in the sense of some higher duty. He saved a life, and he should feel proud of that. “Now, I really don't want to burden you any further tonight, but I have two favours I'd like to ask.” She really did feel awful for what she was about to do, but in this case, there really was no other way.

“Anything for you.” Calvin stood and saluted as he had been taught to many times before.

“First, can we not let my dad know about this? He'd have a freakout.” The first one was a reasonable request, though she did feel bad taking away any glory he might have gained in being the one to save the princess's life.

“Of course. I'd prefer that, actually. The last thing I need is the king knowing I had even let you get that close to the window.” There was no way Calvin had control over such things at his station, but Ana did see his point. Parents can be unreasonable when their child's life is at stake. Especially when they're royalty.

“Second, and this one is a bit more difficult.” Ana let out a deep sigh, trying to think of how she could word this to have it make sense. “I know you're not supposed to let me out of this room, but I don't really want to be near that window right now. I'd like to go for a walk.”

“I think it's only fair, but I will accompany you, your highness.” Calvin understandably knew what the princess was like and knew she was about to run off.

"You know what I'm about to do, don't you?" She asked, and he nodded. "Well, I'm sorry, but there's no way around you losing your job over this at best." She said it with sorrow in her eyes. The last thing she wanted to do was hurt this man's life, but she needed to escape again. Something was wrong, and she felt like she knew the people to talk to. Then, she had a thought. "What were your exact orders again?"

"Don't keep my eyes off of you?" Calvin questioned her logic.

"Well, you won't be. Now come on, let's go. I need someone with a weapon." She said, getting up and throwing her cloak on. Admittedly it would make her stand out more, as the new one she was provided was of the Rexharne colours. She'd have to find a beat-up one when she hit the streets.

"Wait, where are we going?"

"I don't exactly remember." Ana admitted. "But, considering you were given the job to guard me, you don't exactly have a problem with hybrids, do you?" Calvin shook his head. "Good, because we're going to meet some."

"There's no talking you out of this, is there?" Calvin asked, wanting to stick around the castle and not make the king mad.

"Not in the slightest."

"What will happen if I try to stop you?"

"I have no qualms with knocking out someone who saved my life." She walked out on that note and had already given him the choice. Calvin followed behind quickly, just as she suspected.

It was strange. Sneaking out of the castle was much easier with an escort. Most of the guards were told she was sick, so they kept a decent distance away when she was in the halls. Though they were informed that she was to stay in her room at all times, Calvin had the final say. Since he was there with her, she could just walk casually wherever she wanted. Even in the middle of the night, no one gave them a second look. Instead of climbing over castle walls and down the other side, they just left through the front gate. It would have almost been boring, if Ana wasn't already so preoccupied.

"Calvin." Ana said to get his attention.

"Yes, Ana?" He was getting used to using her name but still stalled on it every time he tried.

"You're my favourite person this month. Probably this year." Ana can confirm before that night she had never seen a man swoon and nearly faint. She was happy her royal status was still recognized by at least one person. That was one thing she had to admit. People waiting on her hand and foot was uncomfortable, but it was brilliant when they were star-struck.

She realized it wasn't the greatest thing to say as she had to keep him from falling over. With the pain in her shoulder it was all she could do to keep him from hitting the floor. "Alright, come on lover boy, to the lower quarter!"

"I didn't mean it like that." He tried to defend, but Ana wasn't listening and already moved away from him. "And why the lower quarter?!" He yelled while running to catch up to her.

"It's where my friends are." She said confidently. She was sure that Henry's bar would be the place to go to cheer her up tonight. Her life had flashed before her eyes that night, and she never laughed as hard as when she got comfortable with them.

"Friends?"

"Hybrids, Calvin. They took me in when I left the castle. Keep up, would you?" Ana was saying that to both his walking speed and his ability to follow the plot. Calvin started to realize his best plan of action might be not talking.

It was such an easy jaunt out of the castle. Ana never got to take the front doors, and it was a nice change. She had to admit they were a bit gaudy, though. Two giant steel things embedded in stone that could withstand more than a couple hits from a battering ram. Each one was covered in steel rivets and had no ornate carvings, making them just a couple of intimidating pieces of metal. They had to be at least fifteen feet tall, which made it all the more comical that you had to leave through a much smaller door embedded in the two of them. Of course, it could be locked up with steel bars and practically be a solid piece of steel, but the humor wasn't lost on Ana. After the guards stationed let them out it was just down an oversized curved staircase that narrowed at the bottom, yet another thing designed to fight off intruders, and then a quick walk past the execution theatre and they were on the main street, which lead to both the market and the lower quarter, depending on which way you turned.

They made their way to the lower district, and in her fancy cloak, Ana was happy she had a guard with her. It seemed many individuals were outside for it being so late at night, and all of them had their eyes on her. Likely from the attire, of course. Also, the whole place looked more dilapidated than it did before. More holes in the walls than she remembered, especially buried deep within the alleyways. She chalked it up to being in the castle for too long again. It's easy to forget what imperfection looks like when you're surrounded by a standard of excellence only power can buy.

Ana had to admit, being back out, she did feel naked without a sword. She considered asking Calvin for his as she thought she could use it better but would rather not take something else from that man tonight. Plus it wouldn't come with a lack of insult to his ability, considering she just had her shoulder relocated. There was always the possibility her's was still left in her bed at the tavern. Sure the thing was beat up, but it would be worth carrying again.

Now that they were in the deeper parts of the district, it was time to get lost.

"I will admit one thing to you, Calvin. I have no idea where the place is we're looking for and have never been able to find it on my own. We may be here until sunrise."

"I do dread going back to the castle at this point, so I'm fine with this." The guard had no idea what he had gotten into. Ana knew by the time he met the bar patrons, he may attempt to faint again.

It didn't take hours of searching to realize her hunch from before was actually correct. This place was torn apart, and more than usual. She could tell by the fresh bricks that had been taken out of some buildings, clearly by force. The debris lay everywhere in the back alleys. It was somehow both indiscriminate and calculated. Like someone knew what they were doing, but didn't mind causing a bit of extra damage along the way. Something had happened here. It was just a matter of what.

Ana started running. There was a fear in her heart she hoped was wrong. The consequences if that fear was right were too much to handle. More than once on her way, she tripped over a brick looking for the bar that night, but it didn't slow her down. Everywhere she ran past, she made sure to check the holes in the walls. There was no sign of the bar, but there were signs of people's homes. These holes lead to kitchens and dining rooms, bedrooms and living areas. Whoever did this was nothing short of a monster, willing to rip lives apart just for a single selfish goal. She really hoped she was wrong on who it was.

Calvin was having a hard time keeping up with her, but it didn't matter. Ana had to find that bar as fast as possible. She started to get worried because she couldn't hear a single noise coming from those back streets. Around this time, Henry should be leading some kind of chant about how great he is, and she couldn't hear it. The situation felt like it got more dire by the minute, but it didn't feel solid. Didn't feel real.

That was until she found the hole. The biggest one yet. Broke into the side of a hiding spot for hybrids. The bricks tore about the streets like some wild animal attacked from the outside. The inside, Henry's bar, and much, much worse than that.

Bodies. Countless bodies. Not passed out. Dead. Ana froze and looked away. This couldn't be real. She must have fallen and died, and this is the hell she had to face. No, there was no ignoring it anymore. She turned and looked in once again. The wood was stained red. Barely a bit of the original colour could be seen through. The bottles at the back were all broken. Glass covered the floor and was embedded in some of the bodies over the counter. Ana, shaking from her head to her feet, stepped into the bar slowly. She still couldn't believe it was real. She had to get closer. Had to confirm this wasn't some hallucination.

Once she was in, she wanted to get out. She had killed bandits and ferals that week, but it was nothing like this. Those kills were as clean as they could be. There was no remorse here. Hybrids, regular patrons that she had seen, and some she had met briefly. All of them, their lives ended. Ana fell to her knees. There was nothing left here. There was no solace left in the world. There was no safe place for her to hide. No. She had gone through this spiral before. She wasn't going to do it again that same night. There was a small, very, very small amount of hope. She hadn't seen Drake or Henry's bodies. There was no doubt she didn't want to search for them, but she needed to confirm that they weren't here. She got up off of her knees. The time for mourning had not yet come, but instead, the time for action had.

It was disgusting. There was no attempt to hide the cruelty of what happened here. Whoever did this wanted it to be known. It was clear from the number of buildings that were broken into, to the bodies being left on the floor. They didn't even bother to clean up their mess. This was left behind as a message. Looking around, the attack wasn't recent. It was at least a night before as the pools of blood had stained the wood. Upon Ana's look at the first body, her sorrow turned to anger.

She didn't want to believe what happened here in the first place, let alone who attacked. The body she was looking at was that of a Rexharne soldier. This was an ordered attack. This is why no one stopped them when they tore through the district. There would have been too many of them. Ana had to face the music. There were only two people in this city with the ability to call out such an attack. Her father and her brother. Though she couldn't know for sure, the fact her brother warned her those weeks ago led her straight to the king himself. He wanted them dead. But why? The question was important, but not as important as the issue at hand.

"What happened here?" Calvin asked, stepping into the room after finally catching up. He was sick to his stomach.

"A slaughter." Ana turned and narrowed her eyes at Calvin. "Did you know about this?" The anger welled up inside her. He was a guard. She was a hybrid. A war was started here. Was the man who saved her life the one that would take her out? She wouldn't let it happen.

"No. I'm just a castle guard, not a soldier." He said, the look of shock on his face not going away. It appeared genuine. Ana stood and faced him with fists clenched. She was weaponless, so she didn't know how she was going to handle this. In a straight fight, she would likely lose. But again, if she was wanted dead, there's no reason he would have saved her. He clearly wasn't paying attention either. Caught up in the carnage around him, he didn't notice Ana get aggressive. She relaxed only the slightest bit at this realization and came to a different plan.

"Drop your sword, Calvin." She said coldly.

"What? Why?" He was confused.

"Drop your weapon. On the ground. Out of reach." Ana knew he wasn't the fastest to pick up on cues, but he had better be quick this time. Luckily, it appeared he was still loyal, as he soon untied his scabbard from his belt and slid the weapon across the floor. "Any others?" He shook his head. She had no way of knowing if he was telling the truth but had to take the chance.

Ana approached him quickly, grabbing Calvin by his arms, ready to shake the information out of him if she needed to. She was weak, dealing with both pain and suffering, but dammit if she couldn't still intimidate. "Who do you work for!?" She asked aggressively.

"You!" He said, thinking it was the answer she was looking for. It wasn't, so she pushed him back, ready to strike. The predator in her was getting hungry, and she was closer to the sword than he was.

"No. Not me. Who do you report to?" She asked. She didn't even know it, but her foot was already making a move to grab the weapon.

"For this particular project, it's the king." He started, "but normal-" Before he could finish, Ana held his own blade to his throat, seconds away from ending him. She caught her mistake quickly enough but wished she didn't even get this far.

"Finish the sentence." The black orbs of her eyes still glowed with rage. She was still hungry.

Calvin was shaking. He had to swallow his fear before he could get his next words out. Ana was getting impatient, but he got to them quick enough. "Normally I… I…" He was shaking with fear, and his eyes couldn't peel away from the edge of a blade too close to his throat. Ana noticed this and pulled down the weapon. Calvin sighed with relief. "I report to the captain of the guard, Kasibel."

This relieved Ana. She was almost entirely sure her brother wasn't in on this. It only made sense Calvin would listen to Kasibel, as there was no other way Kasibel would have made it into her room. She threw down the sword next to the guard. The room was silent save from it clanking back and forth on the ground faster and faster until it came to a full rest. She owed Calvin an apology for almost ending him but didn't have it in her to get it out just yet.

"I need you to help me." She said, calmer than she was a moment ago.

"Anything, princess." His loyalty seemed to know no bounds. It was both refreshing and sickening. It would have to do for now, but eventually, she had to get him some backbone.

"We're digging through bodies. We're looking for a man with a bear arm and one almost entirely covered in white scales."

Chapter 16

Hours passed. The late night gave way to sunrise as they overturned body after body. It was the hardest thing Ana ever had to do. Just a few weeks ago, she saw these people drink, sing, and laugh at the same tables together. Now they were lifeless. They lay on the ground as a symbol of the hatred felt towards something the people didn't understand. It wasn't fair. They didn't choose this. It was who they were. They were killed for who they were.

Ana didn't want to admit it, but each body she went through gave her more hope. Every body that wasn't Drake's or Henry's was another chance they were alive somewhere. She knew they wouldn't have some magic answer to this. If they knew what she told the king, they would probably want to kill her, and rightfully so. They still deserved to know what happened and who to blame. The least she could give them is the chance for revenge on the kingdom, and this time would gladly accept her death as punishment.

She knew she was being too hard on Calvin asking him to do this. Every now and again, she could hear him gagging off in the distance. At first, she was surprised that she didn't have the same reaction. It must have come with being part rodent. The smells didn't bother her as much as they should have. The scene was far from lost on her, though.

They had gotten to the point they were checking every room. Some had been torn into, others not so much but not a single door remained standing, most of them nothing but splinters. If the main room was difficult to look at, this became hell. Every doorway they looked into was its own personalized room. A quick portrait of what that person's life once was. It would be the last image symbolizing them, as they couldn't go on any further. There were rooms with paintings on the walls, stories written on the tables, fabrics and wares from other countries, and collections of various stones or works of art. These were all places that showed what each person had to offer to the world. It was painful to know that it had all been taken away from them.

Even without looking into the lives of those who lived here, it was a brutal sight. In the bar, at least the hybrids had a chance to fight back. There were fewer guard bodies in the living quarters, as many of the patrons here were murdered in their sleep or just upon awakening. They didn't stand a chance. Every body lay near a bed or on it. Even above the smell, it was the most sickening thing here.

Then Ana came across the most painful room she would find that day. Hers. Her eyes instinctively closed once she realized it was what she was looking at. She wanted to do nothing more but to turn and run, but even if it was the right thing to do, she had nowhere to go. Not wanting to shelter herself any further, she opened her eyes as quick as she could and let the room come into view. It was kept the same as she had left it, sans door. Not a candle was out of place, and her sword still lay in the bed where she placed it. Ana had to take a moment before walking in.

It felt like her heart sank further with each step. She could have stayed here. She didn't have to go back to the castle. If she didn't make that decision and left her blade behind, this wouldn't have happened. Even if it did happen, she would have been here to fight back. She could have died in honour, protecting something she believed in. Though she had missed her chance and had to walk in shame among the restless souls, she wasn't going to miss the fight again. She pulled back the cover and picked up the old, beaten relic she had used before. It was then Ana realized that this room wasn't kept exactly the same. Her sword had been cleaned and polished, awaiting her return. She had to thank Henry when she found him. It was just a matter of where he went off to.

"I think this is it, princess." Calvin had a hard time calling her by her name in these stressful situations.

"Don't call me that." Ana said coldly while clutching her blade as hard as she did the first time she walked into that bar. Just the very mention that she was royalty right now made her want to vomit. "I want nothing to do with that bastard of a king. I am not his daughter. I can not be. I can not be related to someone so heartless."

"I just don't see how or why King Rolfe would do-" Calvin was cut off by the sound of a loud crash. Ana had buried her sword deep within the desk in her room out of sheer rage.

"Don't you *dare* refer to him as king again. If you're under Kasibel, you're under the heirs to the throne, which in extension means me, correct?" Ana waited for Calvin to respond with a nod. "Then hear my declaration. Rolfe Rexharne is wanted for the murder of innocents, lawful under his *rule* or not. He is no longer to be considered a king but a tyrant that wears the face of one. Do I make myself perfectly clear?"

Calvin didn't know if he agreed or not, but just for the want to keep his own head, he answered. "Yes, Ana." As fast as he possibly could. It was still strange to not have a title for her. In the current circumstance, though, he suddenly accepted it.

"Good." Ana pulled her sword out of the desk. She would have to find a new one soon, as this one wouldn't be much use in battle anymore. "Our goal doesn't change. We are still looking for the man with the bear arm and the scaled one. It's clear their bodies don't lay here, so it's a matter of finding where they ran off to."

"In all due respect, Ana." Calvin chose his following words carefully with the glare that he received. "But where do we start? The city is going to be overrun again looking for you."

"They won't be in the city. If we're lucky, they'll be in the desert nearby. If we're not, they'll have gotten to Ingress by now and have left this place behind."

"How do you know they won't be in the city?"

"Because they're not idiots, Calvin. They don't want to die." Ana did wonder why they weren't here. Henry and Drake didn't seem like the type to abandon the bar when a battle was happening. Maybe they weren't here when it happened, but even that would be strange since Henry never seemed to leave this place.

"The desert is still vast, and of course, so is Ingress." Calvin stated the obvious. "Where do we start?"

Ana hated to admit that he had a good point. Combing the whole desert wasn't exactly a viable option for one escaped princess and one throw-away guard. She needed something to go off of. If only the answer was right in front of her. There was a thought of hitting her desk again in anger, but that's when she saw it. The answer right in front of her. They left a god damned letter on the table. Ana walked over immediately to pick up the two halves of the paper she had cut.

It simply read one word. That one word was all she needed.

Bandits.

"Calvin, I'm sorry I had to drag you into this, but we're about to take a day-long trip through the desert."

"Wherever you lead, I'll follow." With a newfound perspective on the kingdom, Calvin had officially decided he would stay with the one member of the royal family he knew he could trust. Even if she did try to kill him a few moments ago.

The two of them decided to scrounge up for rations in the bar. Luckily they weren't hard to find. The storeroom had barely any damage to it. In Ana's mind, that made them worse than bandits could ever be. At least bandits kill for something. For food or gold. This was senseless. This was beyond senseless.

With their stores prepared, Ana covered herself in her cloak and tied her dull blade to her waist as best she could. It may not be sharp, but at least it was something. She wasn't granted claws and began wishing she was. At least she had a trained guard with a sharp sword. For a moment, she reminded herself she should find a way to stop needing escorts.

Unfortunately, the sun was damn near high noon. This problem was twofold. First, if they noticed Ana was missing by now, there would be a search force out already. Second, Ana couldn't see very well and had to navigate Calvin to their destination. That left two options. One of them was to leave immediately and hope they don't get caught or lost. The other was to stay here and hide out. Considering the mess of this place and the weight that would leave on Ana if they waited any longer, they hit the desert immediately.

Though the last time she left, it was through the market district, Ana decided to escape through the lower quarter and loop around. The last thing she wanted to do was have to pass by the castle. Running this by Calvin, he agreed with the plan, which was no surprise. He was still lost on how she understood where they were going, but Ana was adamant about staying silent until they were far enough away from town.

There were no guards upon their exit, which made it clear the princess wasn't found to be missing yet. Her father's lack of care for her recently had turned into an advantage. Even luckier was the fact that he didn't care about the impoverished in his own city either, even though these citizens were often the ones that stocked his army. Ana was already considering some kind of assault on the castle, and the residents' loss of faith in the ruler was a crucial part of her starting strategy.

It took them no time to get far away enough from Arid Retreat to get out of any guard's sightline and loop around the town. This was mainly due to Ana walking much faster when she was angry. She didn't exactly walk in a straight line as her path in the sand made clear, and since she had to keep her head down the whole time, but the distance was what mattered.

"So, where are we going?" Calvin asked. Ana had to praise him for his optimistic tone. She threw his life into the fire almost as hard as she had been.

"A cave, about a day's walk away from the town." Ana said. She tried to look up to speak to him, but the sunspots left in her eyes proved that a mistake. She cursed her eyes that day as just another thing out to get her.

"How did you get that from a single word?" Calvin almost sounded impressed. Ana explained to him her time with Drake being a mercenary in little detail. Her mind wasn't on the past right now, though Calvin was more than shocked by what he heard.

"You? The princess of Arid Retreat, off being a sellsword? If it wasn't for everything else today, I wouldn't believe it." He laughed to himself at the thought. That was a mistake.

Ana snapped. Not because he laughed at her, but because he called her princess again. "That title is dead!" She began by yelling but brought herself back down a little. "I am to have no relation to that tyrant. Before, it was a preference. Now, you are not to call me princess under any circumstances." She had certainly made the command like she was still royalty.

Calvin swallowed his pride and responded. "Yes, miss." but it still felt wrong. "Is there anything else I can call you instead?"

Ana thought about it for a moment. Not many would listen to her without a title. She had every plan to start a resistance to take her father down, so perhaps something a resistance soldier might be called. The question was what role she would play. She wasn't much of a frontline fighter, so that wouldn't do. There were a plethora of military strategies in her head from the history books, so perhaps something along those lines.

"Commander." She finally decided.

"Commander?"

“Yes. Commander Ana.” She paused for another moment. She might be in battle for a long time if she goes through with this, might as well have fun with a full title. “Commander Ana of the Hybrid Liberation Front.”

Chapter 17

It was an arduous trip. A lot weighed on Ana's mind as they made it back to that cave she and Drake hid in on their first day out. The possibility still lingered that they would kill her the moment she showed up. The moment they found out it was her that let out the secret to their tavern. It wasn't going to make her turn away. She would accept the death as it was deserved. In the best-case scenario, she would get chided.

Then she remembered that chiding would be from Drake and decided she'd prefer death.

It wasn't lost on her that she had a town guard with her either. It would take some convincing that he wasn't some kind of spy. She just hoped she had the time before he was eaten alive. Depending on which hybrids survived, that might even be in the literal sense.

"Why you?" Ana asked, accidentally thinking out loud.

"Why me what?" Considering there was nothing but silence for the last hour, of course, Calvin would wonder what she meant.

"Why were you selected to guard my door?" She figured she would turn her mistake of a question into an actual answer. "Out of all the guards, why not one of the tyrant's men?"

"Well, his guard is small and usually of some kind of noble bloodline. If you get what I mean." Ana did. It didn't take a genius to figure out nobles would want nothing to do with hybrids. Not to mention that gossip was an issue.

"But you were selected by him, weren't you? Even though you're one of Kasibel's, my brother didn't get to know about me until he came to see me."

"Oh, that's easy." Calvin seemed to understand the question now. "My sister is a hybrid, and I make no claim that she isn't."

"So the tyrant knew this?" Ana had already taken to his new title. King was too good for her father anymore.

"Yes, of course. Everyone did. Most soldiers looked at me with detest." he hung his head low. Being a hybrid supporter wasn't exactly easy in the Retreat.

"That still doesn't make any sense." Ana thought out loud. Calvin had to wait through quite a long silence, not understanding what she meant. Eventually, she turned and looked at him directly, which was much easier now that the sun had fallen halfway below the horizon. "Why wouldn't they have found and killed her?" The question was to the point but cold. Ana had crossed a line, yet she had stopped caring about such things upon seeing that tavern. If she needed information, she was going to get it.

Calvin was clearly uncomfortable with the implication but answered anyway. "She doesn't live in the kingdom. She lives in Ingress. It's not the best life, but it's better than here. I still write to her." His heart sank when he realized getting a letter out there wouldn't be easy.

"I'm still surprised you wouldn't have been fired for being, like, a supporter." At least some things were starting to add up.

"Some of the nobles had tried to get me ousted, actually." It was concerning how Calvin could say these things with a smile still on his face.

"Then why did you stick around?"

"Kasibel. Your brother said he appreciated my loyalty and hard work." If he was smiling before, he was beaming now. Ana could have sworn it got harder to look at him. "He said he wanted to keep his soldiers on their merit as a soldier, not what their beliefs were."

"Remind me to thank him for keeping you around." Ana said, hoping she would get that chance. Though admitting to her brother that he had indirectly saved her life would be something she'd never be able to live down.

It was then they saw hope on the horizon. Ana's heart felt like it was pumping a thousand times a minute when she looked up. There was smoke. Smoke coming from the mountains. They were there. There was someone alive there. She knew it wasn't guaranteed to be them, but that damn well didn't matter. Her feet started moving at a full-on sprint. She could have stopped them, but she didn't want to.

"Commander, wait!" Calvin yelled ahead. He liked having a title to call her again. He didn't like having to chase after her, though. The girl was fast.

The hope grew on every bit of sand she packed down with her foot. The idea that she would see her friends again. They might not consider her one, but if they were the last thing she saw, that would be perfect. Much better than just falling off a balcony and never knowing the crime she had committed. She was close now. The cave was in view. The light of the fire was the only thing left brightening up the night.

Eventually, she was so close the fire had begun to hurt her eyes. It was impossible to see into the cave before they adjusted, but it was only a matter of time. They finally cleared, as if the fire had pulled itself back to reveal what laid in that cave for her. Any optimistic feelings she had sunk as the sight before her came into view.

There was barely anyone left. Henry was stoking the fire. Drake was standing watch. There were maybe four or five others, Angui being among them. Every last one of them, besides Drake, stared at the fire or the ground. All life had gone from their eyes. They were broken. They had lost their home. They had lost their friends. All because of one mistake made by an ignorant princess.

Ana fought back the tears that began welling up. This was no time to cry. She had no right to. Not in front of these people. They had everything taken from them. She swallowed her pride and walked up to Drake. He had already noticed her, but for some reason, refused the acknowledgement. He would never admit it, but he didn't think she was real. It wouldn't have been the first time his mind had played that trick on him since they left.

"Drake?" She greeted, unsure of how he would react. At first, he thought he was just hallucinating more vividly. He didn't want the embarrassment if he responded but still had to know, so he asked back.

"Ana?" His eyes widened under the cloak of his hood. Though he would have still said the hope was lost on him.

"Take a break." Came Henry's voice from the side. He stopped staring at the fire and began walking over. "You're seeing things aga-" He paused upon seeing the new figure in front of them. "Nevermind. *We're* seeing things."

"You're not." Ana responded. She wanted to say it happily, but it was nigh impossible.

"I thought you were dead." Drake stated, still not believing his eyes.

"If I was, wouldn't you have hunted me down and killed me?" She asked sarcastically. It was then that both of them realized she was real. Much to her heart's pain, Henry immediately started celebrating.

"Hey, everyone!" He yelled back. "Ana's here! Ana's alive! We have another one!" Though his enthusiasm was always the highest in the room. It was clear that her return lifted spirits. It was tragic that a miracle for this small group was seeing one more of their kind alive.

She caused this. If she had never come into their lives, they might have never been found. Perhaps one day, those lost lives would have finally seen a peaceful society in which to live. Something had to be done so this could never happen again.

"Don't celebrate me." She spoke coldly. Though she knew she didn't deserve it, a tear found its way down her cheek. She trembled with emotion and wanted nothing more than to be struck down where she stood. "This is my fault."

The words were quiet but resonated through the whole cave that night. Even Henry, his usual overjoyed face, was twisted with feelings he couldn't process. She had to say more. "I was the one that told my father the bar was in the city. I thought we could work together to move forward, to make a more integrated world. I was wrong. My failure has cost the lives of your friends. If you wish to strike me down, then do it. I would not blame any of you."

For the first time since she showed up, Drake moved. He walked towards her, a look in his eyes of anger. Anger for the friends that she had lost. Anger for the lives she had destroyed. This was it. He was going to be the one to take her out. It was fitting.

He reeled back his claw, like he had with so many of his enemies before. Ana closed her eyes, as she already knew the thing was at neck height. Even staring death in the face, she leaned her head back for an easier blow. She then felt the hardest slap she ever had. It felt like her face had been hit with a hammer, almost causing her to fall over.

"Don't wallow in what you've done." Drake said, the words seething off of his tongue. "It will carry with you forever. You will remember this moment in your life, and you will be haunted until the day you die. If there is an afterlife, it will follow you past that. Dying now, though? That would be pointless. You still have to fix this. That's your responsibility, and I'm not letting you run away from it."

Ana didn't know what to say. She didn't know what she expected, but it wasn't that. It was her fault, and it was her responsibility. She never looked at it as running away before. If anything, she now felt more guilt for the selfish decision of wanting to die.

"As long as you'll let me, I'll shoulder that burden." Ana answered with her hand on her heart.

"Then come in and eat. We don't have much, but your travel must have been long on your own." Drake offered.

"Oh, I'm not alone." She said without thinking. This made half of the camp watching this interaction raise an eyebrow. "I had a guard escort me." Those were the wrong words.

Talons, claws, and blades were raised. As if on cue, Calvin showed up behind her in a half sprint, practically out of breath. He didn't even notice the pack of half animals bearing down on him.

"Hold on!" Ana yelled out. "He's not one of the king's men!" she wanted to use the word tyrant but would rather hold off on the confusion for now.

Only a couple lowered their weapons, be it blade or body, before Henry intervened but standing between the pack and Calvin. "If Ana says he's good, then he's good! Besides, we're not going to let him leave our sights."

"Not by a longshot." Echoed Drake, the skepticism in his voice was evident and he already had his eyes following every one of the newcomer's movements. Calvin wondered what he had gotten himself into once again. He knew he should have tried denying the princess guarding job, everyone knew she was trouble..

"There's no man more innocent in the castle than him." Ana tried to explain. It took some time for the ambient growling in the background to stop. "Allow him to eat with us, and I'll try and shed some light on his situation."

"Yeah, that's right." Henry went along with it. "Get some food in your bellies, you crazed animals."

Dinner wasn't exactly luscious or luxurious, but it still felt better than what they had in the castle. Sure, the food was astounding there. Perfect in every single bite and made with nothing less than exact science. Ingredients delivered from all over the world to make the best dish, just for you and your palette. Yet, that still couldn't beat sitting around a raging fire, eating some kind of meat that you didn't even want to ask about. It was so overcooked to the point of having a leathery texture, but for the sake of their health it was probably better that way.

It was that feeling of camaraderie that Ana was missing. She just wanted to be part of something, around people that understand. Everyone around her likely hated her guts right now, but they went through the same kind of thing she had. They were all from different walks of life, and no matter if you were a princess or a commoner, being a hybrid would throw your life for a loop. It's in that similarity that they shared a bond. Except for Calvin, who spent his time darting his eyes around to make sure no one was trying to put him up on the menu. It wasn't an unsubstantiated fear, as there was a woman with tiger paws who was thinking of that exact thing.

This meal made something clear to Ana. The divide between the two sides was far too great. Calvin had done nothing wrong but he was looked upon as the enemy of these people. Ana, on the other hand, had single handedly caused the slaughter of what must have been a hundred of their kind. That didn't matter here. What mattered was what they looked like. One looked like a guard, one looked like a hybrid. This was what Ana decided she was here to fix, even if it just started with getting the hybrids to like Calvin, which would be far easier than what was to come.

Though they were all together, dinner was silent. No matter who quelled the fire, dinner would be awkward with someone who just put your life at risk. Henry made sure to threaten anyone who even looked at Ana or Calvin strangely. That was what hurt the most that night. Someone who had lost their livelihood. The only one who made that safe haven for hybrids all around, and he was the one defending her the most.

"So, what's your plan?" Drake asked after giving time for Ana to finish her meat on a stick.

"Huh?" Ana asked, having been too caught up in thought.

"For fixing this. For putting our lives back on course. I assume you have a plan." He knew she didn't.

"I..." She paused. "Have no idea." It was the truth. She had a vague fever dream in her head, but it was nothing they could ever pull off.

"Well, that's a shame. Better start thinking of something fast." Drake voiced, uncharacteristically laying back and relaxing.

"I thought you did have something, general." Calvin chimed in, trying to be helpful. It was the first time he had spoken since arriving, and he realized that it may have been a mistake. Now the princess looked like she was the one who was going to eat him.

"General?" Drake asked, excited to hear what hole she had dug herself.

"I swear to god Calvin." Ana narrowed her eyes at him.

"You're away from the lizard for a month, yet you still have his temperament." Henry rolled his eyes and beamed them at Drake. "I need to make sure to keep people away from you. I swear you have some way to corrupt them when I'm not looking."

Ana laughed a bitter laugh. Again, it hurt that Henry could stay so joyful in the worst of times. She did appreciate seeing the brooding look on Drake's face in response, though.

"Well, can't call yourself a general if you don't have a plan." Drake said, trying to change the subject back. "What are you even the general of?"

Ana spoke under her breath. "... hybrid liberation front."

"Hybrid liberation front, eh?" He made sure to say loud enough for all the cave to hear. They all paused for a moment with varying looks on their faces, unsure how to take the title.

"Well, I like it." Henry said, though he did like everything.

"You'll still need more than that to win the masses over." Drake motioned to the small group they had in the cave. It was then Ana had an idea. It was the same one she already had, but pieces started coming together. It would take a night of thinking, but she thinks she could get there confidently enough to say it out loud.

"You know what, I do have a plan." She said confidently, the ears of her friends all perking up to listen. "Overthrow the kingdom."

Chapter 18

It was the best night's sleep Ana had in a very long time. Sure it was on an uneven rock floor in a cold desert with a barely stoked fire, but to be fair she was starting to get used to sleeping like this. The crowding was a bit of a problem, though. This cave was small for the group, even without the two new additions. Yet she knew she need not fear from her life from the desert or otherwise. There was no more competent group for battle than her present company. She knew when she woke up, things would be uncertain. Questions such as where breakfast would come from being important, for example. She began to look at her situation in a new light and decided things were far more interesting now than they had ever been.

Even if she needed a taste of the castle, Calvin was there. She could just talk to him and feel praised for everything her hand touched. Ana usually hated that feeling, but there was something about Calvin that made it feel better. He was undyingly loyal, but it was just in his nature. It didn't feel like everyone else who worked in the castle, who only did it since they were getting paid. He might have worked there for free, given the opportunity.

Ana woke up on the wrong side of the rock that morning. As the first thing her eyes opened to was the blinding desert sun making its way in. It was enough for her to let out a slightly shocked sound of pain before turning over and covering her eyes. Once things got back to whatever normal could be attained, Ana decided she was going to sleep through the day and stay up through the night. Remembering that she was part bat, she didn't know why she hadn't reached that conclusion earlier.

Work had been divided up among the few that survived. Henry would cook and clean, similar to how he did back at the bar. Angui and the tiger lady, who Ana soon learned was named Lex, hunted desert animals. They dragged Calvin along with them, kicking and screaming. The rest of the group either stayed behind to help Henry or were too injured to work. This left Ana and Drake, who were to keep watch. Drake for his combat prowess and Ana for her heightened senses.

"So, come up with a real plan yet?" Drake asked. It was strange for him to start the conversation, but Ana supposed since he wanted something out of her, it wasn't too far off from normal.

"Partially." She admitted, not wanting to go into detail since it wasn't yet fleshed out.

"Well, let's hear what you've got." She knew she wasn't getting away with that.

"It's a long shot, but many wars have been lost on the division of a kingdom. I think that's our easiest route."

It was more than Drake was actually expecting and also something he put into question. "How are we going to do that, exactly?"

"There's already a start to it. You know Calvin?"

"Stupid question, of course."

"Right, well, there's a reason he's trustworthy." Ana paused for a moment to wonder how much she should actually trust him. She put faith in her father at one point, and that bit her in the behind. Then she remembered his concern and lack of hesitation saving her life, and she could do anything but. "He's not part of the king's guard. He works under the guard captain."

"Isn't that the same thing?" Drake asked, genuinely curious.

"Not at all. Sure, the king technically has control of Kasibel's soldiers, but in a pinch, they would listen to him instead. It's just a matter of dividing the two sides of the guard. If we're able to do that, Kasibel's troop is larger than my father's but less experienced. Hopefully, the group we have here would be able to do enough to tip the scales."

"I have to hand it to you. I was expecting less." Drake admitted.

"Thanks?" Ana said questioningly. "It's by far not a foolproof plan. Honestly, I would suggest running far away from this place before even thinking about it. The border guards are my brother's. They'd let you through without issue."

"I hate repeating myself, but I'll remind you." Drake started. Ana knew she was in for a lecture. "This is the home of these people. Thankfully, more hybrids survived than just us and hopefully escaped past the border. There weren't many of them, though, and the rest are here, not willing to give up on the ground they grew up on. Even though they can't see them, they're not willing to give up on their families that live here."

"I could run for the border right now." Ana said, thinking out loud.

"No one would stop you."

"I wouldn't be able to live with myself." Ana started kicking sand to distract her from the thought.

"Do you think you can accomplish enough here to bear your burden?" Drake was confusing her. First, he wants her to fight. Now it sounds like he'd rather she run.

"I don't think I ever can, but that doesn't mean I shouldn't."

"Very well. What are we up against?" And again with switching sides so easily.

"My father's army is small but well trained." Ana started running through her head, trying to remember everyone she knew, what kind of weapons they were good with, that kind of thing. Unfortunately, she preferred watching her brother's soldiers fight. They were more entertaining and fought as if it was for their lives. The king's men had some kind of noble rules to their battles that kept each other from getting hurt. That wouldn't help them now. "I suppose I shouldn't discount Kasibel's guard, though. They've seen combat more recently."

"Well, that's something." Drake scratched his head, wondering if the fight would be worth it or if it would just lead to more slaughter. "Either of them have any aces up their sleeve?"

"Now that you mention it...." Ana's mind filled with images of The Red Guard. She had never seen a single one of them without their masks. It was the smallest but most effective regiment of the king's army. They had never failed in a task nor lost a member in their years of running. There wasn't even anything in the history books about them, as King Rolfe was the one to put them in place. "My father has a small group, four members that I know of. No one knows what their deal is, but they're dangerous. The kind of fighters you only hear rumours about."

"Rumors are usually exaggerated."

"Not by a pride-filled client they're not. King Rolfe gets what he pays for out of them, and he pays a lot." Ana wondered if they would be the cinch in the plan. It was then she gazed around the camp, noting that they would also have their own task force. Knowing Drake wouldn't be quickly taken down put her mind at ease too. She knew her enemy well enough. It was time to get to know her allies a bit better. "So, Drake." Ana had a tone that somehow conveyed her intrusiveness.

"What is it?" Drake caught onto it.

"So, part dragon? How exactly does that happen?" Ana still couldn't believe it as the words were coming out of her mouth. She still didn't but was interested in the story.

"Think you can swallow it this time?" He was skeptical.

"Absolutely not, but I want to hear it anyway." Ana knew that being playful would annoy the ever-loving crap out of him, making him more likely to talk.

"Fine, I mean, it's not a long story." Drake leaned back against the cave wall as if it was his last time to relax before getting pelted with questions. "I hear a call, I go to it, I become a hybrid. It's anyone else's story only with what people assume to be a mythical beast involved."

"Well, I mean, that's the important part. Where was it hiding?" Ana was peeved at his way of throwing off the question.

"The northern tundras." Quick answers were all he was willing to give.

"A dragon? Big, fire-breathing creature? In the ice? Are you trying to see how gullible I am?"

"No, I already know that." Drake's words proved to be a backfire in Ana's plan of annoying him. He found out how she ticked and was using it to his advantage. "Turned out this one liked the cold."

"But the real question is how did you beat it?" Ana couldn't wait to hear this one. "Sure, you might have been able to prepare, unlike I did with my little bat friend, but we're talking about a dragon here. How could you have possibly won that?"

Drake was mad. It was the first time she had seen him mad. The look on his face was worse than when they were attacked by bandits or ferals. It was even worse than when she first came to this camp. A nerve was hit. "I didn't. We leave it there." His words were seething with rage.

Ana knew when to back off but couldn't help but wonder what he meant. She wanted to ask him more, but that was a bad idea on both a friendship and a survival level. Then Henry came to her mind, and she realized he probably knew the answer. It would just take a bit of alcohol and Drake not being in the room to figure that one out. Though they had no alcohol, and there was only one room. It turned out that Ana needed a strategy to find out about her allies, which might be a more challenging task than actually taking over the kingdom.

It was soon after that the away team came back with a couple of slain hyenas. Calvin was left carrying the desecrated corpses and looked way more tired than the other two. Ana would have to make sure they didn't take advantage of her personal guard *too* much.

It wasn't quite exotic or sought-after meat, but it would do. Somehow Henry managed to pull spices out of the bar with him. He either had messed up priorities or kept those things in his pocket. One way or another, Ana was glad they were there.

Then she remembered she didn't get the full story on Henry, either. Or Angui, or anyone else who was out here. She didn't know the pasts of any of these people. It must have boiled down to having to throw your old life away. Whether it was good or bad didn't matter. Looking back on it would only bring regret to anyone here. Be it the good times lost or the actions of their past selves. No one wanted to talk about what brought them here. They just wanted to live a peaceful life in the now. Ana realized she owed Drake an apology.

"So, any new ideas general?" Henry was the one to ask this time. Everyone sitting around the fire he had made to cook dinner had their eyes on Ana. Their eyes were filled with both hope and despair. That was when she realized this was her calling. That look they laid upon her. She was the one to grant these people their future. It overwhelmed her in the best of ways. It was bittersweet, as she caused this situation, but something awoke in her that day.

"This is going to sound insane, but all resistance plans are. Hear me out...." She gladly went into the same detail she did with Drake about dividing the kingdom.

"That's great and all, but are we going to go in on blind hope that half the soldiers will join us?" Angui was the one speaking up this time. She was one of the ones filled with more despair than hope. Her cynicism was crucial to Ana's strategizing. She needed someone not afraid to point out her mistakes, though she was already prepared for this one.

"Of course not." She confidently announced, shutting out the question. "We start with a small group, maybe two or three, that go in there to talk to Kasibel. Obviously, I would have to be one of them since I have the best chance at conversation with him."

"And how do you plan on not getting caught? The guards will be out looking for you again, and they know what you look like." Drake reminded her. It was a good question, and Ana took the time to think about it. The idea came to her pretty quickly.

"I initially didn't think of it since the barracks are right behind the main castle walls." Ana started thinking out loud. "But it's good that you brought that up, as the barracks can be manned by *both* kinds of guards. Usually, the king's men avoid training. Usually isn't good enough, though, so we need a backup plan. I was first thinking of going over the wall, but that would leave us with no way of explaining ourselves."

"How are we going to explain ourselves if we get caught anyway?" This time Henry chimed in. Having the conversation with the whole group made this feel real, and it helped with understanding the plan.

"That's where Calvin comes in."

"Me?" The guard asked with a mouthful of hyena. The guy sure could eat.

"Yes, you. Though you're not exactly instilling confidence in me right now." Ana shook her head. "Regardless, if you bring us in you could still say you found me and you're bringing me in to see the king. This would leave the group being only the two of us, though. Not many ways out if things go wrong." This time Ana with the objection, and Henry with the answer.

"Simple, I'll go with you." He said, with absolutely no reasoning.

"How are we supposed to explain you?" Ana asked.

"I was found with the princess and taken in for questioning." he was already prepared. Ana could have sworn he was going to leave that until he was questioned just so he could feel smug. And smug he looked.

"Now that you mention it, that wouldn't be a terrible idea. We wouldn't have to cover much of you, either." Ana looked Drake up and down, noting his problems with being concealed. "I think that settles it, then."

"It's just a matter of when you leave." Drake brought up.

"That's simple. Night is the best for us since my eyesight is better than any of the guards. As long as that works with you two?" Henry and Calvin both nodded. "Easy enough, then."

"Can I make one request on this mission?" Henry asked, raising his hand as if he was in school. Of course, it was the bear paw he put up.

"Of course." Ana allowed it, wondering why he would ask first.

"We stop back at the bar as long as we have time."

"Why would we need to do that?"

"Booze." And it suddenly made sense as to why Henry wanted to come along. It would definitely compromise the plan, but morale was just as important as a sound strategy. Wars had been lost over not treating your soldiers right.

Ana did share her discontent with a long sigh but said, "Fine, as long as we have time." As if Henry was a kid asking to see his friend on their outing to the market. She had wondered time and time again what she had gotten herself into and who she got into it with. Perhaps on the trip, she could pry Drake's past out of Henry, though. That was too juicy to just leave on the table.

"I would suggest you leave tonight and not wait a day if you were planning it." Drake joined back in on the conversation, causing Ana to jump, considering she was thinking of talking about him behind his back. "The longer you're away from the castle, the further away the guards start searching. This camp is time-sensitive."

"You make a point." Ana noted the sun in the desert was at its highest point. She couldn't actually see it but knew by how much her eyes burned even looking away from it. "I say we rest now until nightfall, and we should be able to make our way in before dawn breaks."

"I still don't think I understand." Calvin piped up. "Why me?" It sounded like more of a rhetorical question, wondering why the world was bearing down on him.

"Expendability." Angui joked. It made Calvin back away from her. Ana wondered what happened on the hunting trip.

"You really should have said no to guarding me." Ana said, "I can be a bit of a handful."

"I will say the job description didn't include any of this." Calvin said, disheartened by his surroundings. "I was thinking of staying home that day too."

"You just have all the luck, don't you?" Ana chuckled. She made sure to enjoy that moment, as their mission for the night was a dangerous one. It might be the last time she experienced joy in what could be a short life.

Chapter 19

The night came all too fast. Neither Calvin nor Ana were able to sleep well. Henry, on the other hand, was nearly impossible to wake up. You could swear one of the traits he inherited from that bear was hibernation. They were finally able to rouse him after Drake stepped in and gave him a swift kick to the head. Now it was just time for them to sneak into one of the most heavily guarded city's this side of the continent, bringing in a known fugitive, a guard who abandoned his post, and a princess who had all but forsaken her lineage. This was a stupid idea.

That didn't matter, though. At least not with a crew this stubborn and lazy. No one willing to back down from their plans, and no one willing to change them. The time crunch was starting to feel real, as they could already see a guard from the campsite. They were getting dreadfully close, and it was only a matter of time before they got hacked down, and someone would need to go looking for them. Things were looking grim.

"So, we ready to party or what?" Henry said after finally crawling out from the rock he hid under. Ana and Calvin were already packed and ready to go. Meanwhile, despite his demeanor, Henry was still rubbing sand out of his eyes.

"If that's what you want to call it." Ana returned, all too ready to begin walking without him. The anxiety she felt was deep, and she knew it would only get worse the longer she stood around. The idea of going in to sabotage her own kingdom's army was insane. It was something she never thought she'd have to do, but what that tyrant pulled was inhumane. There are some things you just can't ignore.

"Cool, cool." Henry started stalling. "Let me just get a bite to eat, and we'll hit the ro-" He turned around to walk to their tiny supply corner, but Drake stopped him, already holding a wrapped up meal in his hand.

“You’ll eat on the road.” He said coldly, shoving the meal into his friend’s hand.

“Fine, fine. Sheesh.” Henry took it but didn’t forget to stick his tongue out at Drake in the same motion. Drake ignored the immaturity, just happy he didn’t have to tag along.

“I swear the soldiers I have to work with....” Ana said, trailing off in thought.

“What? Did you expect a fully trained army to be at your feet?” Drake asked condescendingly.

“I’m a princess. Of course, I did. As a matter of fact, it would be weird if I expected anything else, but here we are.” Ana looked at her two travelling companions. Though she did trust both of them, she had to realize this was a sad-looking squad. “I’ll just have to work my magic with these two on the way there. Get them some idea of field experience, y’know?” She said directly to Drake as if she had gone out and fought with him a hundred times.

“I swear, you newbies either run away or get too confident and get yourselves killed.” Drake shook his head. “I at least know where you fall.”

Ana considered getting the last word in before she left but knew that he’d have some comeback. She decided to stoop to Henry’s level and just stick her tongue out at him. Both of her travelling companions joined in. Henry immediately, and Calvin soon after, not wanting to feel left out. If nothing else, the two of them were loyal.

“Best be off then!” Ana started off sounding much too optimistic. This was, of course, to hide her fear.

“Remember what I said last time.” Drake reminded her.

“Right, if I go and die, you’ll hunt me down and kill me. Got it.” Ana rolled her eyes and turned back to Henry and Calvin, saying more quietly. “It would at least be better than hearing him try and lecture me for the thousandth time.”

Henry got a good chuckle out of it, and once again, Calvin followed along. If they were going on a suicide mission, might as well have fun along the way.

The trip started with jokes and bits of food but quickly changed into planning. Luckily the three of them knew the city inside and out, each with their own specialty. Ana knew the castle grounds, which overlapped with Calvin who was also used to the upper quarter, and that left Henry, who mainly knew about the lower class and the market districts. Honestly, if there were three people to raid Arid Retreat, they had the best chance.

It didn't change the number of contingencies they had to run through. Even with the half day march to get to the city, there wasn't enough time to go over all of them. A good chunk of this plan fell on the hope the castle and its grounds would remain lightly guarded due to the continuing search for Ana. It was just a matter of dodging the patrols on the way, and every gate guard, and everyone walking the streets on the way there. There were holes in this strategy, but it was too late to back out now.

Once the town was in clear view, the three of them went completely silent. Each one of them had to prepare themselves for what was likely to come. Calvin's fear was the most pronounced, but he reminded himself he was still in service of the crown. Henry made it look like this was just another day even though the threat of death lay before him. Ana knew this was no time for hesitation and resigned herself to thinking this was the only way forward.

They had already put aside the idea of leaving unscathed. That was the best-case scenario, and you never prepare for the best. None of them showed any sign of backing down, though. They knew this would go haywire somewhere along the line and just hoped it was later rather than sooner.

Their fears were doubled by the patrol circling around the city walls. It was much larger than the last time and spread out to cover more ground. There would be less time to make it past the gate guards, and since they had no time to spare, they couldn't loop around to the lazier lower quarter workers. It would have to be the ones that earned their keep enough to protect the market district. The next move was crucial, getting in without being noticed, or noted as suspicious. There were two plans for their story. If they weren't asked to take down their hoods, they would act as merchants looking to set up. If asked about their wares, they would say they worked with one of the merchant lords who didn't stick around too often. Ana knew which houses were free and what a couple of them were full of, so it should go off without a hitch if they take the bait.

The second story was a bit harder to believe but might still work. It would involve Calvin mentioning he was on a secret assignment from the king to take Ana out of the castle and see the world just a little bit more. He would, of course, have to act as if his daughter was missing and not just out for a stroll due to her current condition. There were holes all around it, but they were hoping they wouldn't have to use it. There was a lot of improvisation required, and Ana wasn't entirely sure Calvin was up to the task. Hell, she didn't know if *she* was up to the task.

It then came time to move in. They had stayed back long enough to tell when the guards were coming around, but not too long that the sun crept over the horizon. It wasn't too far off, though, so they'd have to move fast.

"We should run, our window is small, and no matter which story we go with, we can say we're being chased by bandits." Ana advised. Both of the boys agreed with her, so they booked it as fast as they could. The sand was luckily soft on their feet, but it was slippery and caused Ana to nearly fall more than once. Henry and Calvin were behind her, so she couldn't tell how they were faring. She just had to trust they were alright. If this story were to be believable, they would be running for their lives.

The problem with hasty plans is that they have unintended side effects. Upon reaching the gate, the guards already had their weapons at the ready. Ana didn't expect that, as it wouldn't exactly be a smart feat to try and take on the city with only three people. Sure, that's exactly what they were doing, but the guards shouldn't expect that.

"Halt!" Came the first yell before they even got close enough to the gate to try charging in. Ana stopped first, followed by Calvin and then Henry. Each one of them kicked sand up as they skied to their stop. "What's your business?"

"We are merchants, sir." Henry started. He was the one with the most charm, so he had the greatest chance to make it through as long as they didn't ask to see their faces. "Being pursued by a group of marauders. We would really like to get inside so we can fall under the city's protection. I know I would feel safe being protected by guards such as you." Not even passed the introduction and he was already laying it on too thick.

"Where are your wares?" Came the second question, ignoring the note of bandits.

"Can we please talk about this inside the gate?" Henry pleaded.

"I see no bandits anywhere nearby at the moment. For now, it is safe to speak here." The guard was stern and backed Henry into a corner. It was as if his crutch got kicked out from underneath him.

"I do feel much better being reassured by such capable guards." Henry leaned into the compliment while trying to think up the next part of the story.

"Well? How can you be merchants without anything to sell?" He didn't have much time.

"We work for a lord within the city. He stays at his home very rarely, so we already have our wares there." Henry started, realizing he should probably speed things up. "The sun is close to breaking, and we would really like to get set up beforehand if we could."

"Which lord?" The guard asked. Ana had this one down.

"Lord Gaura." Ana immediately snapped to it before Henry tried to think up a fake answer and got them into more trouble.

"And what do you sell?"

"Relics from the wars past." Ana had specifically picked Gaura for that reason. He was one of the best relic sellers in the market and happened to not be home right now. "We could show you fine gentlemen if you'd like." She had to lean on the charm as well. A good merchant won't pass by any opportunity to make a buck, and she was hoping the story would hold together.

The two guards looked at each other and nodded. "Very well, that checks out. Garuda's been gone for a while, I'm sure he won't be happy that the three of you were so late, but that's between you and him. Way above my pay grade to piss that guy off." And with that, they were in the clear. "Only thing is we do have to get you to drop your hoods before coming in. New rule, have to follow it." And suddenly, they weren't.

"I'd really rather not. The damage from the sun and skirmish we had narrowly avoided have done damage to my beautiful face." Ana wasn't keen on going into plan B since neither she nor Calvin could get away without being noticed. Henry was fine, though, as he was rarely ever seen. He took his hood down, and they let him in with no issue while Ana was attempting to make a good excuse.

"Sorry, doesn't matter how much damage. King's orders and all." The guard crossed his arms sternly. "Now, hoods down."

"If you want to talk about king's orders." Calvin started, sounding much more confident than usual. He pulled his hood down to reveal who he was. "I have orders from his majesty to escort this fine lady in without such issues. As personal guard to princess Ana, it is imperative that we be let in."

"I thought you were merchants." The guard was getting suspicious. "And we were told especially to look out for you, as you abandoned the kingdom." Turns out word got around fast.

"Well, that was because-" Calvin couldn't even begin to think up a new plan before the first guard was knocked out by a giant bear paw. In the time it took to process what had happened, the second one went down. Henry motioned for them to run in.

"No one else is around, but let's get there fast, shall we?" He was having too much fun with this. Ana hoped that move saved their plan rather than damaged it. One way or another, it was time to run, and straight into the castle grounds.

Calvin led the way this time, knowing the most about the barracks and the merchant's district. Luckily the two pretty well went hand in hand. It was just a matter of getting inside the castle's exterior walls. There were two main exits that led to the middle of the city and near the lower quarter. Finally, there was a third that led right into the barracks and was normally only used for if the castle was attacked. Calvin was heading towards the third, and Ana wondered what his plan was.

The moment they got there, she understood. The guards waiting were Kasibel's, not Rolfe's. You could tell by the stripe of blue through the regular gold and red colours of the Rexharne flag. The problem boiled down to who they were truly loyal to. If they were loyal to the king, they'd have a problem even getting through the portcullis the two of them stood behind.

"Audry, Otis." Calvin knew them by name. This was promising. "It is imperative that we see Captain Kasibel right away. It's of grave importance." The man was out of breath, making it much easier to believe his story.

"You know the whole kingdom is looking for you and the princess, right?" Otis asked before making any move to open the gate. Even if it was open, the man that stood before them could act as a gate in his own right "There might as well be a bounty on your head."

"Yes, I understand, but the princess is exactly why we need to get in." Calvin was practically pleading.

"Can't we take a message?" Came the question from Audrey.

"Sarcastic as always, aren't we?" Calvin was getting audibly annoyed. "No, you can't. The princess wants to talk to her brother directly."

Both of the guards were taken aback by the statement, and before they could even question it, he pointed over at Ana. Both of them wore skeptical looks, and in the most brazen move he had pulled yet, Calvin brought down Ana's hood without asking her. She wasn't expecting it and immediately pulled it back up, practically growling at Calvin.

"See?" Calvin said. "I already know the rumours going around as to why I was the one sent to protect the princess. They're true. Now let us in, dammit."

It was strange seeing him be so forceful, but it worked. Audrey and Otis started opening the gate almost immediately at the reveal. Ana noted if she were the one to take over the kingdom, Calvin deserved nobility at the very least.

Both guards stepped aside the moment the gate was opened and bowed in respect to their princess. Even though she was being hunted like a mad animal, it seemed Kasibel's army gave respect to any of the royal family. Ana didn't know what his teaching style was like, but it had to be either terrifying or garner so much respect that his soldiers acted like this of their own free will. Not wanting to give her brother an inch, she was going to guess the former and made her way into the guard's barracks.

It was a strange area for a princess to be hanging out in, but she had always loved it here. Between the training dummies, the oversized mess hall, the sheer amount of weapons that may someday become relics of a future war, she loved it. Not to mention for a history buff, this was hallowed ground. Every order would have been taken here. Every time they attacked, every time they had to defend. It was hard not to get caught up in it. The only thing keeping her from it was Henry noticed the stalling and pulled her along. Both of them proceeded to follow Calvin into the smallest building on the premises, the captain's station. A barely hobbled together stone structure that no one in their right mind would ever think it was more than a glorified shed. No one besides Ana, that was.

If outside was hallowed ground, then this was the place where the building blocks of gods were held. It was a small room but served its purpose well, using every bit of space to its advantage. The walls were lined with each type of weapon. There was a shelf filled with books on military strategy and plenty of maps with ink and quills ready to go make plans. In the centre, the most essential part of it all. The war table. The place where the commands were brought to life and pieces moved on the board like some giant game of chess. Ana nearly hugged the table, as it was almost five hundred years old, and saw countless battles atop it. She only wished the old one didn't get burned in the second war of the sand border.

The only thing that soured this room was the only man willing to wear steel armour in the desert heat, Kasibel. Ana had detested her brother for years, but she knew it wasn't his fault. He just had what she wanted, a seat at the war table. She was told princesses should not be the ones giving commands, but she thought differently. The old adage of being careful what you wish for came to her mind that day.

"Calvin?" Kasibel asked, looking ready to rip the kid's head off. "Where have you been!?" He immediately stood and slammed his fist on the table. This wasn't exactly a good start.

"Well, you see sir-" Calvin got cut off before he could answer.

"With me, of course." Ana brought down her hood, and Kasibel started to look even more furious. "He was told to guard me and couldn't keep me from leaving. He did his duty."

"You shouldn't have left in the first place. Do you know what kind of hell I'm getting here?" Kasibel sat back down, knowing he couldn't win this argument in the way he wanted. "What do you want, anyway?"

"Hold on for a moment." Ana decided to stop to give him some perspective. "You think you've been going through hell? No, you haven't. You know who has? Henry." She pointed to her friend, who took the cue to pull out his arm. "This was the man who ran the bar that was massacred. You're lucky it wasn't by you, or I'd be taking you down where you stand." She was furious.

"Oh, you're going to blame me for this?" Kasibel sounded defensive, and unfortunately to Ana, sounded like he was about to have good ground. "I warned you to not tell *anyone* about the whereabouts of hybrids in this city, and what do you do? Go and tell father. That was a smart move." By this point, they were on opposite ends of the war table, bearing their teeth at each other. This might be the first battle this table had seen right on top of it.

"How was I supposed to know dad wasn't to be trusted?" She asked. "I didn't know that tyrant had such a cold heart until I saw that bar." The images came back to her mind. She wanted to be sick. "How could he do such a thing?" She quieted down to ask that question to herself.

"It doesn't matter how. What matters is that he did." Kasibel also began quieting down. "The king is not one for mercy, not for those who break his laws."

"What are you defending him now? For murdering people just for being themselves?" Ana was starting to get heated up again.

"Quite the opposite. I abhor such acts." Kasibel answered, sounding disgusted that she would ever think otherwise. "I've been half considering taking on the throne myself." Jackpot. Ana might not even have to do any convincing.

"If you think you can take it on your own, go ahead and try." Somehow she still wanted to have the upper hand. Now that she knew he already wanted it, she would start playing as if he was doing a favour for her.

"What are you offering?" Kasibel right through her manipulation and got straight to the point..

"I might have a deal for you if you're willing to give me your ear."

Chapter 20

"So you want to use a band of misfit hybrids as well as my men to storm the citadel?" Kasibel asked, his mental anguish coming through in every word.

"Hey, this hybrid took out two of *your* guards." Ana stated, pointing at Henry. "Besides, this was your idea in the first place. I just wanted to lend a hand."

"If it was my idea, why did you come sneaking into the kingdom?" Kasibel had her in a corner. It was excuse time.

"I just wanted you to know I was ok." Ana crossed her arms and put on a snarky face. "A brother should be worried about his one and only sister, after all."

"And a sister, nay, a princess shouldn't have to sneak in and knock out two guards along the way. Besides, they weren't even mine. They were father's."

"Wait, what?" Suddenly a chill ran down Ana's spine. She knew it was a bad idea to assault city staff, but she thought Henry had taken out Kasibel's guards. If that was the case they would have just reported to the barracks, the situation would be explained, and there would maybe be a minor altercation. Those guards being her father's, though? When they woke up, they would report to the king. All entrances would be blocked off and they'd start searching even harder than they likely already were. Their time was shorter than Ana thought.

"Yeah, father decided to staff with his own men. Saying something like 'I don't trust you and your forces with such a task'. He's probably pent up over us turning down the hybrid slaughter." Kasibel's words became heavy on everyone in the room.

"Right, well. Pressed for time here. Assault or no assault?" Ana would jump over the wall to the desert right now if she could. The idea of being captured wasn't one she liked.

"I would need to see your forces." Kasibel mentioned always thinking strategically.

"Great." Ana knew it wasn't great since this would be nearly impossible to pull off, but a deal is a deal. "Tomorrow night. March along the mountains, and I'll be able to call you over."

"Can't you bring them to me? I have an army to run here." Kasibel was getting impatient.

"Nope. Can't afford sneaking in again. You have an easy story. You're going to go out and look for me." Ana's entire back tensed up along with Calvins, as voices could be heard outside. Voices of very angry men. "Right, we've got a deal." Ana picked up Kasibel's hand against his will and shook it before he had the time to respond. "See you tomorrow night!"

"Wait-" The guard captain started, but his three visitors were suddenly making their way out as fast as they could. He couldn't get a word in. Fortunately, she played right into his curiosity. She knew there was no way he'd turn down an offer like this in his time of need. It would be a difficult task, getting out to the desert, but he had every plan to.

Meanwhile, it was a difficult task getting *to* the desert for Ana, Calvin, and Henry. There were already an entire group of the king's guards outside of the barracks. The doors were sealed. It was time to jump.

"You ever climb a wall before, Calvin?" Ana asked, hastily making her way to the exterior barrier.

"Not one as smooth as this." Calvin replied. This brought up questions, but for later. Some experience was better than none.

"Here." Henry had made it forward first, holding his bear paw down to the ground. "I'll boost the two of you and follow up." Neither of them were going to say no to the offer.

Ana let Calvin go first in case something went wrong. It was sloppy, sure, but the aid of Henry got him nearly to the top. It was only a quick vault over, then hopefully not hurting himself coming down the other side. Ana was up next, and it was a bit more smooth, and it had to be. The guards were practically on their tail. She had never had this close of a call before. At least ten men were bearing down on them. Ana wondered how Henry was going to make it over by the time she hit the top, but knew she had no way to help him. In her haste she practically tumbled down the other side. If the sand wasn't there to break her fall, at least a bit, the mission would have been over right then and there.

Ana could have run, but she was too anxious about Henry. She could hear his paw hit the wall hard. The picture in her head from the other side made her think he had punched a hole in the thing for better grip. What came next was the sound of guards shouting at him to get down. Followed by the harrowing scream of the bar owner. He had been hit. It could have been by an arrow or a javelin, but the sound was followed by a solid thud. Ana was beside herself and needed to act fast.

She grabbed ahold of the wall again and tried to climb up it, but there was a weight holding her back. A heavy weight around her ankles. A weight trying to save her life that she was willing to forfeit for the second time.

"You wouldn't come out alive or any better." Calvin reminded her sternly. "We can't go back. The same thing would just happen to us."

"I'd willingly rip them all to shreds right now. Let go of my ankles, Calvin, or you'll be among their numbers." She wasn't willing to back down, but her grip was failing. This time her personal guard was on the opposite side of the wall, doing the same thing he did for her at the tower. Only this time, she didn't appreciate it.

"No. I won't let you die in a vain attempt to save him from the dungeon. Kasibel is there. He won't let another death happen." Calvin's undying loyalty was showing through again, but his confidence in her brother reinforced something in Ana. She trusted him just as much, especially after hearing he turned down the mission to attack the bar against the king's orders. She had to trust him. There was no other option.

Ana got down from the wall and started running immediately. Now was not the time to think out one's actions, as she ran with Calvin as far as they could through the desert sands. The only hope they had of not getting seen was avoiding the patrol and hoping the gate guards were inside, taking down Henry. There was no looking back for either of them as it could spell certain death or worse. They would have to assume they were seen running towards the hideout. Upon arriving, they would have to act accordingly.

It was some time before either of them ran out of breath. The city was merely a speck in the distance. Both of them had fear to thank for the motivation. It was still a little over half the day's walk to get back to camp, and neither of them had slept in a while, but stopping meant failure. They agreed without any words to continue on and would grant themselves the chance to fall over when they got back to the cave.

Ana wanted to talk to distract herself, but there was nothing to speak of. Henry was captured, that was certain. What they were going to do to him was another question. Before, Ana would assume that Kasibel's pleas would keep the bar owner alive, but her opinion of her father had changed. She somehow trusted that her brother could keep Henry alive, but what did that mean for him? She knew he was going to be in a cell, that was certain. At least the dungeon was the easiest way to sneak in and out of the castle. Even more so now that she had night vision and sensitive hearing.

The problem lay in what might happen in that dungeon. She had seen it before. There were still torture devices down there. She was assured that they were only there as a relic of the past, meant to strike fear in the wrongdoers of society. Now she questioned that excuse. The man she knew from her childhood would never use anything down there. The man she knew now would. Either torture or public execution, those were the two things bouncing back and forth in Ana's mind. The man who murdered a tavern full of innocents would either ignore her brother's cries, even if they would start a war, or twist them into his own will and not *technically* break the promise. This was the most worried she had been in a long time.

"How much pull does he have?" Ana needed an answer to the question.

"Who?" Calvin asked, understandably lost as it was the first time either of them had spoken in hours.

"Kasibel. How likely is it that he can sway the king?" She clarified impatiently.

"Kasibel would threaten the king with war over murder on his own grounds." Calvin assured her.

"Do you think it would be enough?"

"What do you mean?"

"Do you think it would be enough to stop him?" Calvin's questions were starting to get on her nerves. She wanted answers now. They had hours to talk, but her mind wouldn't let it go on that long.

"A threat of war stop the king of a peaceful nation? I would think so."

"Thinking so isn't enough. This man is mad. What is he willing to start for whatever twisted plan he has?" Ana had asked the question to the desert more than Calvin. It was confusing. There was no motivation behind it she could think of aside from pure hatred of the race. Perhaps that was it, but if he hated them that much, he would have shown it upon seeing her face the first time after she turned. Something wasn't adding up. A move like this should only be for significant threats to the kingdom or its citizens.

The law might have had something in it against such a large gathering that wasn't under the eye of the monarchy. But, even then, it wouldn't be justified to uphold it in such an extreme. The king might be going paranoid as many rulers had, followed by bringing their kingdom to ruin in a bout of trying to keep the power. He seemed too young for that to occur naturally, though, and there were no conditions that he had fallen under recently. The medical staff was chatty, so it would have been easy to figure out. So unless it was an attack of something with absolutely no build-up, then sure, it could be a condition, but it was unlikely.

Ana wanted to believe there was a reason for this. She wanted something to hold on to that would make her family feel whole again. There was nothing. Every avenue she searched down couldn't justify what happened at that bar. With the exception of every single hybrid being a spy for another kingdom, no reason held up. Even then, unarmed enemies of the kingdom were to be taken in if they surrendered, and remembering the bodies, many of them tried.

It was an impossibility, as her life had been full of recently. After hours of walking, it was still hard to digest, and it started coming back up when she saw the cave in the distance. What was she going to tell everyone? That the man who put his whole life to running a safe spot for them to stay was captured, and it was her fault. Somehow, the slaughter of countless hybrids wasn't enough for one of them at the camp to kill her, yet she felt losing Henry was. There was something magical about that man's charm and optimism. She felt her actions had robbed the world of one of the best men it ever had.

Her fears came to light the moment they were in eyesight of the camp. Drake began approaching the moment he could see the two of them. He wasn't a man to abandon his post, but seeing only two of them coming back instead of three, Ana knew why he was making his way over. She walked to meet him halfway and stopped in front of him. She expected anger, a lecture, perhaps death; what she didn't expect was him to keep going.

"Wait, what are you doing?" Ana asked the moment Drake walked past her.

"Going to get him back." He responded, not stopping.

"No, you're not. It's a suicide mission. Henry is safe." She didn't believe the words herself but needed time to regroup. She wasn't losing Drake too.

He paused and turned, ready to hear her out for a split second. "How can he be safe if he isn't with you?"

"It was my brother's barracks they captured him in. Kasibel has control of what happens with prisoners caught on his watch." Ana didn't know how true her words were, but they felt wrong.

"Do you really believe that?"

"Not at all, but it's what we have to work with." Ana was far from confident in any of her strategies. Maybe her brother would manage to have the answer, but that was far from an idea she wanted to rely on. Even if he did have a plan, it would involve storming the kingdom. No matter what path they took, someone would shed blood. There was no peaceful way around it.

"Then why should I sit around and wait?" Drake asked, ready to run at a moment's notice.

"I have a plan. We can get him out and work towards our goal in the same move." Ana answered, the ideas coming to her as she talked.

"So why can't we execute it now?"

"Because we have a meeting tomorrow night with Kasibel. We need to be on the same page."

"Wasn't that the whole point of you running off?" Drake was getting heated. "Are you telling me Henry got captured in vain?"

"No. The amount of time he bought us was enough for us to get the meeting in place. We used every second we had and then some."

"Henry is worth more than just buying time." It was clear nothing Ana had done before this had as heavy of an impact.

"We just have to wait until tomorrow night, and-" She was cut off quickly.

"We don't have until tomorrow night. Your trust in your family is what killed most of us. I'm not putting Henry's life in with theirs."

"But Kasibel is-"

"I don't care!" It was the first time she had heard Drake raise his voice. "What little unity that we had left stood on the shoulders of that man. Without him, there's nothing keeping us together. You think I like dealing with Angui? No. Just because we all share one chapter in our story doesn't mean every hybrid gets along, but Henry changes that. He quelled the arguments and made each one of us feel at home. The bar being destroyed was nothing. It was just a physical place that we stayed together. Many died, and it was devastating. But our home was wherever Henry was. You've taken away our home."

Each new word felt like another stone that had fallen on Ana's shoulders. He wasn't wrong. This was her fault. Her fault for trusting in the one person she thought she could trust. Because of that, many innocents died. Once again, that trust was put to the test. Kasibel was supposed to be different, right? She hoped she was right. It would practically be suicide to charge in there and save him. There was no way a plan like that could work, not without backup.

"You shouldn't go in there on your own." Ana said. She wasn't on board with storming the dungeon, but it might be her only option. She was finding herself backed into a corner all too often. "You shouldn't go in there at all."

"You have two minutes to give me a better idea, or I'm gone." Drake was serious. She could even swear he was timing it by the sun's position.

It wasn't enough time. She tried to go back in there, but Calvin stopped her. Should she have let him? So many questions came to her mind. So many people wanted so many different things. It was hard to keep them all satisfied. Is this what being a ruler felt like? Is this what she was destined for? It was like being given a puzzle with pieces that only kind of fit, and you have to leave some out to complete a jumbled picture that you hope you're happy with. She had to focus on her strategy. This time, she had to get the full picture.

She thought back to the one thing she did know, history. The wars fought in the past had many foleys, and those were what she would turn to for inspiration. Battles were lost on the failures of the losing army, and avoiding those failures was the only way to succeed. Suicide missions were usually on that list, though there was something else that came to her mind.

Motivation. The power behind an army lies within how willing its soldiers are to fight. Without Henry, there was no motivation. Or was there? Perhaps storming the castle to get him back would be a critical move that would help them fight their way through. Alternatively, it could be the final straw that broke the hybrids. It was the role that Henry played that would make the decision.

It didn't take much thinking to narrow it down to general or monarch. In either case, the loss of such a key unit was usually not something any regiment could come back from. They would be looking for leadership, someone they respected. If no one of that nature was there to fill that role, they would quickly lose all will to fight. With the remaining group they had, it left no one that could fill that position.

"Alright, I have an idea." Ana had finally pieced the puzzle together. It looked as ugly as she expected and likely blood-soaked.

"Go on then." Drake waited impatiently.

"We sneak in to get him back. You and me." Ana decided to wait for the comment on her plan.

"So all you could think up was tagging along with my idea?" Drake answered smugly.

"Not quite." She answered. "You'll need me as a key member. We sneak in at night when my eyesight is best, and I can guide you. Not to mention you don't know your way around the castle dungeons."

"I could do it fine myself."

"I'm not done." Ana had to assert herself in this. "If we're going to continue by storming the castle, we can't stay nearly a day's march away. We have to take everyone else with us."

"A large group would be easy to spot." Drake was getting tired of Ana's ideas. Ana was getting tired of him pointing out the obvious.

"That's a risk we have to take. We have to stay hidden, so I would say everyone besides you and I take the mountain paths. That would keep them out of the main line of sight. This way, when we meet with Kasibel, the assault can start quickly." Ana was hoping if her brother came while she was in the dungeons, Calvin would suffice as an intermediary for the two groups.

"I've been thinking about this, and I don't see how taking over the castle is going to help us." Drake always found a hole he had to poke his finger in.

"Simple. History is written by the victors. Win the war, rewrite history. Do you want a bar to go back to, or a whole city you can roam freely?"

Drake thought about it for a second and hated to admit that she made sense. He always wanted to pull a move like this. Staying in the shadows wasn't exactly his cup of tea. It wasn't any of the other hybrid's either, and the idea of freedom was an idea worth fighting for. "Alright, you've convinced me." He finally admitted. "I suppose we should go tell everyone what happened." He turned to walk back to camp, but she stopped him the moment she could.

"We can't tell them." She said strongly.

"Why not?" Drake was skeptical. Ana explained her rationalization. It didn't sit well with him, but it again made sense. "So what do we tell them?"

"He stayed inside the city as an informant. Watching how the guards move so we would know when to strike."

"So we lie our way through until we get him back?" As much as Ana didn't like how condescending Drake could be, but at least he got the point.

"Pretty much. It's between you, me, and Calvin." Ana turned to the guard in question. "Are you alright relaying our battle plan to Kasibel if we don't make it back in time?"

"Yes, of course!" Calvin stood at attention right away. "I've studied strategy in excess."

"Good, just make sure you don't get us killed." Ana was starting to feel like an actual general. The lives of these people were in her hands. She had lost the first battle, her mistake being that she didn't even know it was happening.

She had no intention of losing the war.

Chapter 21

It took some convincing to get the rest of the hybrids on board. Lex, in particular, had many questions about why she should trust Ana and already appeared to have no faith in Drake. Things were starting to look up when she agreed as she was the hardest to convince, if only because Henry was currently in enemy territory. It reinforced their need to get him out of that dungeon, assuming he was still in there and not listed for execution or worse.

Their group was far from sizeable, but looking at what she had to work with when the time came pleased Ana. She had already seen Drake in combat, and though he acted aloof, Calvin was a seasoned fighter. Being under Kasibel meant that he had seen at least some kind of action, even if it was just wrestling a thief to the ground. Angui turned out to be exceptional with her swords and used her own venom to coat them. It was savage, but effective.

The rest were new to her, and not a single one could be considered a pushover. Lex had the arms and legs of a tiger. It made using weapons, or even utensils, nearly impossible for her though her claws made up for that. Ivan was fused with a bull, his muscles being the one thing that stuck out as inhuman. He had the horns as well, but they weren't nearly as prominent. That left Talia, who wasn't much for combat, but her vulture wings were large enough to lift her off the ground. Ana had to admit she was jealous, but her use for scouting was incomparable.

The small team mixed with Kasibel's army should be enough to take the castle. Ana was hoping to take King Rolfe by surprise, but that man had proved his might and knew what he was doing. If anything, they should expect an ambush from *him*. The plan was laid out, but there were contingencies set for even if scouting went wrong. Ana and Drake were to take the desert to the castle, and the rest were to hide in the mountain range. Talia flew ahead to check if the path was clear while the rest started making their way around. It would take longer for them to get there, which was likely a good thing. It gave more time for her and Drake to do a jailbreak.

Ana had stated that the war had already begun. If either group found one of the king's guard, they were to be taken out. It was the only way to keep from getting caught. Bodies in the desert tend to get buried, and it would take longer for someone to find them than it would for the battle to begin. There was some pushback about the idea, but at least Angui assured Ana she had no issue with killing. It made Ana concerned about who she was helping, a problem that would have to be tackled later.

Ana had wished she could have gotten some rest, but nightfall was already upon them by the time she was done explaining the plan. She and Drake also had to go over any strategies they had for the dungeon. Once the first group split off, they began talking.

"Our main problem is going to be the bars. They're buried inches into the stone, made of thick steel, and the keys aren't easy to find." Ana was speaking her qualms out loud, hoping that would help her come to a conclusion.

"I could try breaking them," Drake said. "I'm no pushover when it comes to strength." Ana almost laughed.

"I'm sorry, but I don't think you could just pull these things apart with your bare hands. We'll likely have to lockpick or find a key."

"A key would likely be deeper in the castle, correct?"

"Yes, and well guarded. It would put us in a dangerous spot." Ana didn't like the idea. Only one guard held the dungeon keys, and a request had to be made for him to even go down there. Ana had always known their prisoners weren't treated well, and at one time, she had no issue with it. That was before she found out what people could be imprisoned for.

"Do you know how to pick locks?" Drake asked. A question that concerned Ana.

"To be honest, I was hoping you would know how." Ana sighed as she tried to think up a new way through this.

"How hard is the dungeon to get into?"

"Not terribly on a normal day. I'm sure that's not the case anymore." It was another problem she hadn't had the time to think of. It was likely they'd have to take out a guard or two before even getting past the first door. "You know, this might be the end for us.

Once we go in there."
"Not very promising words coming from our general." Drake's tone was sarcastic.
"At least they're honest." Ana looked up at the sky as the first stars became visible. It might be the last desert night she'd get to enjoy. That feeling was reinforced with each step she took. The sand falling between her toes like her own personal hourglass. She didn't like the idea of it ticking down so quickly.
"You might as well have confidence in this, even if you don't have a plan." Drake said, trying to reassure her. Even with the fear of death being so close, that was the thing that scared Ana the most.
"But what if it does go wrong?" She was willing to voice her concerns. If not now, then when?
"Then we'll be dead, and you don't have to worry about it." And there it was. He was right, but she really wished he wasn't. Going into this with confidence was the only way. Hesitation was a death sentence. As gloomy as he was, Drake was the one who found her when she transformed. He explained everything to her and introduced her into his world. Ana figured he regretted that decision greatly, but he never stopped being kind in his own way.
"Thank you." Ana had wanted to say those words for so long but never got the chance to. This wasn't the best opportunity, but it might be the last.
"For what?" He was genuinely confused.
"If it wasn't for you, I may have been executed by guards a month ago. If anything deserves thanks, it's that." Ana thought about what she said and continued, knowing it wasn't enough. "But you've helped me through a lot of this. If I don't get another chance to say it, I figured I should let you know I appreciate you."
"I'll save the 'you're welcome' for after I save your life in the dungeon." Drake really knew how to tone down an emotional moment.
"How about we have a bet?" Ana asked, a smirk coming across her face.
"Go on."
"We keep track of how many times we save each other's lives. Whoever is lower has to help Henry clean his new bar for a month." The idea of that sent shivers down her spine, more than her life being at risk.

"Heavy cost, but I'll take it. Zero isn't a hard number to beat." She could have smacked him then and there but knew it would hurt her hand more than it hurt his scales.

Any lighthearted conversation they had came to an end as the city walls came into sight. There was something different about it this time. The view Ana usually had of this place was of home, of the market stalls, of the residents. She saw a bustling place with so many nooks and crannies that creatures or back-alley deals could be taking place in. It was a living, breathing kingdom.

Now she stared upon a fortress. A solid rock in the middle of the desert no easier to penetrate than a boulder. The walls high enough that climbing them was a disadvantage. An army that was constantly on patrol looking for her. The sands around it a battlefield named after the amount of blood shed on it. The task was nearly impossible, but that was just possible enough. Any chance to right the wrongs she had done, she would take. Her path was already drenched in blood. Now she would spill it in return. It felt wrong, but there was no other way forward.

Conveniently the moon was thin that night, making the desert particularly dark. That was the other problem with staging an assault on this place. You could see for miles on any side of it. If humans had night vision, it would be impossible to move forward without being noticed. The torches near the gates were the only things to burn brightly, which would work in their favour. As before, they were planning on going over the wall, away from the light. It also made the guards' eyes less used to the dark, meaning they had a larger area to work with.

"We go in through the barracks wall." Ana broke the silence.

"What? Why?" Drake felt like that was one of the worst places to make their way in.

"I can only imagine that the tyrant is expecting us to attack. He's been paranoid since I left. He's going to have the force spread thin between scouts and the city. The only guards that are likely in the barracks are my brother's"

"How can you be so sure he wouldn't station one of his own there?" Drake was getting more concerned by the minute.

"No one is stupid enough to break into the barracks." Ana said with a smile.

"Except us." Drake hated this idea.

"Now you're getting it." They were getting close enough that a guard could spot them. Both of them knew this, and Drake in particular, resented this, as he wanted to remain silent. The worst part was he didn't have a better idea.

As always, there were guards stationed at each gate and also on patrol. This kind of thing was becoming a common occurrence. Ana already knew their pathing and timing. She never thought that she would be the next one stupid enough to take on the impenetrable fortress, but here she was. They had silently agreed on the same strategy as before. They hugged the mountain range to keep as out of sight as possible on the approach. They reached the wall without issue, but then came the questioning.

"Are you sure this is going to work?" Drake asked, not knowing what kind of fight he was getting himself into.

"Not in the slightest." Ana responded. "This is a hail Mary at best."

"Then why are we doing it?"

"It's already a suicide mission. Might as well take some risks that, if they pay off, lower our odds of dying." Ana didn't like having to do things like this. She'd rather be trying to raise odds of success, but she had to work with what she had. "I'll go first." She began to mount the wall.

Her ears were open from the time they could see the glimmer of torchlight coming off the city walls. Now she heard guards talking on the other side of the wall. Typically, this would be worrying, but she already knew the voices. She had heard them not a day before, and they belonged to Audrey and Otis, the same two that let Calvin in. After what she felt were one too many slip ups due to this district's wall being much smoother, she straddled the top and confirmed her suspicions. Kasibel's guards were at the same posts as before. Instead of just jumping down the other side and causing a scene, she had an idea.

Ana stayed atop the wall for a moment and found the nearest pebble she could. She picked it up, and luckily they weren't too far away, as she wasn't exactly good at throwing things. She went ahead and chucked the stone as hard as possible in their direction. It skipped along the ground and stopped right in front of Audrey. Exactly as Ana hoped, the noise and movement was enough to alert her, but no one else. Unfortunately, she had to throw another, as the first was just enough to get the guard's attention on the ground. The second attempt was a bit more vigorous than the first and hit Audrey right in the shoulder.

Ana froze for a moment. The worst thing that could happen is Audrey calling out, asking if someone was there. Most guards were not okay with getting assaulted, and Ana was hoping she found the exception. The first part of the response wasn't great, as Audrey pulled her spear and started looking around with purpose. Another stone would definitely cause her to call out, so there was only one move left.

Ana quickly climbed down the other side of the wall, barely doing anything more than hanging off and letting herself drop. It hurt her legs, but it was barely noticeable with the amount of adrenaline running through her. Her head snapped up the moment she could make it, darting her eyes around to make sure the only guards near were ones she knew. The only one she could see near her was the shocked Audrey. Ana held a finger up to her lips to indicate silence, and Audrey only half obeyed.

"What are you doing?" She said in a hushed tone, walking over to the infiltrating princess.

Ana mimicked the volume. "We need to get our friend out."

"Who's we?" Just as the words left her mouth, Drake finished climbing over the other side of the wall with considerably less stealth than Ana had.

"The bear-armed man, where did he go?" Ana asked.

"The dungeon, I presume. The king's guard got him pretty fast." Dammit, Ana thought. Her father was trying to take control of the situation. It was just a matter of how much he managed to wrestle from Kasibel.

"Are there any around?" Ana ignored the inquiry eating at her and left the priority questions first.

"All of his are either in the castle or out looking for you. There's also a bounty for your return. Hefty sum."

"You looking to cash in?" Ana asked snidely.

"It's tempting, but I respect your brother too much. Just a friendly warning, the city is out for you, and they know what they're looking for."

"That's fine. I expected as much." Ana lied. She didn't expect him to get citizens involved. "Do you know if anything happened to him?"

"We got banned from the dungeon the moment he was locked up.

Even the king's regular guard isn't allowed in."

Ana threw her hand out preemptively to stop Drake from storming right in. He did indeed try but respected the move and held back. A good thing, too, as he would have broken his way straight into the dining hall from here. "Then who could be guarding it?" Ana asked.

"It's privileged information. They're considering it a prisoner of war situation." That was going to cause even more problems. The king was expecting a war. Whether or not he expected his two children to be the ones leading the charge was a separate story. He was at least suspicious of them both, so they couldn't rely strictly on surprise. "There is a rumour, though." Audrey continued.

"Well, go on then." Ana was impatient.

"They say a single Red Guard is staffed there." Those words sank Ana's heart. An unknown enemy that has theoretically never failed in a mission. That was the last thing she wanted to hear. "Anyone who has seen them walking the castle has only seen three, their leader included." That news was like finding out the poison you just drank takes two hours to kill you instead of one. Still, Ana counted her blessings.

"So there's only one guard stationed there?" Drake asked, not being nearly as quiet as the other two.

"You could say that." Audry replied.

"I wouldn't, though." Ana had to think about this one. "Whatever we're up against isn't going to be easy."

"Waiting around isn't going to make it easier." Drake was practically tapping his foot with impatience. Ana wondered if you could buy a leash for a dragon. It might make these outings more bearable.

"Right." In the end, she had to agree. "You didn't see us, right?"

"I'm under orders to not see you." Audrey replied.

"Told you he was good." Ana said, turning to Drake. He didn't appreciate the comment as much as she wanted him to. She looked back to Audrey. "Will opening the gate raise any suspicion?" She asked, referring to the one leading out to the street. Clearly, it wouldn't, as Otis was already at the crank inching it up for them.

Ana and Drake pulled their cloaks over their heads and slipped their way through as quickly as possible. Though it seemed odd to Drake to leave the castle walls only to circle back in, Ana explained to him earlier on that there was a public execution stage. It wasn't something she liked to think about, but sometimes a monarch did have to put someone up there to prove a point. It was a powerful tool used throughout history, and unfortunately, it worked.

The reason this was good for them was it needed to lead to the dungeon somehow, so one of the castle entrances led right into it. It was a public area only populated when an "event" was happening and brought them exactly where they needed to go. Avoiding guards along the way wasn't as challenging as Ana expected. It seemed most were outside the walls, keeping any break-ins from happening. They were doing an awful job.

The execution square wasn't the most comfortable place to be on a regular day, but the lack of civilians living nearby made it perfect for two people who didn't want to be seen. The setup was morbid as the stage was a theatre for death. The constantly sharpened guillotine hung menacingly against the faint moonlight. The nooses swayed back and forth in the slight wind. Ana could swear the bloodstains were fresh. It was a strange place to be safe, but she still hated it enough to move through as fast as possible to get inside the dungeon. Drake had no complaints about this.

They stood in front of a staircase downwards, with two daunting metal doors blocking their path. They were likely locked, but they were set if that was the only complication they ran into.

"You ready?" Drake asked.

"Nope." Ana said, letting out a long sigh. Nothing could ever prepare her for this. "So let's go."

Chapter 22

There was only one thing worse than the doors to the dungeon being locked. They weren't. Drake pushed his claw against the blackened steel door and it scraped the ground loudly as it opened. The sound echoed through the dungeon so loudly that Drake might as well have knocked before coming in. Whoever was in here definitely knew they had company, and they were expecting it. They were either very cocky, had set a trap, or both.

Ana took a look in first. They both knew to expect something. It was just a matter of what. Her eyes helped as they quickly adjusted to the darkness. Not a single torch was lit. Theoretically, whoever was on guard needed to see, so it signalled them to be cautious. She scanned the room top to bottom, and nothing seemed out of place. This was even more concerning. She took a deep breath and stepped in.

The room was just as she remembered. A long, wide corridor with cells on either side. Both the cells and the hall itself were rather large for something used to house prisoners. Most of the empty space was taken up by various torture devices. Once upon a time, Ana believed her father that they were never used by him and had been kept for historical value and to set fear in the prisoners. If she didn't already discredit that excuse, the bloodstains on the stone table in front of her hammered it home.

She had to keep herself from charging in to make sure Henry was okay. She knew the answer. He wasn't. That's why they were here. She was just lucky Drake couldn't see it; otherwise, he would charge in and land in whatever trap was waiting for them, be it a blade or a pit. Inching her way forward, Ana pulled Drake along behind her, as his eyes still weren't adjusted to just how pitch black this place was.

As they walked along, most of the cells were empty. Actually, all of them were. Something wasn't right. There were usually thieves from the market that were kept here for a week. The whole reason Ana didn't like sneaking out this way was due to the comments of some of the more vile men placed here. So where were they? The place was quiet, save for a faint sobbing in the distance. The question fell from her mind the moment she saw a cell occupied. He was curled up in a corner and shaking, but she could tell from the back of his head and the bits of fur lying about his cell that they were looking at Henry.

"Here he is." Ana whispered to Drake. "He's moving." Drake would never admit it, but he could have jumped for joy just at the fact that man was alive. He settled for walking over to the cell bars and trying to see for himself.

"Henry." He called out quietly. Henry didn't turn. Something was wrong. Drake couldn't even hear it at the bars, but Ana could. Henry was crying. It sounded like he was out of breath. "Henry." Drake called out a little bit louder. The figure in the corner stopped shaking and turned his head. With it came the rest of the upper body, and finally, what was wrong. Drake still couldn't see, but Ana could. She held her hand over her mouth to keep from screaming, vomiting, or both.

Henry's arm was gone. His bear arm. There was nothing left but a barely bandaged bloody stump. His other arm was wrapped around him, holding the spot where it used to be. Ana could tell by the look on his face that even he was still in denial that it was gone.

"Drake." Ana barely managed to say it. It was as if Henry's shaking had been passed on to her. "It's gone. His arm."

"What?" He asked quietly. He didn't believe the words that fell on his ears.

"They cut off his arm, dammit!" She practically screamed. There was nothing that could keep her quiet anymore. The pain she saw in Henry's face was more than words could convey. The man didn't have the will to speak. What had been done here was beyond inhumane. This was demonic. A demon controlled this damn city, and she was ready to storm inside right now and go kill him with her bare hands. Drake was already on it. Except there was one problem. Upon seeing what had been done to their friend, they had forgotten that this place was likely trapped. Though both of them tried to move, their feet were stuck to the floor. Ana looked down to see a sticky white substance that was keeping them in place. She scanned the room quickly but still saw nothing. She tried breaking free again but to no avail.

Ana decided it was best to close her eyes and listen. If anything was coming for them, it wasn't right on top of them yet. As she focused, every sound nearby became amplified. She could hear Drake and Henry breathing, and when listening close, she could even hear Henry's tears hitting the floor. Then there was something else. She could only describe it as a scuttling sound, like a large group of bugs were making their move across the floor. It was getting closer. She really didn't like the idea of being eaten by a swarm of cockroaches, but it was sounding more and more likely.

Once it got close enough, she opened her eyes again. At the end of the hall, shadowed by the darkest corner, she saw what she had feared. A red cloak. A mask menacingly covered the guard's face. A well-trained fighter walked over to them slowly, knowing they were stuck to the floor.

"He's here." Ana spoke, not knowing if Drake could hear or see him yet. He could not.

"Yes. I am." The voice that responded was one of dignity. The same you would hear out of a highborn noble that hadn't missed a lesson on etiquette. "And it seems the king knows his daughter well."

"Don't call me his daughter or him a king." Ana spat at the ground, as there was not much else she could do in response. She could feel the substance around her feet moving and Drake breathing a bit heavier. He was trying to break out. Whether or not it was going to work, Ana would have to distract their new friend until he could.

"All he wants is to be reunited with his family. Is that much for a father to ask?" If Ana could have punched this guy right there and then, she would have, but he had stopped half a dungeon away.

"It's too much for a tyrant to ask."

"The prey is loud as it realizes the corner it's backed into. Your words echo, yet they're hollow and unheard." He was clearly trying to badger Ana on. It was working. "If you don't cooperate, I was given permission to bring you back in pieces."

"I think I'd rather that." Ana tried to call his bluff, but the red guard was all too quick to pull a long thin blade out from under his cloak.

"A shame. I would rather chat more. It's rare to converse with someone who was once so dignified but fell to the common folk." The man ran the blade along his teeth. Was it a scare tactic? It seemed risky, to say the least, and all it did was confuse Ana. Until she started piecing things together.

Prey. An unknown substance that kept them stuck to the ground. The lack of torches, indicating an ability to see in the dark. The sound of bugs crawling about and the final tell. Ana had seen that move before. One of the best sword fighters she had met in recent days had a way of poisoning her blade using her own venom.

"You're a hybrid!?" She had to stop thinking out loud. The idea of the king even having one of them under his employ was insane. This could mean all four of them were, but there was no time to process that. Not with the situation she had in front of her. Though he hadn't revealed anything yet, this guy was clearly a spider. She didn't want to think about where his web came from, but whatever kind he was, he was venomous.

"I'm surprised it took you this long to guess that." In the dramatic fashion of a noble, the man threw off his cloak to reveal six extra legs curled up behind his back. He unfurled them one by one, clearly having a flair for the dramatic. Each one of them looked as sharp as the blade in his hands. "I do hope you're not afraid of me."

"He's a spider. His weapon is poisoned. About thirty feet still ahead of us." Ana ignored the noble's dramaticism.

"What are you saying? Of course I am." Typical that he was completely full of himself. Ana had used this to their advantage. The guard didn't expect the punch to his gut from a dragon claw. He was too fixated on Ana as his 'prize' capture that he didn't notice Drake had been freed.

The spider hissed and quickly scurried around a corner, out of sight. In typical highborn fashion, he shouted from the shadows, "How *dare* you interrupt me like that? You're just lucky you won't see your death coming."

"Can you see anything?" Ana asked out to Drake.

"My eyes might as well be closed in here." He answered. That's what she figured. He was a good fighter and all, but that wouldn't help if he couldn't see. She couldn't break free to help him, either. She had to act as his eyes once again, just like fighting the coyotes.

He was quiet for all too long. Likely savouring the moment or trying to make one of them lose focus. Drake kept trying to look around, but it was no use. Ana listened carefully and heard scuttling, but it was going too fast and sounded like it was coming from so many places that she couldn't pinpoint the exact location.

"He's moving. I don't know where." She kept Drake informed. The moment she said anything, the sounds stopped. Ana looked around to make sure he wasn't anywhere nearby, and at first, didn't see anything. Then, the slightest sound of an exoskeleton scraping along stone made her look up. "Above you!"

It was almost too late. As the spider creature fell from the ceiling, all Drake could do was try and keep his arms over his head and face to block the attack. He barely managed but was able to push off the enemy before he could wrap his spider legs onto anything too important.

Certain death was almost guaranteed if he tried any harder. It wasn't long before he did.

"Left side!" Ana yelled out, though the spider heard it too and changed his attack at the last second. The poisoned blade tried to dig into Drake's right side but stopped short as most weapons did. There was a disappointed grunt from their opponent before he had to dodge a swipe from one of Drake's claws.

The strategy was too obvious. It was no sooner than Ana had called out to Drake again that the spider made its way toward her. She barely had time to react, as the moment this creature let his eight legs touch the ground, he was able to move at incredible speeds. Her blade was barely out from under her cloak when his envenomed edge tried to find its way into her neck. There was a brief illumination in the dungeon as the two swords met. Ana tilted his blade away but couldn't do much about the legs that found their way around her. The creep's teeth were almost into her shoulder by the time he was pulled off of her.

The spark gave off just enough light for Drake to see where he was and save Ana's life just in time. She noted since she was his eyes, they were currently even. She kept her blade drawn and was unsure of where he ran off to this time. This fighter was clever and had abilities almost unparalleled among hybrids she had met so far. This was worse than she thought.

"Where is he?" Asked Drake furiously. He didn't like these conditions.

"I don't know." Not exactly encouraging words. It was hard for Ana to even pinpoint where he was running. Those legs each echoed through the hall as if they were all over the place. It was two against one, but it was hard to see a way out with such a significant disadvantage on both sides.

"You could have just come home. He would have taken you back, you know." His voice sounded like it came from every corner. Even for a spider, he was good at being creepy. "Now I have to bring his daughter's lifeless body to him. It's a shame."

"That's the only way that bastard is ever getting me back!" Ana yelled into the abyss.

"Don't talk." Drake said to Ana. She was about to protest but realized what he was trying to do. The more she talked, the less she could listen, and he could get closer without her noticing.

"Clever, clever, clever." The echoed voice came again. "Too bad it won't amount to much."

He was too fast. Ana couldn't call it out this time before the creature was on top of Drake. Though many of the sharpened legs went to strike him, most skidded right off of his scales. One of them did manage to find his face, and it was the first time Ana had heard Drake scream out in pain. It was lucky Drake was quick; otherwise, it might have made its way straight down his throat.

Even in the dark, Drake wasn't going to take something like that lying down. The moment he knew where his opponent had hit him, he reached up both claws and grabbed hold of the leg quicker than it could retract. A loud snapping noise filled the cave, as well as the screams of a terrified noble as Drake bent the leg back as hard as he could. Just like any pest's would, the leg broke right off like a snapped twig. It was left dangling in the air like some gruesome tree branch.

Ana could see the creature inching forward to attack again but backing off out of fear. The spider legs retracted onto his back as they were when he first showed up. He realized they were nothing but a weak point in this fight. Ana was overjoyed at the pain on his face trying to pull the broken one back.

"So this is why mother told me not to play with my food." He said, trying to pass off the pain. "No matter." What was a moment ago primarily spider, now stood on two legs as a trained noble. Though this was a threat, especially with an envenomed weapon, the agility was gone. This would make things much more manageable.

"Left!" Ana called out. Drake blocked the blade with his arm before it found its way into his face.

"I know." Drake called back. His eyes were adjusting. This would be an even bigger problem for their opponent. He couldn't see much, but just being able to react to movement directly in front of him was enough.

The blade came in for a second strike and was blocked once again. Drake only had one known weak point, and it made things much easier for him when it came to predicting where the next attack was coming from. He even kept his arms above shoulder height, already prepared for whatever was coming.

If Ana had any questions that Drake's scales were those of a dragon's, this night had cleared that for her. Attack after attack and he barely budged from his position. At one point, the spider gave a short attempt at trying to saw his sword through Drake's arm, but it didn't work. If anything, he may have dulled his blade further.

Ana could see the creature look back at her as if to consider that line of attack again. He quickly threw it out of his mind since no matter how little he could see, turning his back on Drake wasn't exactly the best idea. One broken leg and a dulled sword later, the Red Guard began to withdraw.

"Two against one is hardly fair." He said from the shadows, giving a pompous holier than thou stance as he angrily shoved his blade back in its sheath. "No matter, you'll be surrounded before long." He uncurled his legs and went scuttling away from the pair of them. The best thing Ana had seen yet was that creep limping with one of his eight legs held off the ground.

"I hate to say he's right. We'll have to get out of here quickly." Ana said, trying to break free from the web underneath her. It still felt tight, and she couldn't get her sword in at an angle that wouldn't cut her foot.

"Not without Henry." Drake said in a matter-of-fact way.

"I included him in we." Ana replied and was frankly offended that he would think otherwise. As if Drake appreciated the sentiment, he went over and cut the web away from Ana's feet as his claws were much more precise. "Now, it's just a matter of how to open this door."

"I'm sorry…." The first words came from inside the cell. "Leave." You could feel each word shaking as it made its way through the air.

"Don't think so." Drake said, making his way over to the bars. His vision still wasn't the greatest as he almost walked right into them.

"There's no point." Henry's voice was weak. He sounded as if on the brink of collapse. "I can't help them anymore."

"Yes, you can." Rare words of encouragement from Drake. "Just seeing that you're alive would be enough."

"I wasn't done..." Henry trailed off. He never turned his face away from the wall. He didn't want to look at either of them. "I wasn't even close to done...."

"You're still not." Drake added in. "Even if you were, you've done enough for us. You've made up for it a hundred times over by now."

"I wasn't done...." He repeated. There was nothing left for Henry to say. He couldn't help but continue sobbing.

"I don't want to say this." Ana butted in. "But we don't have time. The three of us have to get out of here." She specified to keep Drake's mouth shut about her potentially forgetting Henry. Drake agreed.

Ana figured the metal bars would be the hardest part of the process, but the strength of a dragon came in and surprised her once again. Drake was able to grab onto the metal cell door and pull just hard enough around the hinges for a couple of the rivets to snap off. A couple of quick moves like this, and the door was off.

"How many prisons have you broken out of before?" Ana asked. He did it as if it was second nature.

"You don't want to know." He answered as he made his way into the cell. Henry wasn't hard to pick up, but Drake made sure to take off his cloak and wrap it around Henry's stump before he did. It was still bleeding. The damage was fresh and not taken care of. It was even hard for Drake to look at. He picked Henry up by his back and legs, and there was no protest. Henry was too weak to protest. He looked so much smaller without his arm. Ana couldn't look away for a moment, getting lost in the damage she had caused. It was only Drake walking straight by her for the exit when she snapped to and followed along.

Thinking strategically, Ana realized this would be a problem. Henry was a broken man, and in no way could lead a group of hybrids into an all-out war. If anything, showing them his state would terrify them. One or two might be driven into vengeance, but Drake is the only one she could count on doing so. It would be nearly impossible to get him back to his inspiring self at this point, but Ana was going to try anyway.

Upon reaching the metal doors out into the city, she spoke up. "We should split up."

"Why?" Drake asked.

"We'll be harder to spot individually. We'll meet on the mountain pass" Once the moonlight crept in as the door swung open, Drake could see her sly smile. "Plus, I have an idea."

Chapter 23

Drake was able to make it out of the city with little resistance. The Red Guard clearly wasn't able to sound the alarm fast enough. It was still relatively difficult to make it around the extra patrols, but it was no different than on the way in. The only major issue being the guards watching the gate. Since a war was about to begin anyway, he had no quarrel with putting down Henry, knocking the two of them out from behind, and continuing forward. As long as Ana was fast enough, she'd be able to enjoy the same exit.

Once he was out of the walls, Drake sprinted, Henry's legs dangling in the air as if he was a dead body. He was so weak he might as well be, but Drake kept habitually checking his pulse for signs of life and would know if he actually went. Out of everything Ana had done, it would be the hardest to forgive her for this.

He put Henry up against the first safe rock he could find. He could hear the faintest clamouring up the mountain path next to him, and knew the others made it. They were barely out of sight of the patrols, and he was even able to see the guard's unconscious bodies lying at the gate as the early sun broke the horizon. Another pair found them quicker than he had hoped, but it wasn't going to matter. That spider would let the king know the moment he could that an attack was launched. Two nobodies at the gates meant nothing.

Ana was taking longer than he had hoped. As much as he didn't like her right now, he didn't want a key part in their new strategy to die. More than a few times, Drake contemplated running Henry straight to Ingress and abandoning the idea of an attack, just for the safety of his friend. The problem was the moment he woke up, Henry would never forgive him.

Right before he was starting to write her off as dead, Ana practically vaulted her way over the wall that led to the barracks. It was a good thing she was smart enough to not take the main exit.

Drake didn't have that luxury. This meant that they would start moving again soon. He didn't want to show Henry to everyone else. It would break their hearts, and Henry would likely blame himself, but there was no other option that wasn't running away. Drake didn't like to run away.

Ana was practically out of breath when she arrived back. She had a bottle in her hand. "Sorry that took so long." She said through bated breath. "They're crawling around the place like ants."

"This isn't the time to keep us waiting." Drake stated. His words could send a chill through the desert air.

"I didn't know what else to do for him, so I brought this." Ana passed the bottle over to Drake. It was dusty and full of a dark liquid. Bourbon, it looked like. "It was the only one fully intact I could find in the bar."

Drake inspected the bottle. It was practically full, and the cork was still in good shape. It wasn't the best answer to Henry's problems, but he'd appreciate it. It would numb the pain as well. "I give you his thanks. He might not be able to speak after he wakes up."

Even after seeing what she had seen, groups of soldiers and hybrids lay dead in the sand for their choice of life. The innocents who died from what was nothing more than a political move. It was Henry sleeping against that rock, half of who he was lost to the world, that hurt the most.

"Should we take him into camp?" Ana asked.

"No." Drake answered. "We should let him go in with some dignity. We'll wait for him to wake up."

Strategically, Ana couldn't disagree more. Time was not on their side, and they were being searched for. The whole city would be on lockdown in a matter of moments. An attack had to be sprung fast if it had any chance of making it inside the walls. On the other hand, Henry was resting. He was hurt and wasn't going to recover if constantly woken up by the rabble around him. Though you could see the pain on his face even in his sleep, he needed this. He likely hadn't rested since he was brought into that dungeon.

"He probably wouldn't want to see me when he wakes up." Ana said, taking a look down the mountain pass. The early morning lights made their way through the tight passages, and she couldn't help but admire the beauty of a rocky path that led up to the source of that light. "I should go into camp."

“No, stay here.” Drake practically ordered. “If anything, he would want to thank you when he wakes up.”

“Why?”

“Don’t know. It just sounds like something he’d do.” Drake knew Henry well, but could never understand him. Ana had no qualms sticking around. If anything, it would give her a chance to notice any changes in the guard pattern. Or at least it would if she could ever take her eyes off of Henry.

What she was looking at was war. A man taken and traumatized for the sake of a political movement. She stared into the face of discrimination. The lengths that man will go to just to show he’s superior. She didn’t want to start a war. She just wanted to find peace for both sides, and maybe society would take in what it had once forsaken. It was clearer than ever that there was no way it was going to happen without a fight.

It was far too long until Henry’s eyes opened. They once looked as bright as the sun, but now they were empty. Two void orbs that gave a glimpse into a broken soul. He blinked at the sunlight a few times before looking up to Drake and Ana. His head turned slowly between the two of them before his gaze found the ground once again. It was clear he either couldn’t or didn’t want to talk. Either way, they respected this.

“I know what you’re thinking. And stop blaming yourself.” Drake said while looking down at Henry, though he also turned his gaze to Ana. “Both of you. It will get you nowhere.”

“Amazing words of encouragement, sunshine.” Ana replied. The idea that he would start the morning with a lecture bothered her. She couldn’t help but notice the corner of Henry’s lip turn up for a slight second at her shot at Drake.

“All I’m saying is we have a war to win, and I can’t have you two bringing yourselves down.” Drake clarified.

“I’m sorry…” Henry spoke up. The same words he had said in the dungeon. His voice was still weak. Each word sounded like it was a strain on his body. “I won’t be of much help.”

“Maybe not in a fight, sure.” Drake agreed, “But that’s not all you’re good for. As a matter of fact, you proved to be pretty bad at it.”

“Hey!” Ana interjected on Henry’s behalf. She was ignored.

“I don’t think you realize how many lives you’ve touched, Henry.” He continued. “Every one of them worried about you the moment you left. The moment you came back, I was ready to storm the castle by myself, but thankfully Ana came with me." This was clearly serious. Drake was admitting he needed help. "Just seeing you will be enough."

"You think they'd want to see me like this?" Henry asked. He couldn't help but look over at his missing arm. It was painful to see him start crying at the sight of it.

"Of course not. They want to see you in one piece. I want to see you in one piece. But you're better than dead."

"I think that's..." Henry shifted so he could sit up. "The nicest thing you've ever said to me."

"Don't bring it up." Drake looked away. Mostly because he couldn't handle an emotional moment.

"Take me to them." Henry said, much more seriously than he had ever sounded. "I have something to admit."

"You think now is the time?" Drake asked.

"If not now, then when?" He responded. Ana couldn't even begin to imagine what they were talking about, but the strategist in her wanted to get moving, so it all worked out. While she had the chance, Ana offered the Bourbon to him, and he graciously accepted a swig with her help opening the bottle. Without another word from any of them, Drake picked up Henry again. He insisted on trying to walk, but both of them knew the once bear-armed man wouldn't be able to hold himself up.

The wind had never been calmer in the mountain pass. The path was smooth. Not even a pebble out of place. Even the sun itself seemed to be shining its light a little more softly this morning. Everyone could feel a fog surrounding them. A fog of uneasiness, of not knowing what the future was going to hold. It was thick. They couldn't see the minutes in front of them. What lay ahead in the path of their lives could be a pit that would end it then and there. The same feeling was shared across the whole camp, Ana, Drake, Henry, Calvin, and even Kasibel. Even if they won, they didn't know if their futures would be bright or bleak.

The entourage making their way in didn't help. They were spotted from a distance by Talia, as she did routine flights to make sure no one was sneaking up on them. She had a preemptive glimpse at what was arriving but didn't want to believe her eyes. She didn't dare relay any information aside for their arrival. She lied to herself about what she saw. It only made it worse when she realized she was right.

A look of horror washed over the camp as Drake, Ana, and Henry got closer. Every one of the hybrids staying there turned pale. Kasibel had arrived recently, and even he and Calvin couldn't believe what they were seeing. Jaws were dropped, and a lack of motivation surged across the camp. The exact opposite of what Ana wanted to happen. It seemed like a selfish hope, but a lack of encouragement would cause more problems than just two royal siblings not gaining the throne.

"What?" Henry was the first one to speak up. "Am I that beautiful that I've rendered you all speechless?"

No one knew how to react. Even in the face of some of the worst torture a person can go through, Henry still managed to make a joke. No one dared laugh. It was too hard for them.

Henry made his way down from Drake's arms, though Drake didn't want to let him go. The dragon helped the ex-bear get his legs back on the ground and brought him over to a nearby rock to sit down. Internally, Henry felt like he was being a burden.

"Do we have a plan?" He asked Kasibel directly. Even the guard captain had a hard time responding.

"Somewhat." He finally managed to mutter after shaking the shock of the sight in front of him. Once he came to, a wave of anger washed over his face. It was clear he didn't know what the king had planned for Henry. "We need to move fast to keep any element of surprise. The king doesn't expect my troops to turn against him yet, but he is expecting all of you. Our assault will launch first from the inside of the castle as a distraction, followed by your group coming in just as the king's guard gets pulled back. It will be easy to take them when they don't know what front to cover."

"I was thinking the same thing on the way over." Ana spoke up as her sibling rivalry instinct came to life.

"No, you weren't." Kasibel returned. He was right.

"Honestly, I don't see how we could pull something like this." The tiger lady Lex spoke up, sounding quite disheartened. "I mean, just look at him...." She couldn't bear to look at Henry for any longer than a few seconds. The rest of them seemed to follow her sentiment.

"Now, don't go backing out just because of me." Henry tried to lighten the mood. It didn't work.

"Even I'd find it hard fighting knowing that you're back here like this." Angui spoke up this time. "If the world could attack someone as kind-hearted as you, it might not even be worth fighting for."

"Big words coming from a professional assassin." Henry returned. Angui admitted he had a point, but it didn't change her mind. "Look, you don't have to worry about me. If anything, I've had this coming for a long time."

"How could you have?" Ana was next to speak up.

"Remember how I told you about my brother and I? When we met our first hybrid?" Ana nodded, reminiscing about her short time at the bar, wishing it wasn't so short. "I didn't tell you the full story." Henry pushed himself up with his one arm. Drake tried to help him, but the look he got in return even made him back off. Henry was shaking, clearly still weak, but he stood upon the rock where he once sat.

"I know a lot of you think I'm just a good person. That I went and ran a bar to keep you all safe because that's who I am. That's who I've always been." Henry spoke out to everyone in the small crowd, including Drake and Ana. "Well, I haven't. And if karma should come for anyone, it's me.

A long time ago, while I was still fully human, I was part of a noble family. Low ranking nobles, sure, but we still had the same beliefs." Henry took a deep breath. "Of course, that means like many of you before you turned, we hated hybrids. We're all guilty of name-calling and staring from before we knew any better. That's just normal, it shouldn't be, but it is." Everyone nodded along. It was a common sentiment. "Only... my brother and I took it a step further.

We once found a man in the woods. Part wolf, if I'm remembering clearly. Blood loss and all that." He motioned to his stump. "All I know is he had four legs and was rather fast, so we took it as a challenge."

"You threw rocks at him, didn't you?" Ana interrupted. Something about the way Henry spoke made her want to join in the conversation.

"Yes, that's how it started. That's what made him run from us." You could see Henry's face shift as he thought back. "It would have been bad enough there, but eventually, we hit him hard. I think it was my brother's throw that got him right in the back of the leg. It was enough to keep him from running any further. So we managed to catch up to him, even in the middle of the woods on our human legs." He had to stop for a moment to catch his breath. He looked away from everyone for a minute as he tried to compose himself. "He was just lying there on the ground. We did enough damage that he couldn't run, not for a while anyway. But then we…." He stopped. His lip quivered. "We…" Henry's face turned bright red. He held his hand over it to try to keep some dignity. "We each grabbed the nearest… Big rock we could find…." His lips were uncontrollable now, and the words were coming between hard sobs. It was hard to get the rest out. "We… beat him… until he stopped moving…." It was nothing but tears at that point. He couldn't say any more. Drake had to come up and support him, both emotionally and physically. Henry wiped the tears away from his eyes and looked out at a captivated group. He needed to finish getting his point across.

"This is why I deserve what happened to me. None of you should feel bad. None of you should feel like you caused this." He looked over at Ana in particular. "I ran that bar as a way to make up for that sin. It has carried with me ever since. It's only now that it's finally caught up. I could never forgive myself if it was my state that stopped this revolution. This fight could determine your place in society as people, not just some animals to be hunted. You go out there and fight. Not for me, but for the hybrids that couldn't make it. Like the ones who fell at the bar. Like the ones who died in the forest at the hands of some stupid kid."

There were no words left to say. Not a single person at that camp expected a story like that from Henry, the nicest man they had ever met. The only one unfazed was Drake, who likely already knew. Ana couldn't help but think back to her father. Many people have many different faces, and they can change throughout one's life. Was the king one of those men? Had something changed with him? One way or another, his actions were still condemnable, and Ana had every intention of being his judge.

It made everyone think. Ana was right to bring Henry back as the first course of action. Though he had been broken physically, his spirit was still intact. He still wanted his vision to go on, even if he couldn't fight. After enough silence had passed, Agui drew her blade and pointed it directly at Kasibel's neck.

"Well?" She asked. The atmosphere changed in an instant. Everyone was ready to fight on the drop of a dime.

"Well, what?" He asked, standing his ground. Even staring death in the face, the guard captain wasn't one to go down without dignity.

"Get going, guard boy. We don't have much time." It was a rather aggressive way to get her point across, but it wasn't unlike her. Everyone slowly started nodding their heads in agreement.

"I think that would be best." Ana spoke softly. It was hard for her to take all of this in.

"Very well." Kasibel agreed. He stepped over towards Henry before he left, causing everyone to get even more tense. Angui and Drake, in particular, were ready to cut his throat out if he laid a hand on the man. "I wish I could give a speech like that." He said to Henry before leaving down the mountain path on his own. Once he was gone, Ana took a spot standing beside Henry on his rock.

"A dark thing has happened today." She said over the crowd. "These are bleak days where innocents can be murdered in their home without recompense." She was beginning to get louder than she ever had. Every word that came out of her carried her every being. "These days *must* come to an end. If they are, we have to fight through the darkness. There will be blood. There will be more death. There are only a few of us, and some won't be here tomorrow to see their next sunrise, but you are fighting for a future. You are fighting for the lives of those that died before you and those who have yet to come after you. Without our victory today, those lives went in vain and won't have a chance upon reaching this world. We are doing something more important than ourselves." Ana took a moment to take a deep breath to stay strong and not break down on the podium. "Before we march on that castle, I want to say thank you, and I'm sorry for the damage I had caused. I want to say you'll all be here with me tomorrow, and we can have a celebration, but that's just wishful thinking. So I'd like to take this chance, in case I or any of you fall, to say goodbye." Her eyes started to water, but she blinked it away. If she was going to lead this, there had to be strength.

There was a strategy to her words. She had thought the fear of death would make one or two of them leave. The reality of battle was too much for some, after all, and those wouldn't be worth having on the battlefield. Much to her surprise, everyone stayed captivated, waiting for her next words. There was only one thing left to be said.

"Prepare your weapons. Battle is upon us!"

Chapter 24

"Talia, you're going to keep a lookout for when the strike begins. Can you perch on the mountain top?" Ana asked. Talia nodded. "Good. When everything begins, we should each work in small groups supporting the soldiers inside. Most of us can individually take out multiple guards, so we can turn the numbers in our favour. No one goes in alone. No matter how strong you think you are, you need someone covering your back at all times."

"Alright, so who's with who?" Angui asked, clearly concerned about getting stuck with someone she might not like. Drake agreed with the sentiment and didn't want to be anywhere near the snake.

"We should have groups who have worked together before. This battlefield isn't the place to learn something new. Do you have any issue fighting with Lex?" Ana asked Angui directly.

"Not at all." The snake lady looked over at the tiger, who agreed with almost too much enthusiasm.

"Drake, you work particularly well with anyone?" Ana asked, already knowing the answer.

"Nope." He crossed his arms in a brooding fashion and looked over to the sunrise.

"Good, then you're stuck with me since I haven't had the pleasure of fighting alongside anyone else." It rolled off her tongue sarcastically. "That leaves Ivan and Talia. Any complaints there?" Nothing came from the ox or the vulture, but the bear did speak up.

"What about me?" Henry asked.

"Are you crazy? We're not bringing you along." Ana answered. She already knew he would try and be a part of this battle, despite suffering a very recent and very major injury.

"Then I'll have to go in on my own." As stubborn as ever, the man wouldn't budge.

"I could always take your legs off too." Drake threatened. Everyone thought it was a bit too harsh, but Henry laughed it off.

"Fine." Ana rubbed her brow in frustration "There's no sense arguing with you if you're planning on getting yourself killed. One more for your party Ivan?" Ivan snorted in agreement. He wasn't a man, or ox, of many words. "Good enough. Just make sure he doesn't get himself killed."

They went over strategy for the rest of the morning. Each group would be coming for each of the three main entrances to Arid Retreat. Angui and Lex opted to take the lower district, while Ivan, Talia, and apparently Henry were going to be going in from Market. That left the line straight up the middle for Drake and Ana. King's road is what they called it, primarily where nobles from other countries would come in with all their fanfare to show off.

"There's one last thing to look out for." Ana took a breath and prepared to warn them of their biggest threat. "There are four soldiers in red cloaks. Do not take them on if you can avoid it. Each one is part of an elite team known as the Red Guard. Drake and I ran into one on our way to get Henry out. He turned out to be a hybrid. Part spider. We don't know what the other three are, save for one likely has a horn."

"So? From what I understand, we have more overall soldiers and six hybrids to their four. If anything, this should be a piece of cake." Came the rebuttal from the tiger, though she looked to Henry and apologized after realizing what she said. "Sorry." Henry shrugged in response, trying to keep his feelings hidden, though he was clearly hurt.

"Don't take them lightly." Ana reiterated in the most severe tone she could pull. "Is everyone clear on their strategies?" Silence. "Good. Make whatever last preparations you need. We'll split up immediately and surround the outer walls as best we can. They're on edge but not enough to go out and actively attack cloaked travellers." Ana double and triple checked her sword at her side. It was about to be a necessity. "Talia, take to the skies and cry out the moment you see an attack. Everyone else, let's go."

Talia spread her wings, carrying nothing but a spear brought by Kasibel and made her way to the top of the mountain. Things were starting to feel real. At any moment, the call could come to charge in. Ana was just hoping everyone could get in position in time.

"I just can't stop getting stuck with you, can I?" Drake complained while throwing on a new cloak, making sure every part of him was covered.

"Unless you want to go in on your own." Ana stated.

"I think I'd rather that."

"Well, you don't get to make that call." She should have expected such a response. "Now, let's get going." Ana couldn't tell if she was eager to get this fight started or anxious to get it out of the way.

The waiting was the most painful part. Not just for the call to battle, but they had decided they should leave the pass at a staggered time to not pull much attention. Ana had set up the groups in order of who needed the most support. Angui and Lex in the lower district will have the most problems out of the gate with the lack of Kasibel's guard currently stationed there. She and Drake didn't have it much better and were likely to reach the castle first. From there, Ana could navigate better than anyone in this fight, save her brother. Lastly, Ivan, Talia, and Henry would be getting the most support as they'd be storming in next to the barracks. Ana hoped nothing would happen to Henry, but it was too late to change strategies now. The time for planning was over. The closest thing she'd get to that now was improvising on the battlefield.

Once Angui and Lex were out of sight, Ana and Drake began to make their move. She had walked with him a few times now, but it felt different. Before, she had felt like a burden to him. Now she felt as if they were on equal ground.

"Still keeping track?" She asked him on the way. "We're one to one, by the way."

"What?" At first, Ana thought he had forgotten what she was talking about. Soon she wished that was the case. "We're clearly two to one in favour of me. Does breaking that creep's leg count for nothing?"

"You only strictly saved my life once by pulling him off. I had you cleared when he was on the ceiling. Didn't matter who landed the last blow."

"You're only saying that because you didn't land any blows."

"Only because you didn't free me sooner."

"Oh yeah, I also freed you. Make that three to one."

"Stop making up excuses for points! I would have made it out of there by myself eventually."

"Before a guard found you?"

"That's speculation." Ana was getting heated, making it even more infuriating that Drake didn't even raise his voice.

"Speculation that's correct." He didn't even give an inch.

"Fine, you get two. One for pulling him off and one for breaking his leg. Cutting me out doesn't count."

"I don't think it's fair, but I'll take it." Drake said with a sly smile.

"You're damn right you will." It took Ana all too long to realize he made an extra point just to negotiate her down to where he wanted her. It was a stupid game anyway. They shouldn't be keeping track of who saved whose life more. Though Ana did have every intention of winning.

The argument was a good distraction for the task at hand, though not for nearly as long as either of them would have liked. They had reached the outside of their gate all too soon, with nothing but a mid-sized sand dune to cover their location. Both of them had to duck behind it to stay out of sight, which was awkward to do without drawing attention.

If they had thought waiting for their time to leave was bad, it was worse when they had no more walking to do. This was the last moment of peace that would be felt for a long while. It might be the last one they would have before they hit the ground lifeless. The sand usually comforted Ana. Between its warmth and willingness to shape to the form of anyone who sat in it. Today it scorched her, begging her to get up and go do her duty.

Time had no meaning. Minutes could have passed though it felt like hours. Perhaps hours did actually pass, and they had no idea. Ana's head was running wild with things that could have gone wrong. Was Kasibel somehow not able to make the order? Did someone find Talia on the top of that mountain and take her down? They couldn't have had the time to climb to the top, but they could have shot her with a longbow. Ana started thinking about all of the archers in the castle and who could potentially make that shot.

Though the waiting felt like forever, everyone involved wished for more time the moment the screech of a vulture echoed over the mountain tops.

Chapter 25

Angui and Lex had already taken out the guards stationed at the lower district's entrance when Talia let out her cry. Patience wasn't something either of them had and it showed. They justified it by saying it would be easier not getting caught if the guards were dead. At least they both knew what they were doing.

"Finally, I was starting to get bloodthirsty." Angui stated while refreshing the poison on her scimitar by running it along her tooth.

"Starting to? When aren't you?" Added Lex, bringing her claws back out. Her fur was already soaked in red.

"When I'm drunk." She answered with a smile, slithering her way into town.

"Let's hit up the bar when we're done then, shall we?" Lex followed her in. Neither of them were moving particularly fast. Though impatient, they knew running headlong into a war wasn't the smartest idea.

"This whole place is prone to ambush." Angui stated while keeping her eyes on every back alley they passed. She was right. If the king expected an attack from this side, they were given the most dangerous one to start out with. Neither of them had any issues with this as they enjoyed a good hunt, but there were too many places to hide. If they weren't careful, their death would come quicker than they could see it.

"You thinking what I'm thinking?" Lex said while taking a look down a particularly dark alley.

"Now I am." Angui enjoyed the idea. Without words, each of them sunk into their own separate alley. They stayed close enough to cover each other if things went wrong but made sure to hide. Angui found a very narrow and dark passage that had no exit. It was perfect, as her snake body barely fit in, and she could poke her head out just enough to see well. Lex took to the rooftops, and though none of the buildings were particularly high in this district, was able to find one she could hang out on the very corner of without being seen. Her claws hung over the edge a bit, ready to pounce on top of an enemy at any moment.

It was clear this district wasn't where the main fight began. Word might have not even gotten this far. There was potential if they had left the guards alive, they would have run in and alerted the others in the area, but they didn't. This left for what they considered a fun game of cat and mouse. Or at least cat, snake, and mouse.

The first attack went to Lex. She kept her eye on the main street, and it didn't take too long for a couple of guards to come rolling in to make sure nothing had started. They counted their blessings initially as nothing had, but regretted their decision to come to work that day. Both of them were wielding spears and holding them straight up, which was an issue with Lex's angle of attack. All it took was some patience, as thin as hers was. The moment she had the chance, she pounced on one from behind.

The attack was made with *heavy* prejudice. She had wanted to attack one of these idiots since the moment the bar was raided and had to wait way too long to do it. The guards were wearing helmets which meant she couldn't kill on the first strike, though she was able to topple one over. From there, it was easy. He didn't know what hit him before her claws were at his throat. And then his chest. And arms. Anything that wasn't bleeding when she started was at the end. She got so caught up in the attack she almost forgot there was another guard. When she looked up, Angui had already run him through the back with her poisoned blade. He was already limp and falling onto the ground, but it was clear her life was just saved.

"Don't get distracted." Angui instructed, looking annoyed.

"Sorry." Lex said sincerely. "I just wanted to enjoy it."

"Well, that won't be a problem now." Angui turned Lex's attention over to the small battalion of guards that followed in behind the two they had killed. If either had any foresight, they would have realized there was company only a couple blocks away.

"You going to keep count?"

"Only if you don't cheat this time." Angui responded, but Lex was already gone. They were both outnumbered by a good five to one ratio, so they took to the alleys. This place had become a death trap. A death trap that slithered and pounced.

Angui made sure to take a confusing path, which wasn't too difficult considering the district. Around here they fit in a building anywhere they could. No luxuries, just space for bodies to lay down and rest. This gave way to plenty of winding paths that anyone would be hard pressed to tell if they were a side road or an alleyway. She was being chased by six guards with varying weapons. Each one adorning the red crest of Rexharne, which was something they were to look out for to make sure they didn't kill a friendly. Most of the reason Ana sent the two of them to the lower district was due to the lack of Kasibel's guards. She knew neither of them would actually pay attention to who they were killing. Anyone with a weapon was fair game.

After slithering down enough strange paths, Angui managed to break up the troop following her. At first, they had to split into two groups of three because they didn't see one turn that she took. A couple of turns later and one of the three that was actually on her tail took a different path since he thought he saw something. He did. And that something was a half-snake woman who sliced his neck open before he got a chance to call for help.

She slithered her way back to where the other two split off. They were stalled out in one spot, not knowing which way she went. This was a problem as they lacked any distraction she could take advantage of. They were both looking for her. She picked up a pebble off the ground and threw it around the corner, hoping to only get the attention of one of them. Unfortunately, she alerted both, but wasn't entirely unprepared, as she situated herself in an alley where only one person could swing a weapon comfortably. She would have preferred a wall to her back but it opened up on the other side. It would have to make do.

Both guards were carrying short swords. Easy enough combat for someone who had mastered the art. They were cocky, though, as the moment they turned the corner and saw her, one of them rushed in as soon as he could to take her down and had some words to go along with it.

"Accept your death half-breed." He said while taking a battle stance. As she expected, he was classically trained and wouldn't go down too easy.

"How about I accept yours on your behalf." She held her weapon up defensively and was ready when the first attack came. There wasn't much room to maneuver, so attacking from the side was nearly impossible. She deflected the overhead strike that came her way, though the strength behind the blow surprised her. She tried to go for an attack but had to remain defensive. The man she was fighting was experienced.

She hated to admit it, but she was on the back foot. She didn't expect swing after swing to be dealt. The attacks started coming from a place of hatred, and he acted as if he was trying to chop down a log. It was poor form, and she could easily kill this guy at any time, but not without getting damaged in the process. Angui didn't want to be knocked out of the fight that fast, so she had to think of something.

Instead of trying to beat him in a test of strength, she used his forward movement against him. On each swing, she would back up a little bit less, inching herself towards him. Eventually, she got close enough that on the next upswing, she would make her move. Before the sword could find its way towards her, she used her snakelike form to fire herself forward and buried her teeth into his neck. It was quick and painless for the receiver, as her venom acted fast as it reached his veins. His muscles locked up, and his sword fell to the ground with a sad clank. The body soon followed as it went as limp as it could and acted now as nothing more than an obstacle in the alley.

Something was off. Angui was expecting another battle right after. She was about halfway down the passage she had chosen, but the other combatant was nowhere to be found. It was nearly too late before the snake turned and dodged a stab that was aimed right at her back. It nicked her just enough that she could still feel it through the adrenaline. Her eyes narrowed at the prey who would dare attempt to attack the predator.

When angered, Angui's fights were much shorter. She should have cared more about the potential of a counterattack but got lucky this time. She used the same technique to hurl herself forward, this time with her sword forward and aiming at whatever it could hit. Her gambit paid off as it ran the guard through the stomach and out the other side. With the surprise still in the unfortunate woman's eyes, Angui made sure to use her free hand to knock the opposing sword away. Then she pulled hers out, made a slash for the third guard's throat, and that was that. Now, there were three more left to hunt.

On the other side of the district, Lex had her own strategy going. Her group of four wouldn't break up no matter how hard she tried. Even down single file alleys, they managed to march in a perfect formation. This was a problem initially, but then she had an idea.

She found the shortest loops she could circle around. With no way to drop these fools out of formation, she would have to split them up herself. It took a couple of tries, and luckily they weren't seeing what she was trying to do, but the moment she ran down one passage, she kept going in a circle as fast as she could. Once she got the timing right, that left three in the first alley she ran down and one straggler just making it in. She pounced in quickly, knocked him to the ground, used her claw to free his throat from his neck, and ran off down the next alley.

Lex questioned why she had to get the smart ones. The moment she pulled that stunt, they broke formation, but in a way that they were hunting her, not the other way around. She didn't like being the mouse. She didn't like mice. But she had to deal with it for a moment while finding a new way out.

The three remaining showed their knowledge of the area by walking down paths that would link them back up. It was no surprise to Lex when she realized she was being blocked in with how they were making her run. As much as she was cocky and thought she could take more than one, there was more hunting to do after this, and she didn't want to take the chance.

She knew she would have to think faster the moment a spear found its way clanking on the ground behind her. They were willing to throw their weapons and likely had more on them. If she let them keep going, she'd get hit. She had a risky move at the ready but had to take it. The moment she turned the next corner, she knew she was hitting a dead end. That was part of her plan. She ran straight to the end of it, where none of them could be waiting for her, and climbed up the wall as fast as possible. She figured she'd be seen but didn't expect the one right on her tail to be fast enough to have picked up his spear again and almost hit her in the leg with it on the way up. The narrow misses were starting to humble her, but the next kill brought her back to hubris.

Once she hit the top, she knew her opponent's weapon was below her. She kicked off the edge of the roof, which gave her the momentum to perform a backflip to line herself up over her opponent. Like all cats, she landed on her feet, claws out and ready to tear the guard to shreds. The only merciful thing was he didn't see it coming. The remains of the body after Lex had gotten on top of it were indescribable.

This still left two behind her, but luckily her method of combat was enough to make them think twice before attacking. Just enough time for Lex to turn around, dodge a spear thrust, and throw her body into the side of the shaft to break the wooden weapon. She had no time to indulge herself, so she went for the guard's throat with her left claw, and after following through, pounded her shoulder into his chest. There was no chance for quick retaliation.

She would be surprised if she could make it out of this combat unscathed. Her last opponent made sure that wasn't the case. While Lex was busy killing his friend, he managed to stab his spear into her leg. It went in deep and was hard to pull out, which caused Lex to scream out in pain. The problem is he missed what he was aiming for, a finishing blow. All he did was lower her mobility. This didn't matter much as they were in such close quarters. The last thing the guard saw was a tiger paw before his head made too personal a relationship with the stone street.

Lex wanted to take a moment to lick her wounds, but there was no time. There could be more guards on their way, or Angui could have gotten herself in trouble. She limped back to the main street, though she still moved faster than any human would.

It was clear her worry was unfounded, as she found the snake pulling her sword out of a soldier that couldn't have seen her coming. There was only one thing that bothered Lex about this.

"And not a damn scratch on you. I swear." She said in a sour tone.

"That's the advantage of fighting with finesse." Angui wiped her blade off on her prey's cloth pants so she could proceed to poison her weapon with her fang once again.

"Any more?" Lex asked, trying to keep herself from panting. She was in worse shape than she had thought.

"None that followed me. Can't hear any movement either." Though her words sounded confident, Angui couldn't help but dart her head around. Something was wrong. There weren't nearly enough soldiers to guard a whole district. Sure, they had some help on their side, and a good half of this kingdom's army were fighting for them. But only twelve? The city should be swarming with hundreds. Either they *really* didn't care about this district, or there was something else.

"You think it's strange too, don't you?" Lex asked.

"To say the least." They were both wise to keep their guard up, as Angui saw something out of the corner of her eye. Movement. Fast movement. She guarded in that position and turned, her blade finding the end of a sharpened spider leg coming out of a red-cloaked figure.

Chapter 26

"Are you sure about this?" Ivan asked in his gruff but well-meaning voice.

"Wouldn't miss it for the world." Answered Henry, his face as white as a direct look at the desert sun. The blood had barely stopped from his severed arm. His remaining human limb was carrying a spear, one of many weapons left behind by Kasibel for the weaker hybrids before he left. Henry never thought he'd again count himself among those that can't defend themselves, so he felt he had something to prove. It didn't matter the state he was in. He wanted to be part of this battle. Live or die.

"Well, we have a while if you need to change your mind. No one would blame you." Ivan reassured him, but Henry's mind was already made up. It was made up years ago.

"It doesn't matter what anyone else thinks." He was already getting irritated at the idea of leaving. He wouldn't be able to live with himself if he sat this one out. "Besides, I've already had to settle for the safest position. We're the only team of three, and we're the only ones with full backup from any of the knights."

"But if something were to happen-"

"If I were to die here, it would be an embarrassment." Henry nearly snapped back. "I have a reputation to uphold." He knew he had gotten a little too heated, so he attempted to calm things back down with humour. It seemed to work, as Ivan chuckled it off. "What about you?"

"What do you mean?" Ivan asked, visibly confused.

"Do you want to do this? I mean, your life's on the line here."

"Are you kidding me?" Ivan laughed again. "I'm strong as an ox! Like I'd ever stay on the sidelines."

"Exactly." Henry was comfortable that his point was made and turned his attention back to the entrance they were meant to take.

There were two guards stationed on either side of the door. Each one wielding a spear and a shield, as if to insult Henry for only being able to use one. They each planned on taking one down when they heard the screech, and it shouldn't be difficult. In their positions when combat started, they should be distracted enough to be two easy kills.

That's when it hit him. That's when Henry realized his problem wouldn't be fighting with one arm or dying in combat. It would be killing again. Something shot through him and made him feel sick. Even if they were the enemy of the hybrids, was this really the best way to get their point across? He didn't have much time to make his decision. The battle cry would come at any minute. Though he was the one that endured the torture of this terrible king, how many of these guards actually knew? How many of the army they were about to try and kill were aware of what they were representing?

The call came so much earlier than he would have liked. The screech of Talia's vulture voice echoed out over the hills. Maybe if he just waited a second... No. Ivan was already rushing in horns first. He'd have to deal with the moral consequences later. Henry got to his feet and ran towards the desert outpost. It was time to take his bar back.

The start was exactly what they expected. The noise near the barracks distracted the two guards long enough for Henry to get his spear through one's neck and Ivan to take the other down with his bare hands. Ivan's wasn't a clean kill, but it got the job done.

It didn't hit either of them until they took their first kills and stood in that entry. The battle had started much faster than either of them had anticipated. The barracks were being held down by Kasibel's soldiers as they were already surrounded. The king's guard seemed too prepared for this. It was such a mass of bodies that, if there wasn't an obvious partition between them, it was hard to tell who was who. It was just a lump of swords, spears, armour and blood. This made it clear what Henry and Ivan were to do here.

"Same as the guards. Charge in from behind, knock out their force, allow Kasibel's men to spread to the rest of the city and the castle." Henry planned. Ivan nodded. "We're the first choke point. We fail, so does everyone else." The weight of his words fell on both of them.

"So we don't fail." Ivan stated.

"Exactly." Henry readied his spear in his one hand. It was an awkward weapon to wield, and he didn't know how well he'd hold up. Even if he could take out one or two before going down, that's all he needed. Both of them shared the slightest moment of a break before entering the fray in full sprint.

The hope was that no one would notice them, and they could take a couple of kills before combat came their way. This wasn't how it played out. They were seen only about halfway between the entrance of the market district and the wall of the barracks. An officer of some kind called out the new threat, and some of the soldiers in the back turned to face it. Henry's heart sank, thinking about how quickly this might end. Ivan also thought this wouldn't take long, but in a much different way.

Henry still didn't have all of his strength back, so the beast of a man called Ivan got in there first. It didn't matter that he was unarmed, as the main takeaway he pulled from the ox he fused with was muscle. Almost too much of it.

Ivan's first opponent wielded a spear and tried to stab him with it, but Ivan was too fast. He moved out of the way and grabbed the polearm before a second strike could come. Before the soldier knew what had happened, his weapon was broken in two. Without hesitation, Ivan wrapped his hands around the man's neck and crushed his windpipe. It was likely enough to kill him, but even if it didn't, he wasn't getting up from his slump anytime soon.

Though the first kill was easy, that wasn't going to be the same for the second and the third. After seeing what one-on-one was like with this beast, Ivan found himself surrounded by three of them. Two with swords and one with another spear. Each one ready to strike, but no one wanted to make the first move, even with the numbers on their side. So Henry went ahead and made the first move for them.

His strike was weak as he wasn't one for combat. What mattered was that it hit. One of the guards took the spear to their arm, though it was barely a puncture. They didn't expect the one-armed man to attack. This gave just enough time for Ivan to take advantage of the situation.

The ox took the heads of the two men who weren't injured and hit them together hard enough to knock them out, if they were lucky. That left him one on one with a swordsman who had taken the tiniest amount of damage to his good arm. Much like the loyal guard of a king does when faced with such a situation, the combatant ran out of the city as fast as he humanly could, sparing his own life.

Distraction was the name of the game that day. Though there were more king's guards here than anywhere else in the capital, it was clear they were the greenest of the bunch. The sight of Talia's talons coming down from the sky scared a couple off. She managed to land on a third before he even had the chance to strike, incapacitating both his arms with deep wounds. The crowd to the barracks was quickly clearing, with only a thin line of soldiers left to get through. Things were going way easier than the three of them could have ever expected.

For a moment, the three hybrids helped by flanking the other side of the troupe attacking the barracks. This caused the last few soldiers to scatter off in whatever direction they could find without opposition. There was a small victory celebration from inside and a quick glimpse of Kasibel as he made his way away from the front lines. The morale of these soldiers was in no small part to his willingness to fight alongside them.

"Well, that could have been worse." Ivan stated, seemingly unbothered by being covered in blood.

"War is never that simple." Henry reminded him while greeting Kasibel's soldiers with a nod. They returned the gesture slightly but maintained vigilance and didn't move from the front line. "What are your orders?" He asked one of them.

"To keep the enemy from crossing this line, sir!" Came the response, which threw Henry for a bit of a loop. He thought nothing of it yet, as he had information to get.

"What are we using the barracks for?"

"The sick and wounded. This is our last line of defence for those brought to us, sir!" Again with the sir. Not something a hybrid was used to being called.

"Should we push forward?" Ivan asked Henry, itching to continue the fight. It was clear in Ivan's eyes that he had been waiting for this for a long time.

Henry thought for a moment. All they were meant to do was secure this side of the city. He expected it to be much more challenging than this, but it seemed they had the most support here. "No." He said after a short silence.

"Don't you think the others might need some support?" Ivan asked, almost angrily.

“I absolutely do.” He answered. “But it’s barely started. Anything could happen in the next few minutes, and this is a key strategic point. We hold out for now until we know this place is clear.”

“I could do a flyover to see if there are any forces approaching.” Talia added.

“Not a bad idea. Keep an eye out for arrows.” Henry all but gave the go-ahead no sooner than Talia took to the skies. The interim period gave him and Ivan a chance to look around.

The market district was completely empty. Not a single soul in the street outside of ones that had just left the bodies they were attached to. It was strange to see, as this was the busiest place on this side of the continent. Clearly, everyone would have cleared out once the fighting started, but something still didn’t feel right.

Henry’s eyes made his way to the market stalls. He hadn’t paid attention to them upon entering, but now he had a sick feeling in the pit of his stomach. “He knew. They’re prepared.”

“What do you mean?” Asked Ivan, not one for vigilance. Henry motioned over to the stalls. Empty. Every single one of them. This could only mean two things. Either the merchants managed to pick up every one of their wares before departing town, or…

“They knew.” Henry spoke heavily. “No civilians on the streets. This city was set to be a battlefield before the fighting started.” He gave a look back at the carnage behind him. Still no more threats than what they had taken out. “Keep on guard.” He said to Ivan before turning back and repeating it to the barracks. The battle felt too easy. There was no way this wasn’t a trap.

This was confirmed upon hearing the screams of a vulture off in the distance.

“Talia!” Henry yelled as he ran off in the direction of the cry, spear in hand. Ivan didn’t follow far behind him. Both of them keep their eyes up to the sky despite the desert sun burning their retinas. There were no signs of her. Something took her out of the sky.

It wasn’t long until they encountered the same problem. An arrow landed right at Henry’s feet from an unknown source. Startled, his eyes darted around from street to street and rooftop to rooftop. There was nothing to be seen. Before he could say anything, Ivan covered him with his muscular body not a second before another arrow came flying through, nailing the ox man square in the back.

“You idiot!” Henry cried out as he got out from under the man grunting in pain. Not only did he get himself hurt, but he broke Henry's sight to the target. It wasn't until a third arrow came flying that he caught a glimpse of a red cloak making its way into the sky and falling back down behind a building. Henry dodged it in a way that would have made it bury itself directly into his arm if he still had one on that side.

"Cover. Now." Ivan wisely suggested as the two of them ran to the closest wall blinding them from their assailant.

"Red cloak. Likely another hybrid, part of that special force Ana was telling us about."

"We have to get Talia out of there." Ivan stated urgently.

"We have to assume she's already dead." As the words came out of Henry's mouth, they tasted sour. He didn't want to have that attitude, but he was right. They had to take on the threat first and worry about the injured and deceased later. This was war. Ivan understood, but still let out a low growl.

"How do we proceed?" Ivan asked, looking up to Henry for advice. Figuratively.

"We move through the alleys. We'll find them eventually, especially if they decide to shoot again. Keep your back to a wall, and be careful when you get close. That bow may not be the only threat." Henry clutched his spear tight to his chest to feel safe.

"The way you're talking, you sound like we'd be splitting up." Ivan pointed out.

"We will be. A flank is the best way to take this situation."

"But what if you make it there first?" Ivan asked, grave concern in his voice.

"Then I fight. Same as you." Henry's sheer dedication was enough to back the ox man off. There was no waiver in his words. This was going to happen whether he liked it or not.

"Fine. Just don't die."

"Right back at you. Don't go pulling any bull." Henry winked. Ivan groaned as he made his way down the nearest alley, hoping those weren't the last words he heard from the ex bartender.

Henry was terrified, stepping forward into the opposite alley. His movements were slow and deliberate. He hugged the wall so tight he might as well have not been moving. He kept his spear swinging around him, keeping any potential threats at bay. The truth was he didn't want to fight in his state any more than anyone else wanted him to.

But he had to.

This was a matter of pride. As much as he hated to admit it, Henry was an inspirational leader for this resistance. His personal strength on the front line didn't matter. What mattered was that he was there. He gave the rest of them something to fight for. The truth of this war was that, without Henry, there was no war. It would be replaced by the history of hybrids being stamped out in the kingdom in one fell swoop.

He heard another shot from the bow. Though unsure where its target was, the sun was in his favour. Henry could see a shadow fly across his alley and then fall back down. He was close. A couple more turns, and he would be there. One on one combat. With a hybrid that still had all their parts together. Henry never thought he would miss that big, clunky claw.

Every step was carefully calculated to make no sound. If he was going to do any damage, it was going to be by surprise. He turned the next corner slowly, his heart stopping as if it too wanted to stay silent. Upon looking at an empty road, he took a deep breath and moved to the next logical corner. Nothing again. No more shots to pinpoint the location of this creature either. He'd just have to keep moving and hope he'd get lucky.

Another turn, nothing. He kept moving forward, sacrificing his cautious movements for speed. Nothing after the next corner. Henry knew this city well. He had lived here for years and knew the darkest corners where new hybrids would hide. It brought back memories of scouring the alleyways like this. The only difference now was he was looking for prey instead of another to join the pack.

After a few minutes of searching, it started to feel strange. He had run into no one. Not Ivan, or Talia, or whatever was trying to kill them. It was too late when Henry realized this was a distraction. The sounds of footsteps marching through the street echoed in his ears like war drums. The barracks were about to be under attack, and their hybrid support wasn't going to be there to stop it.

Chapter 27

Ana and Drake entered the main gates of the city with barely any resistance. Two guards were stationed, same as any other entrance, and both were knocked down easily. The main street straight up to the castle was barren. Not a civilian or a guard in sight. Just two straight rows of middle-class housing that mostly kept castle staff.

"Even on a slow day, this street is bustling." Ana commented.

"The king knows a war is going on, and he's opened the way to his castle." Drake replied, keeping an eye out for any potential threats. "Something is wrong."

"Perhaps he moved all of his forces inside already?" Ana pondered out loud.

"Is he the kind of man to wait for his enemies to come to him?"

"No. Not in the slightest."

"Then we'd better be prepared." Drake nervously retracted his claw and brought it back out again, as if making sure he didn't forget how to use it.

Their plan was to go in through the dungeons. There might be guards there, but there were also prisoners. Prisoners who would likely do anything to get back at the ones who put them there. If they were lucky, they might release a hybrid or two. The problem was supposed to be getting there in the first place.

Once the gates to the public gallows were in sight, there was at least some opposition. Two guards at either side of the gate, each standing at attention and wielding spears. Drake and Ana decided to hang behind a nearby building to check them out.

"He must have holed himself up then." Drake concluded. "I suppose this reign hasn't had to deal with much in the way of battle on home turf."

"Take a closer look." Ana advised. Drake didn't catch on to what she meant and shrugged. "Their position isn't that of the king's personal guard. It's lazy, and inattentive." She was right. It was as if these guards didn't even care to be there. These weren't soldiers waiting for a war. These were workers waiting for the day to be over.

"Do you think they know?"

"If they don't, they're about to find out. Ready?" Ana asked with a smirk on her face. She was enjoying this way more than she should be. Drake nodded, and on the count of three, they rushed in at full speed.

Ana pulled her sword out before they got anywhere close, but it didn't matter. Drake was faster. He managed to knock them both out before they even knew what hit them. He wrapped his claw around the first one's face and knocked him against the wall hard enough to leave a dent. Before the second one could react Drake was already moving towards him and made a matching dent in the street. Now it was just a matter of getting into the dungeon. They quickly pushed open the gate to the public execution ring.

Also empty. Only two incompetent guards blocking the entrance. Ana and Drake shared a glance and continued cautiously. They peered over the staircase that led down to the dungeon. The doors weren't just unguarded. They were open.

"We're being invited in." Ana commented. There was going to be something down there, likely one of the Red Guard. The question was which one.

"Far be it for us to pass up the gesture." Drake responded. He was right. What else were they going to do? Ignore their plan entirely?

They made it down step by step. Each one felt like an eternity had passed since the last. The ordinarily dark room came slowly into view, but this time it was well lit. Every torch had to be burning down there. Even the cracks in the flagstones were clear as day. If that wasn't bad enough, Ana could see the first cell come into view. It was open. They had no vision of any threats, but as it all came into view, it was clear every cell was open. The prisoners were already let out. Best case scenario, they were set free so Ana couldn't rally them against her father. Worst case, they were already rallied against her. This was going to be a problem.

Drake shared in Ana's fears, but that was the least of their problems. There was one clear threat looming directly on the other side of the dungeon blocking the only door into the castle, and it was wearing a red cloak. Whoever they were, they were waiting for this.

“Which one are you?” Asked Ana from across the room. It was only a matter of time before they found out, but she would like to know ahead of time.

“The one to stop you both in your tracks.” Came the answer. A masculine voice, one to match the overwhelming stature of the creature. It was impressive that his cloak covered everything but his mouth.

Drake took that as a challenge, and Ana quickly followed up. They both raced in headfirst. This was no time to wait and think. Drake went to deliver the first blow, clawing at the creature’s face. He was swiftly blocked, which was to be expected. What wasn’t was the fact his claws did nothing. They scraped off the man’s arm harmlessly. Ana soon found the same problem with her sword. Their opponent hadn’t even moved, and he had them both worried.

The first and only blow came to Drake. He caught a fist to the chest that practically knocked him onto the ground. The dragon barely keeping his balance left Ana worried, though no similar blow came to her. As a matter of fact, the Red Guard ignored her and kept going for Drake, leaving his back completely open.

It was a mistake to assume Ana wasn’t a threat, and she wanted to end this as quickly as humanly possible. She let out a battle cry while thrusting her sword out into the man’s back. The blade stopped dead in its tracks and sent a wave of pain up Ana’s arms and straight into her spine. The sword barely caught on anything and didn’t take much effort to pull out. There was armour under that cloak, but Ana couldn’t hear any metal scraping. Whatever it was, it was natural. A turtle maybe?

Drake prepared for the next blow, but it wasn’t quite enough. He had blocked it with his arm, but all that did was hurt and push him back even further. Drake attacked his opponent’s chest and faced the same deflection as with his first. This was going to be a problem. An enemy he couldn’t even damage? It was unprecedented.

It concerned Ana as well, but she wasn’t about to keep going for the same attack that didn’t work. She was still being ignored. Whether or not that was because of her father’s wishes or that she didn’t seem like a threat. What mattered was it worked in her favour. She pulled her blade up and sliced straight down the back of the creature. Not to do any damage, that ship had sailed. She wanted to tear his cloak in half and succeeded in her endeavours.

The red fabric tore unevenly. The cloak pulled back to reveal a rigged armour, light brown in colour like that of the desert sand though lacking its beautiful glisten. Five main plates of natural armour went up the creature's back, revealing him to be part armadillo. This revelation left no solution. What's worse is the guard knew that and continued his assault on Drake.

He couldn't be attacked head-on and was too powerful for even a dragon to handle. This was worse than they thought. The only thing Ana had on her side was his lack of interest in her and knowledge of armadillos. The front of his body should be soft, so it was just a matter of getting one good strike in. As she watched Drake get nearly knocked over yet again, it was clear that wasn't going to be an easy task. Now Ana had to figure out how Drake would get the upper hand if she couldn't work as a distraction.

The battle continued, and it was clear it wasn't going to last long. While she thought, Ana decided to come to Drake's side. Perhaps he couldn't ignore her if they fought together. She held her blade in front of her and rushed into combat. Not a moment before the armadillo noticed this maneuver, he quickly grabbed Drake and threw him backwards, once again turning his back to the princess. This left the dragon prone for the first time this fight, and it was the first real threat Ana had ever seen him face. She felt powerless.

Wait. That was it. She kept trying to think how he could get past the armour, but maybe Drake wasn't the answer. She looked around the room to the torches once again. Burning brighter than ever. One thing this hybrid didn't get were the eyes of an armadillo, or they would be burning in this bright of a light. Human eyes. Eyes that can't see in the dark. This was going to be easier than she thought. She tried to give Drake a knowing look but was unsure if he noticed. Hopefully, he could hold out for just long enough.

Ana had to turn her back on the fight, which wasn't something that came to her easily. Even for the most amateur fighters, it was hard to know you didn't have vision of their assailant. With any luck, the armadillo would have to encounter that same problem soon. Ana looked around the room and quickly found a snuffer cap. She grabbed it and started her run along the eastern wall. It was time to put out the lights.

One after another, she put out every flame she came across. The room slowly slipped into a darker and darker shade. Hopefully, Drake was putting up enough of a fight so she could get them all out. Upon reaching the end of the room, she turned and started going up to the other wall. Unfortunately, her plan was noticed, and she was face to face with a seven-foot-tall armadillo man who didn't intend on letting her move anywhere. She threw down the snuffer in what appeared to be a panic. The clanking of the metal hitting the flagstones echoed throughout the hall in a rare moment of tension right before the first strike came.

The man immediately bashed Ana to the ground. It was clear he held back, as any attack that might have been meant for Drake would have knocked her out on the spot. She didn't know what his plan was from here, as he could only do so much without permanently damaging her. At least she assumed his orders were not to do as such. The king still cared about his 'precious' daughter, after all. What was he planning?

Ana played her role as helpless for a second before picking up her sword and going for a strike directly at the armadillo's chest. She didn't expect it to land. He was much too attentive for that. What he didn't expect was her plan to continue. Before either of them knew it, the dungeon went from its usual dimly lit chamber to the absolute pitchest of black. Ana smiled, knowing that Drake understood. Throwing the snuffer cap behind the Red Guard worked like a charm.

"I've got this from here." Ana yelled out as she sprung to her feet. The fake fall did wonders. Hopefully, Drake was still on the same page as her. She hoped he would continue further in to help Kasibel. Upon letting out a soft, but high-pitched screech she had been working on, she knew Drake was gone. It was only her and a blind Armadillo.

"This will get you nowhere." He stated. The second time he spoke, and he already sounded panicked.

"Afraid of the dark?" Ana asked in the most sinister voice she could muster. It felt good having the upper hand for once. No response came. Chances are he had balled up. There would barely be a chance to hit his soft stomach. Ana had already prepared for this, though.

She ran up to the last location she could see through sound. Her eyes still hadn't made it back to the darkness yet. The earlier torchlight was too bright and left her temporarily short on vision. With her weapon ready in one hand, she brought the other out to feel where the creature was. Her hand touched his back, and immediately she was struck down. This time for real, as she slid across the floor and her sword made the same clanking sound the snuffer did. He was faster than she had expected, but she didn't intend to make the same mistake again.

Ana sprung to her feet quickly and moved for her sword. She knew it was the only intel the armadillo had on her location, so she grabbed its hilt and purposely slid the blade along the floor, making a high-pitched grinding sound. It was awkward, but she managed to turn quickly in the opposite direction, making her opponent move in to hit her again only to find empty space.

There wasn't much time for Ana to make her next move. Her eyes started adjusting to the dark again, which meant that his weren't far behind. She could see his exposed shell now. He was facing away from her, swinging his arms out hoping to hit a target. All the while keeping his defensive stance.

She saw her chance and took it. While the creature was attacking, he had to bend the tiniest bit forward. This gave her an opening. As quietly as she could, she stepped up behind him. The moment she was in range, she struck. Right between the second and third sections of his shell. They had separated just enough to fit her sword right through. She had felt a bit of resistance on entry where his armour met his back, but it didn't matter. The blade made it the rest of the way through with all her weight behind it. The Red Guard looked confused as the blade barely came into sight for him. The one glimmer in the darkness being from his own blood on its edge as it protruded from his chest.

Weakness overcame him as he fell to his knees. Just being hit was rare for this opponent, let alone being struck by a killing blow. Ana pulled the blade out of his back. A gruesome sight as a bit of connective tissue came with it. She still wasn't used to this, and it was almost enough to make her sick. There was no time to get weak knees now, though. Lying on his stomach might be a defence. She had to make sure her opponent wasn't getting back up.

She didn't know if it was the strategist in her or the predator, but she went for that same stab again, making sure she heard her sword hit the stone underneath the armadillo. Then she did it again. And again. This wasn't a time to let one of the strongest pieces on the board survive.

Once content that her target couldn't get up, she wiped off her blade and inspected it. She had dulled the point to a nub. She would have to remember to pick up a sword from the armoury on her way inside the castle. Ana dare not think of anything besides moving forward. The weight of what she had done, killing an enemy who was holding back, would have to find its way to her shoulders later. For now, it was time to find the one who forced her hand.

Chapter 28

Angui moved back defensively, holding her blade up against the new threat. Seven sharpened legs pointed towards her from an all too confident opponent. A spider hybrid. This must have been the same one Drake and Ana had run into.

"What happened to your leg?" Angui asked smarmily, calling out the one broken limb.

"Fight with a lizard." Came the response that sounded as if it came straight from a noble. "Not exactly the revenge I was looking for, but a snake is close enough." Any thoughts of him being high born were lost when he licked his lips as if he hadn't eaten in days.

"I'm just glad he was kind enough to leave me the other seven." Angui smiled and ran her sword along her fang, leaving a thin trail of venom glimmering on the edge.

"You plan on taking all the fun for yourself?" Lex asked, feeling ignored. She didn't like to miss a fight.

"Yes." Angui said, nodding toward Lex's leg. "Trust me." Lex was frustrated but couldn't help but agree. She would never admit the pain she was in, though going into combat might as well be suicide.

"Oh, how thoughtful of you to not team up on me like barbarians." The spider mocked. He gave a similar show to Angui as she did for him, running leg after sharpened leg along his teeth until they were all coated in venom. He was much faster than she was at it.

Angui readied herself, taking a defensive position in front of Lex. She was sure this creep wasn't going to leave her alone. He seemed to like to type to prey on the defenceless. There was no telling how well Angui could protect Lex, though. She had never seen someone fight with their legs before, at least not like this. It was as if her opponent had seven swords at the ready, as well as two extra limbs. This wasn't going to be easy.

What was worse, he was inviting her. It was a stalemate right out of the gate. He didn't move, not even a twitch. Angui thought he might be setting up a trap, or perhaps he fought on his legs and wasn't used to having one broken off. She took a gamble that it was the latter and went in for a strike.

Slithering at full speed, she threw herself forward with her sword pointing straight at his chest. There would be nothing better than this fight ending quickly. Unfortunately, her opponent wasn't so dull. She expected him to block with one of his many appendages but wasn't ready for him to sidestep with such grace. Working on the assumption his mobility was shot put her at a disadvantage already. She found herself stuck in some kind of sticky substance that was left behind by him. A web. She was a snake, caught in a web.

"Well, that was too easy." He said, shrugging his shoulders. "I suppose I'll have to make my own fun." The spider began to make his way toward Lex. Luckily Angui wasn't the only one making mistakes today. Angui broke free of the web quickly. All she had to do was slither back and forth quickly until it loosened. It would have taken longer if it wasn't for the spider's second mistake. You don't threaten Lex.

Angui charged once again, full of adrenaline. Her opponent almost didn't notice her and could barely deflect the strike with one of his legs. It came close to glancing him, which would have been enough for death. In this battle, the first strike was all that mattered.

"I see." Angui hissed, backing off just enough to get out of range. "You can't fight for yourself, so you prey on the weak. Typical."

"Considering you two are all I have to prey on, I don't really have a choice in the matter, do I?" He chittered back. Lex took the threat personally and slashed out at his human legs.

"No!" Angui yelled out as she rushed back in. She was just in time to distract the spider from attacking back.

"Not willing to team up on me, are you?" He asked, keeping Angui at bay but not moving from his position between her and Lex. "I guess I'll have to go one by one." Angui didn't notice one of his legs left combat to attempt a stab at Lex. Luckily the tiger was paying attention and rolled out of the way. There was seemingly no way she could stay out of this fight, which worked in the Red Guard's favour. It was a matter of keeping the snake distracted with protecting her friend, and all it would take was one slip up.

Angui had already caught onto the plan, though she didn't know how she would get around it. No matter how hard she tried, she couldn't help but sneak a peek at Lex whenever she got the chance. Every time she did, she would lose some footing and come that much closer to taking a strike. Her arms were tensed, her tail was coiled. She would have this down if she wasn't distracted. It was time to try a different approach.

It was a simple move, but hopefully effective. In the middle of protecting herself, she began looking for an opportunity. It had to be at a specific spot, directly into his face. Eventually, she got her opening. Not one her sword could get through, but one she could fire a ball of spit through to hit her opponent in the eye.

The spider let out a noise of disgust as he began to lose his footing. He backed off and almost let a blow in but regained composure almost as quickly as he had lost it. She tried again, but he began dedicating one of his legs to keeping his eyes safe.

"Nice try, though absolutely disgusting." The spider mocked.

"You going to keep that leg up there forever?" Angui asked, bringing attention to yet another weakness she would attempt to exploit. One of his legs was broken, another set to keeping the injured tiger away, and now a third protecting his face. This left five. Now she just needed to find a new distraction for each and every one of them. Not an easy thing to do while your life is on the line.

Though Angui didn't want her in combat, Lex was definitely going to take more than one leg to keep off. Especially while he was still turned away from her. The tiger pawed at his legs much like a housecat would, but with much more deadly claws. The only thing keeping her from connecting was his defensive positioning. There was no opening she could take that wouldn't wind up getting her poisoned on the way there. Even Lex wasn't impulsive enough to go that deep.

For a while, they were at a standstill. Everyone ready to strike but no one willing to actually do it, fearing giving up too much defence. The spider attempted to reposition himself to get his back facing a wall so at least he could see both of them. Angui and Lex made sure to disallow this. Every time he tried, one of them would get there first.

Eventually, there was a break in the position. He couldn't hold like this without somehow slipping up. He tunnel-visioned on Angui, seeing the more significant threat being the one that could kill him in one blow. He took one of his legs off of the defence of his rear and lunged in for a strike at Angui. There were two mistakes to this maneuver. Angui maintained a solid guard and, if anything, was waiting for a strike. This let her react quickly, slithering back before any of those envenomed spider legs came close to contact.

The second problem came in the form of searing pain in the creature's human leg. The moment he raised the protection from his left, he found himself with a tiger's claw digging deep into his flesh. He didn't need to look to see the damage. He could feel his foot wet with blood. Adrenaline kept him from falling over immediately, but he wasn't going to be holding onto that numbness for long. This had to finish quickly.

The spider threw his body forward as if he was trying to land face-first on the ground. Four of his arachnid legs took over the job of holding him up, which in turn was losing four weapons. He didn't have much of a choice aside from a reckless attack on the snake. Even on four legs, his speed was still breakneck. She had no chance of guarding against the three others barreling down at her. Angui raised her sword and lunged forward, hoping for the best.

The two of them found themselves in swapped positions. Neither one of them turned to face the other as the battle was already over. The spider was hit in his shoulder and Angui across her chest. Each of them made contact, though his damage was much worse than hers, it likely wouldn't matter. Venom is venom, and neither of them were bluffing about their potency.

"Good fight." The Red Guard said weakly, his body already feeling the effects. His disposition completely changed while facing death.

"You too." Angui replied. She would rather her last moments come with some form of respect as she let herself sink to the ground. A good chunk of her strength was used just to turn herself over so she could look up at the desert sun. The spider had the same idea. Might as well witness its burning beauty as losing vision was the least of their worries.

This respectful attempt at passing left one problem. One barbaric cat, whose eyes narrowed as she saw what had been done to her friend. Angui's vision began to blur, but she still saw the streak of orange run past her and knew what was about to happen. She tried to grab her friend but didn't have the strength. She could hear the sounds of flesh ripping and screaming. Terrible screaming from an already dead man being dragged to hell by his feet and not lowered down softly. Angui hoped it would be over soon, but she knew Lex. She wasn't going for a quick kill, and it didn't stop. With what remained of her strength, Angui managed to whisper one word,

"Stop."

She didn't expect it to be heard. It was so faint she was unsure that any noise came out, but the cat's ears picked up on it. The shrieking slowed, and Lex returned to her friend's side with anything but understanding.

"Why." It wasn't a question Lex asked. It was the only word to say how she felt. All Angui could do in return was shake her head. She just wanted to go peacefully, not hearing the pain of one last victim in this war. The tiger got the message and sat down next to her friend.

Lex picked up Angui's head and laid it on her lap, trying to keep her eyes focused up at the sun like she wanted. The snake had a new thing to look at, though. She instead chose her friend's face as a better final sight. Though she couldn't see it very well. At least not at first.

It was in that silent moment Angui realized she just might make it. Focus was coming back to her. She must not have gotten enough of the venom to end it, but just keep her out for a while. Her heart filled with warmth at the sight of Lex once again, covered in blood or not. Honestly, it might have been stranger if she wasn't. There was something wrong, though, and it took almost too long to figure out. Angui's heart sank once again as she could make out the fur on Lex's arm.

There was a cut.

A small nick. Nothing major if it wasn't for the venom. If it hit Angui this hard, she knew her friend wouldn't be able to survive even the slightest drop. She had to keep herself from laughing, as she knew the recklessness of the tiger would come back to bite her someday. Just why did it have to be now? Why when she had gained back so much hope for life?

It was then the snake had an idea. She had to act weak, not show that she was recovering, but get more words out.

"Closer..." she said faintly. Angui didn't know if it would work, but it did. Lex brought her head in tighter, so her face was right near the arm of the cat. Angui could already feel her friend's strength leaving and had to act fast without the cat learning about what she was doing.

Angui moved her head just enough as if to kiss the cat's arm and carefully wrapped her mouth around the open wound, making sure not to puncture with her teeth. Still, in a weakened state, she didn't know if she could do enough, but she began inhaling the blood into her body the best she could. She tried to make it seem like a regular kiss, but it went on for too long.

"What are you doing?" Lex asked, her voice broken. She didn't truly need an answer. She already figured it out.

"Saving your life." Angui answered in bated breath. She couldn't pull out any more. Her body wouldn't allow it. The world started to slowly slip away again, as her friend's face quickly became blurry. Lex held Angui tighter and tried to hold back any emotion. It was no use. When she focused on trying not to cry, her body started shaking. When she tried to focus on that, she began sobbing. Every battle is life or death, but this was the last death Lex wanted.

"You shouldn't have." Lex replied. Her voice came out as a whisper beneath heavy breathing.

"I was already gone." Angui lied.

"And I..." Lex stopped herself, or rather her tears stopped her words for her. She couldn't tell which was true. Angui brought her hand up to her friend's face as the last movement she could muster. Lex could feel her going limp.

"Didn't want to go on without you...." The tiger finished her sentence. She didn't know if Angui heard her. She was already gone. Though Lex couldn't let her go. She sat as long as she could, holding the body of the snake she held so dear.

Minutes could have passed. Or hours. There was no concept of time left. Her last moment with her friend was finally broken as she heard guards yelling commands at the sight of her in the street. Lex's eyes narrowed, and her claws made their way out.

Those soldiers didn't realize the mistake they had just made.

Chapter 29

"Ivan!" Henry cried out, rushing back through the winding alleys in a panic. "If you can hear me, get back to the barracks! Ivan!" He hoped he was heard, or at least that Ivan heard the sounds of marching. This battle was going to be fought from behind. The hybrids were perfectly distracted. Worst of all, Talia was probably dead.

Henry ran awkwardly, not used to the lack of weight on one side. The spear in his other hand wasn't helping either. The imbalance left him hobbling quickly instead of running. He couldn't help but think that his body was doing this on purpose. This was a trap set up by the king. There was no way he was going to get in there and come out alive. Not with his reduced mobility or attack power. Clearly, something in him didn't want to die.

"Ivan!" He called out again, expecting no response. Much to his thankful surprise, the ox man turned a corner near him and they met up. Ivan slowed to match Henry's speed. Henry wanted to fight with him to run ahead but knew it would just waste more time.

"Any plans?" Ivan asked.

"Not a one. Get drunk and hope for the best?" Henry tried to lighten the tension. If this was going to be his last fight, he wasn't going out sounding serious.

"Would work if we had anything to drink." Ivan made a painful point that crashed him back to reality. No booze was the worst part of this. Henry knew he shouldn't have left that bottle of bourbon at the campsite.

"There has to be more than one way into that barracks, right?" Henry asked, more of a hope than a question. Then it came to him. It was so stupid it had to work. "The castle."

"What about it?" Ivan asked, perplexed.

"It leads into the barracks." Henry answered proudly. "So we go through there."

"Are you insane?" Usually, when the largest creature you know asks you that question, you deserve it.

"Think about it for a second. Most of their force has to be what's out here, right?"

"You think the king would leave himself without defence?"

"Absolutely not, but his guards will be near him. The ground level will be less defended than the front lines or the throne room. Even if he was tactical enough to overcome ego and spread his guard out more, Kasibel and his main force started this by cutting their way into the stronghold." Henry tried to pat himself on the back for his idea, but attempted to use an arm that wasn't there.

"And what if Kasibel failed?" Ivan asked skeptically.

"Then we're already dead and just postponing the process." Henry pretended like he was joking. He really wasn't. If the main force went down, it was only a matter of time before his men and the rest of them crumbled.

"So our plan is to just walk through the front door?" Ivan had to make sure he was hearing this right.

"Would you expect your enemy to do that?" Henry asked coyly.

"No."

"Then it's just stupid enough to work." Henry turned towards the castle and moved forward with complete confidence, knowing it was the only way to get Ivan to follow. It worked as time was of the essence, and neither of them could spare it to argue.

They laid low, making sure to keep to the side streets. Ivan took up the rear as he was harder to take down, and Henry was a better strategist anyway. As they got farther away from the barracks, the fighting got louder. More and more soldiers must have been piling on. Henry wasn't sure they would be able to do anything even if they did make it through the castle, which was a shaky idea to begin with.

Eventually, they had to make their way out of the alleys and onto the main road. They didn't come out recklessly and stayed parallel to the eastern street, popping their heads out every now and again to check for guards. The stragglers of reinforcements seemed to be endless as every time they checked, there were at least two more running towards the combat. This was at least favourable for their entry point. It did still weigh on them that they'd be abandoning their post.

It didn't take long for them to run out of back roads. Henry and Ivan found themselves in the city centre, the crossroads of Arid Retreat. Much like Drake and Ana found earlier, this seemed to be the calmest of any road.

"Well, this is convenient." Henry mentioned.

"Too convenient." Answered Ivan, but Henry was already making his way out into the open.

"We've got no time to worry about that." Henry answered Ivan before he even tried to question the decision. Ivan was already running alongside him.

"So not only are we breaking into the castle through the front doors but doing it along the main road as well?" Ivan was starting to wish he was one of the hybrids that ran away.

"No other way about it, is there?" Henry answered. It seemed the first half of the journey was over, and it was just a matter of making it past the front gates. That was until the first arrow hit the street near them. Both hybrids instinctively found a wall the arrow would have been shot from the other side of.

"Any other ideas?" Ivan asked, furious, thinking this was going to be the death of him. Henry looked up and down the street and came to a decision as quickly as he could. It seemed the mystery archer was their only real threat.

"Yeah, one." Henry answered. Ivan raised an eyebrow in concern, and for good reason. "Run faster." Before he knew it, Henry was in a full sprint down the main road towards a stronghold in the dead centre of a civil war. It was an awkward run as he got used to not having a second arm to balance himself out. Ivan considered for a split second letting himself get shot before following Henry. In the end, the ex-bear got him this far, might as well see where it leads.

Another arrow landed on the flagstones, nearly hitting one of Ivan's feet. Then another one Henry could hear whistle past his head. No matter how good their opponent was, it was hard to hit moving targets when you only give yourself a short time to fire. Although whoever it was had an arrow with their name on it, and he wasn't going to stop firing until he found it. They kept coming as if at least three soldiers were chasing them. It was going to be a matter of a bit of speed and a lot of luck.

Arrow after arrow whizzed past them, many of them close calls. Henry noticed the angle they came from started to become more parallel to the street. It was clear their assailant was firing from farther away.

"We're outrunning him. Keep pushing!" Henry gave words of encouragement to Ivan that weren't quite needed. The man pushed through like a speeding Ox.

Coming up quickly were two plain sandstone sets of stairs that ran up in a curve to the left and right, leading to the castle's main door. "Left or right?" Ivan asked.

"Split." Henry answered. He could see a couple of unfriendly soldiers guarding the front door. If they attacked from both sides, it would be much more efficient. The arrows slowed down when they started climbing. Clearly, whoever was firing them was either too far away, or at least courteous enough to not accidentally hit a friendly. It wasn't going to matter either way. Henry had a plan for dispatching both of their obstacles.

Surprisingly Henry kept up with the Ox's speed, and they reached the top simultaneously. Both guards wielded spears and held them at a ready position, seeing the attack coming from a long way away. Because of this, they had a decent chance to evaluate their targets. One very angry strongman rushing at them full speed and a one-armed human with a sad looking stick that could barely be called a spear. This is precisely what Henry had counted on.

Both guards turned toward Ivan. Both of them pointed their spears out in an attempt to keep Ivan from running into them and taking them by surprise. Neither were paying attention to Henry. Both of them wound up getting stabbed through the neck by that terrible excuse for a spear. Ivan nodded at Henry and looked impressed for the first time all day. Now all that stood between them and their alternate route were two large ornate doors with a smaller, more reasonable door seated in the centre of them.

This turned out to be the most challenging obstacle so far. Both of them tried to push it open, and neither for a second thought that it might be locked.

"What do we do now?" Ivan asked.

"I don't know." Answered Henry. "Didn't think we'd get this far." Ivan looked like he was about to add a third body to the pile that day. Soon he realized he might not have to, as at the last second, Henry heard something and moved his head barely out of the way of an oncoming arrow. It made a loud clank on the metal doors and fell to the ground broken in two. Both of them took cover behind a low wall meant to act as a railing for the staircases and their raised platform.

"Think we can get in through a window?" Ivan asked.

"All the ground-level ones are barred shut." Henry shook his head. "Maybe if we can climb up a smooth wall one story, we might be able to get in." He didn't say it out loud, but he thinks he could have at least tried if he still had his good arm.

"We'd be shot off anyways." Ivan snapped him back to reality, knowing what his friend was thinking.

"I don't see you coming up with any ideas." Henry snarled back. He quickly found his foot in his mouth as Ivan ran into the door at full speed, and it budged. Just a little, but it was movement. He went at it again, hitting the door at the same time another arrow hit it. With more incentive, the third attempt did it. It took the strength of an Ox, but the door had bust open. Both hybrids ran inside and closed the door behind them. It was still on its hinges, luckily. Henry went to lock it and realized the mechanism had broken off. It wasn't going to be long until their hunter found their way in.

"You are so lucky that door opened inward." Henry chided.

"So are you." Ivan replied as he turned away from the door. They found themselves in an open foyer. Nothing too fancy, especially by castle standards, but it worked for greeting nobles and the like. Doors were lining each side of the hallway, too many of them, in fact, and a couple of main staircases leading up. The most important thing was the lack of guards. Most of them, as Henry rightly planned for, must have been off in some other combat somewhere in the city.

"Now, if only there was someone here to show us around." Henry remarked as he made his way to the first door on the east side. Opening it found nothing but a dead end in the form of a small armoury, likely for guards to grab from at a moment's notice to defend the gate.

"We have to be quick about this." Ivan reminded as he checked the next door. No luck there either. If there was a hall to the outside, it wasn't obvious. It was as if this castle was designed to confuse intruders.

They didn't have time to check another door. They barely had time to check the ones they did. Ivan found himself turning around to the sound of the entrance crashing open and a battle-axe barreling down on him from a creature in a red robe and large, feathery brown wings. He was able to catch the pole right under the axe head and stop it from coming any further. It hovered barely two inches off of his chest.

Henry saw this and immediately ran in to help, but not before another strike came and Ivan found himself dodging. It wasn't normal for the Ox to be on the defensive. He knew if this went on too long, he'd be backed into a corner and would either have to take the axe by grabbing it or by the head making its way into his chest.

The ex-bear proved that three arms are better than two as he kept the problem from arising. He came from the back of the bird and forced an action. Since they were up against a trained soldier, their opponent didn't opt for being flanked and instead flew up into the air to reposition himself. Henry always hated hybrids who could fly, even after he became one. Having three dimensions of movement was far too unpredictable.

Ivan and Henry proved that this wasn't their first time in a fight by immediately putting themselves back to back. As their opponent could attack from any direction, they figured they'd cover all of them. Whatever type of bird they were up against was clearly a predator and went for the weak one first. Henry found himself on the receiving end of an aerial attack all too soon. He knew he'd never be able to block with his spear, especially with only one arm trying to hold back the weight of his opponent. The other option was to move and have Ivan take an axe straight to the spine. Unfortunately, he calculated that outcome all too late. His instincts made him dodge in a direction that would have gotten his arm cut off if there was one there.

A guttural scream came from the ox man as he fell to the ground. Henry attempted to strike before the Red Guard could pull his weapon out, but it turned out he had a sword hidden under his robe, which quickly came to block. A few one-sided strikes and parrys later, and Henry found himself far away from the unmoving body of his friend. It was painful to watch the axe come out as if it had been stuck in the knot of a log. Henry found it clear that he was the only hybrid left of his squad.

It was funny. As the weapon master of a red guard came at him, Henry thought over his position. He was put at what was supposed to be the safest of the attacks but made sure he wasn't. Now it wasn't only him that was in danger. Two of his friends were dead. He held his spear shakily, knowing that his fate was barreling down on him. A fate he thought he deserved. He closed his eyes. There was the sound of footsteps coming closer, but it didn't matter. Likely more of the king's guard, though they wouldn't be needed. Henry was a one-armed man with barely any combat experience. The only thing he knew was drinking.

He was hoping for his death to be swift. It wasn't. He didn't want to open his eyes but couldn't help it out of curiosity. The room came back before him, and what he saw was the last thing he expected. Kasibel's men. They had broken through. They had survived the attack, and now they were in the foyer with him and the bird. He had to have seen at least 20 of them between the ones running around the halls and the ones starting a fight with the hybrid. Henry almost felt like he was going to make it out alive, but again, his opponent was a master predator. If he was going to die, he was going to take a snack with him.

Henry was just about ready to prepare for his fate again, yet found himself quickly surrounded by guards. All of them protecting him. Their various weapons acted as an impenetrable shield the bird couldn't get through. It was clear he was going to survive. Which to Henry might just be a fate worse than death.

"Why..." He muttered under his breath. Humans like this coming to help a hybrid, and one they only just met. Lives laid on the line before him to try and keep him alive. It didn't make sense. They weakened their position to come over here. There was no tactical advantage. Just to keep one ex-hybrid alive.

Out of the five guards around him, the one at the lead spoke first. "Because of my sister." He said, which followed by the rest of them.

"And my brothers." Came another.

"My friends." A female voice.

"My children." An old, shaky voice.

"My wife." Came the last, the strongest of the five. It didn't make any sense. All Henry knew was that he had backup and raised his weapon in defence. The bird flew up above the reach of anyone's weapon as any other move was just too dangerous. He planned on picking them off one by one.

With his newfound confidence, Henry saw the only move he could make. He slid his spear through his hand stealthily until he was gripping the very back of it. It was a clear shot. He made sure not to even scrape any of his saviours on the weapon's way up and threw it as fast and hard as he could. The weapon lazily flew through the air and gave plenty of time for his opponent to dodge. It would have been a fatal miss if it wasn't for the follow-up.

Three more spears came flying from the group, following Henry's lead. Whoever these guards were, they were well trained in throwing weapons. The attack flew through the air, too spread out to run away from and too bunched together to easily slip through. The Red Guard almost made it out, but all it took was a graze of his left wing to make him come tumbling down to the ground. Even an insane member of an elite King's guard knew they were defeated, as they gave up their weapon and put their hands above their head. The two of Kasibel's men that didn't throw their weapons away came to either side of the hybrid, preparing to take him prisoner.

"It's been an honour, Sir Henry." Said the oldest of the group, one of the ones who threw a spear.

"I still don't know what you mean." He was confused by the exchange. "Why would you risk your position like that to save me?"

"Don't flatter yourself too much now, boy." replied the guard. "We would have done it for anyone facing death like that. Albeit, you are a special case to us."

"What do you mean 'special case'?"

"Well, you ran the bar, didn't you?" The man asked, sounding almost as if he was questioning himself in his old age.

"I don't see what that has to do with anything." Henry was still lost.

"My daughter was a hybrid. Jeane was her name. You gave her a place to stay." The man said proudly but solemnly.

"Jeane..." Henry thought back and remembered the woman. Part fox, if he remembered correctly. Didn't drink much but was always a fan of his cooking. That's when it came back to him that she was one of the ones that died in the raid. "I'm sorry I couldn't save her." He apologized.

"Don't be." The man replied sternly. "You were the only thing that kept me able to see her. If anything, she would have died quicker if it wasn't for your protection." He motioned out to the other four guards around him. "Same story with all of them. If it wasn't for you, we wouldn't have been able to live near our family. It's a shame they met the fate that they did, but that's why we're fighting this war."

"Thank you. For both your kind words and saving my life." Henry took the compliment though still was unsure if he deserved it.

Knowing that his work had helped the lives of full humans was an uplifting feeling, only brought down by the massacre faced at that very same bar. He looked over at the hybrid he had just fought. They had bound his hands and wings already and taken his weapons away. The difference between the two sides fighting this war was evident. If it was the other way around, the bird's wings would have been cut off at best. Even so, Henry couldn't help but wonder if it was the best idea to keep him alive. "What are we going to do with him?" He asked.

"Bring him down to the dungeons. Lock him up until we're done." The old man replied.

"The dungeons? Have they been cleared already?" Henry was surprised. He knew it was where Drake and Ana were heading, but there were only two of them. It had to have been guarded better than that.

"Yes, sir. Another one of these buggers that fancy themselves the king's elite guard was down there. Only the one to take out."

"I suppose Drake made short work of him." It made sense to Henry. No matter who you are, a dragon is a strong opponent.

"No, sir. Was our princess it was. Made him look like a right fool."

"Really?" Henry asked, somewhat surprised. "Well, there might just be a chance for us yet."

Chapter 30

The moment he made it out of the dungeons, Drake ran into opposition. Every floor was patrolled with the exception of the foyer since only an absolute fool would attempt to storm the castle gates with no backup. He had never been in a war like this before and found it hard to decide what course of action to take. It was either clear out the guards or go straight for the heart of the castle. As good as he was at it, Drake didn't really care for mindless killing, so he chose the latter option. If he could take down the king, it would end everything early. He just wished he had a strategist like Henry or Ana to back up his decision.

It only made sense that the king would hide in the throne room or his own personal quarters. Considering the show he made of himself, Drake figured the throne room would be the best bet. It was just a matter of getting there undetected, so he kept his movements as quiet as he could. The whole time he couldn't shake the thought of Ana being left alone to fight the hybrid in the basement. He knew he couldn't dwell on it. This was war. He had to do his job and hope for the best.

From the briefing beforehand, he knew the throne room was on the second level. Getting to the staircase was harder than he had expected. Once inside the belly of the beast, the rotation was three guards in a group that maintained line of sight with the patrol in front of them. There was the answer to why the main street was so empty. If he engaged, there would be no less than a six on one, potentially more. The spiral stairs might not be a viable option.

It was then he remembered one more critical detail. The throne room was described as plain, with four windows that backed the throne. Drake just had to make it outside and up the back wall. He was just hoping that they weren't expecting hybrids to make it this far in to begin with.

He made his way back to the foyer and recklessly attempted one of the doors leading towards the back of the castle. Luck was on his side today as he found the kitchen. It was staffed, but not by guards. A short chef was, for some reason, still running around cutting vegetables like it was nobody's business. The last thing Drake wanted to do was silence a civilian.

"I didn't see you. You never came through here." Came the fast and somewhat aggressive voice from the man.

"You're really just going to let me through?" Drake asked, confused. He realized he should have just counted his blessings and ran for it, but his curiosity got the better of him.

"I don't get paid enough for this. Just get out of my kitchen."

"Sure thing." Drake made a half-sprint towards the back door and opened it to reveal the courtyard. Perfect, just what he was looking for. He couldn't help himself from apologizing to the chef like he owed it to him before he left. The words were met with merely a grunt. Drake made sure to close the door behind him on his way out.

The courtyard itself was like a tiny oasis in the middle of the desert. This was good. Plenty of bushes to fall on if something happens and he gets knocked off the wall. That situation seemed likely as two of the king's guard were staring right at him the moment he came out the door.

Drake had no intention of getting into a fight he didn't need to, and he noticed these two were wielding swords. He decided to take advantage of the guards' surprised reactions. Since there were no other weapons clearly on them, he turned and jumped a couple of feet, grabbing onto the wall with his claws and trying to get as much grip as he could with his feet. There was nearly a slip on the first grab, but nothing he couldn't take control of. He didn't even look back to the guards scrambling over to him and just started climbing as fast as he possibly could.

He heard the clank of swords hitting the wall directly where his ankles just were. Drake's scales were pretty defensive against bladed weapons, but they weren't perfect. If they had cut in just the right way, he might have lost all power to his foot. Clearing the thought out of his mind, he raced up the side of the building at the speed of a panther climbing a tree. Four large windows were coming up. Arch shaped things that looked grand as if to let light in, though from this angle, they faced a mountain. It was as if the windows were meant to be more of an escape route than an actual fixture. Too bad that contingency was being turned on its head. Now it was just a matter of if the king was in or if Drake would have to make an appointment for later. Once he got to it, he grabbed the far right window's ledge and vaulted himself over it.

This was definitely the throne room, on account of the throne. Honestly, if it wasn't for that clear feature, there was no telling what this room was for. It was unfurnished, unpainted, and most importantly, unlit. The torches were out, and it was going to take Drake's eyes a moment to adjust. Unfortunately, they never got the chance, as a blinding flash of light followed by the sound of stone hitting the ground a few seconds later interrupted the process. Somewhere in the blurred dots of his vision he could see what had happened. A red cloak and a helmet with a horn affixed. He didn't find the king, but this was just as good.

"Went off and hid, did he?" Drake asked while going in for a blind strike against his opponent. His claw found air, which he wasn't surprised by. The attack was obvious, but he didn't want his opponent to know his eyes weren't doing well.

The intimidation and banter didn't matter, as Drake found himself struck by a metal gauntlet on the back. The blow almost knocked him over and hurt like hell. Instead, he used the momentum from the strike to take a few steps forward and whip around. His opponent held a defensive stance. Somehow it was perfectly timed to when Drake could see the whole room. This was an experienced fighter.

"I assume the horn is real?" Drake asked, putting his own claws up in defence.

"Same as your scales." A confident feminine voice replied.

Drake went in for another attack, this time to gauge his opponent's defence. "So, what are you?" He asked while making a weak swipe, only for it to be deflected and counter-attacked by those metal gauntlets. Drake didn't put much into it, so it was easy enough to defend and gain distance. "Deer? Rhino? Narwhal?" Something about the Red Guard's body language gave away discomfort at the guesses. Pride, perhaps?

There was still the question about that flash of light. Drake didn't see any kind of handheld cannon on his opponent. He had to stay on the defensive until he knew what it was. The answer became clear to him sooner than he had anticipated.

"You're not the only mythical creature roaming these parts." She said upon lifting her hands up to take her helmet off. This was a prime opportunity, and Drake wasn't about to let his foe flaunt in front of him like this. He knew she'd have to be blinded and unguarded for a split second, so he went in on an all-out assault the moment the headpiece was half-way taken off.

This was a mistake. The iron horned helmet gave way to a majestic golden glowing horn underneath. It sparked for a moment as two blades clashing against each other would before releasing out a bolt of lightning that hit Drake square in the chest before he could land another blow. His vision went black for a second before he came to, half-way across the throne room and barely able to move. No one expected the guard to have this powerful a piece, and Drake was paying the price for it.

"Unicorn?" He asked weakly, trying to sound unaffected by the blast.

"Kirin." She corrected proudly, allowing another bolt of lightning to crash on the ground next to him. She was showing off.

"Ah, furry lightning unicorn." Drake responded, forcing himself to his feet. His balance was off as his muscles had spasmed from the shock. This was going to be like fighting drunk. Only his opponent would be dead sober. It wouldn't be the first time.

"Legendary beast of storms, thank you." She sounded genuinely offended as she sent another bolt at him. It barely missed. Drake couldn't tell if her aim was off because his movements had become unpredictable or if his insults were actually working. It didn't really matter which, as one strike could be enough to end it. Hell, the one he had taken might have already ended it and he was just pushing for pointless time.

Time wasn't something he had much of if he was going to win, either. He didn't know much about kirins. Before today Drake didn't even think they were real, just some kind of fairy tale. Horned horses that control storms seemed pretty far-fetched. Then again, so did fire-breathing flying lizards. The only thing he could determine was that the lightning was coming from the horn. As gruesome as it was, he had to find a way to break that thing off before he had any chance.

Drake laid his focus on the horn as he went in for another assault. Maybe if he could lock hands with her, she'd feel the lightning just the same as he would. Though it was far more likely a creature like that had some kind of defence against such an attack. He was out of options, though, and went for it anyway.

She didn't strike back, surprisingly, and held up her gauntlets to catch his claws. He tried to brute force his way through her defences and up to her horn. It didn't work. She was as strong as him, if not stronger. Drake tried to unlock the position by sliding one of his claws out, and then when she went to defend against it using the other one. It still didn't work. She was faster and much better trained in hand-to-hand combat than he was. It wasn't a huge accomplishment, considering Drake had no training.

It was then he realized something, and it was almost too late. If the room wasn't so dark, he might not have noticed, but her horn began to glow. It got brighter the longer they held position. It didn't take a genius to figure out what was going to happen next. Drake waited for a few seconds until he could see the first spark of sudden light near the tip of the spike. The moment he did, he unbound his claws by moving them down and following the momentum to throw his body out of the way and behind his opponent. It wasn't graceful, but the sound of stone cracking as a bolt of lightning hit confirmed his move was correct.

That only left the problem of the following strikes. When he came in, she did more than one, so he scrambled to his feet and started running. As another bolt barely missed him. Drake cursed himself for not counting the strikes upon entry. Before he could blame himself for anything else, he found himself on the ground again with a sharp pain in his chest. It only lasted for a second before he felt his heart stop.

This was it. How it ended. Fighting a fight he somehow blamed himself for. Finding Ana and bringing her in was the worst decision he could have made for his own survival. It didn't matter, though. This was a death that was worth the cost. As long as the grand scheme succeeded, this kingdom would have to turn itself around for the better. Besides, he wasn't the only life lost in this war.

It was about when he could feel his thoughts get slower that life came back to him. Everything hurt like hell, and every one of his muscles tensed at the same time. He opened his eyes to see no time had passed, and he was still in combat, but the guard's horn was dull again. Based on how he felt, it must have been another strike of lightning, and that's where he finally found his opening.

In her attempt to make sure he was dead, the Red Guard managed to do the exact opposite. Whoever she was, she wasn't experienced in killing with her own power. It made sense as she would have had to keep it close to the chest. You can't exactly go out throwing lightning bolts on every mission. Drake still needed a way to win this fight, though, and it came to him without him even knowing it.

He brought himself to his feet the moment his legs would let him and found he almost immediately fell over. It was as if he was standing on ice. Upon a quick glance down, he *was* standing on ice. The information had to be processed quickly. He couldn't figure out what caused it, but he knew the dragon he was fused with was an ice dragon. Now it was just a matter of doing whatever he did when he was dead.

It wasn't long after he stood up before she came crashing down on him, both gauntlets on the attack, knowing that she should have crushed her target's skull in when she had the chance. He had to catch them and lock the position again. Both of them stood staring daggers at each other in a contest of strength until that damn lightning recharged.

He had no idea how he was going to do it. He didn't even know how he did it laying on the ground, but Drake had the way to summon up the power of frost. Staring at his hands, he focused all his willpower on trying to freeze her gauntlets closed. It didn't work. He could see the glow from her horn start to come back, but instead of focusing harder, he got angry. Apparently, that was the right thing to do, as both gauntlets started to freeze over. Drake would have stopped to admire his new power if it wasn't for the fact his plan still didn't work.

All he succeeded in was forming ice crystals on the end of her fists. Once the Kirin realized this, she unlocked the position and took two steps back, just to come barreling back in once again. This time her weapons weren't only hard and metal, they were covered in spikes. Drake had to dodge to the side. He couldn't risk whatever ice he made having the ability to pierce dragon scales. The whole time he was still focused on creating more, and it was working. Somewhat.

He ran in circles around the room, trying to not be a stationary target as he knew that lightning was coming back. Shards of ice were left in his wake, falling from his palms as he attempted to gain control of whatever power this dragon had. He could feel the clumps getting bigger and bigger, and worried that running around would continue to not be a viable option. Especially considering last time, he might have died for a few seconds.

Drake could hear a faint crackling sound, meaning there was no time left. His decision was quick, and he made a complete stop. Planting his feet, he made a stand against the first bolt of lightning with his palms held together in front of him. He wasn't fast enough to block the first blow, but his opponent had expected him to keep moving, so it flew past him and cracked an interior wall. By the time the second bolt came flying, he had formed a small shield of ice, hoping it would deflect the next blast. It was only about a foot in diameter and a few inches thick. Luckily this was barely enough, as the next bolt hit the top and deflected over his head. Unfortunately, it left the ice cracked and unusable as it fell to the ground.

Turns out that saving your own hide is a good motivator, though. As the next bolt came very quickly, trying to penetrate his defences, Drake already had another one up that was slightly bigger than the first. It cracked and fell apart but kept him from getting hit. He started a third but abandoned it upon noticing the Kirin's horn was dull once again. Now it was time to find out how this power was on the offence.

Drake came in fast, preparing his own fist in a spiked covering of ice shards that had to be dodged. This put his opponent in an unfavourable position below him. She attempted to come out by punching upward, but he expected that. He fell back and threw a hand at her horn in response. It was finally the position he wanted. He had the horn in his hand. He pulled her head down with it to make sure all of her weapons were pointing away from him, both her hands and lightning. Now it was just a matter of breaking it off.

It should have been easy. Just grab it with both hands, pull in one direction and push with the other, then snap. Done. No more threat and one less death. Albeit one from the enemy side, but it was a better way to turn out in war. It was then he hesitated. Not because the task itself was difficult. It was that it reminded him of Henry. If he broke this hybrid's horn off, it would be no different than what they did to his arm. A part of him wanted it to get revenge for his friend. Another part knew that this was just bringing himself down to their level. Taking the weapon away, even if it meant taking away the life of the one who had held it. He was on the verge of just knocking her out instead, but he could feel it. Through his fingers, he could feel the static building. There would be no way to block the attack besides letting go, with the exception of…

Snap.

Going purely on instinct, Drake found himself in the position he was after, but it wasn't the one he wanted. The pain shrieked out by the guard found its way into his very soul. She had fallen to the ground, defeated. There was no way she would be a threat anytime soon, but was it worth it? Holding that horn in his hand made him question himself. He was in this city to help hybrids, not tear them to shreds.

As much as he would have loved to stay and apologize, Drake knew there was a war going on. Though cruel, he had to convince himself it was someone who wanted him dead mere moments ago. He didn't look back. He couldn't. A crack of light shined through as he opened the throne room doors to exit and faded into darkness as he left as quickly as possible. If nothing else, his trophy would make a nice gift for the king.

Chapter 31

Kabel wore the face of a ruined man. He was covered in bruises, cuts, and his armour wasn't looking the same as it was that morning. His sword was chipped and quite possibly bent. He had lost count of how many soldiers he had made it through to get this far. 23 soldiers had died beside him on the way through. That number he would never lose count of. As they died, he could feel their names getting burned into his memory for the rest of his life, and he knew these were just the ones that he had witnessed. If he survived this next encounter, his first action would be to identify every body that was strewn about the city. He never wanted to forget the men and women that laid down their lives for the future of Arid Retreat.

He found himself with a small squad consisting of Calvin and one other guard by the name of Laura. Both of them were just as beaten as he was, but they were at the final step. The moment they finished their climb to the top floor of the keep, they knew Kasibel's hunch was right. There were four guards stationed outside the doors they were after. The king's chamber. The leader of the most war-ridden kingdom known to history, and he hides at the first sign of battle. That was reason enough for a coup, but the atrocities he had performed with the same human shields outside his door were the real reason this fight had begun.

The three soldiers looked to each other to confirm everyone was still accounted for, and without thinking, charged straight into battle. They were quick. None of the guards knew what had hit them before they hit the ground. They didn't even have time to take a defensive position. Even four against three very tired soldiers, no amount of experience could have prepared them for the sheer anger and efficiency of Kasibel's forces.

It wasn't that the enemy meant nothing to Kasibel. Quite the opposite. He knew they were steered in the wrong direction by the king, but there would be no winning them over. The loyalty held by the king's guard was infallible. Keeping any of them alive wasn't an option, as much as he would have liked it to be. Anyone still standing after the king had fallen would still push forward into their deaths. Kasibel knew this because he once felt the same way. Someone finally snapped him out of it, though, and all he hoped was that she was still alive.

The three of them stood before the massive ornate doors that led to the largest bedroom in the castle. They knew that they would face opposition going in. It didn't matter if the king had one hundred men or if it was just him, the fight wasn't over. Kasibel took a deep breath and uttered the first word to come out of his mouth since they had stormed the gates.

"Ready?"

Both Laura and Calvin did nothing aside from nod and grunt. Their gaze was fixated on the door. This was the last step. Something neither of them ever knew they were going to be a part of, let alone be this close to victory. What happened in this next room would change the very shape of The Scarlet Sands for years to come, but they were ready. After what they had seen, they would rather die trying to take over this kingdom than continue living in it the way it was.

Kasibel took a deep breath before ramming his armoured shoulder into the door at full force. He had expected a barricade, but the door flung open effortlessly. He had expected guard, but the room was empty save for one man in a massive red regal robe, sipping from an ornate glass of wine.

"You could have knocked." The king stated distastefully.

"How dare you." Kasibel chastised. "After all you've done, how dare you."

"I had a perfectly run kingdom until you went and threw together this little rebellion."

"The only thing that 'threw together a rebellion' were your actions." Kasibel fired back.

Rolfe gave him a calm, disappointed look in response. He took a sip of his wine as if he were just having guests over. "You don't understand, my boy. You see-"

Kasibel stopped him in his tracks. "Don't you dare call me-" Rolfe had lifted up a finger to ask for silence. Years of training made

Kasibel stop just long enough for him to continue.

"These creatures that you defend are the largest threat this kingdom has ever seen." The king conveyed this with heavy conviction. One that you knew you'd never be able to reason with.

"I'd say you're the bigger threat here." Kasibel was on the verge of rushing his father down with blade in hand. He knew there was something more at play here, though. The king would never leave himself completely defenceless.

"That's the point, boy." The king continued. "We're a nation built on conquering. We were put here by the gods to claim this world as our own piece by piece. If we are not the strongest, this would not be possible. So I had to eliminate those who may stand in the way of the throne."

"If you were going to take someone on, it should have been me!" Kasibel yelled out emotionally. "I'm the heir. I'm the true threat to the throne."

"No, you aren't, boy. You're human. You wouldn't have a chance against me!" The king threw his glass right past Kasibel, who didn't move. The glass shattered against the back wall, which began to be stained by the wine.

"So what? You're getting on in years, old man. And you consider yourself the strongest human?" Kasibel mocked, his sword at the ready.

"Far from it." The king requited. He slowly undid the gold-coloured thread that laced together his robe around his neck and let it fall to the floor. It revealed below it a white silk attire showing through the muscles of a strongman, but more importantly, what Kasibel could only describe as a mane. A thick layer of hair that made its way around his father's neck and puffed out brilliantly.

"This isn't possible." Kasibel's face became as white as silk "This whole time. This is why you never let us see you outside of your royal attire."

"Correct." The king retorted, adjusting his mane. "If we are the only hybrids, there would be no chance for opposition. No one could overpower us, even though they'd try. Like you are now." He prepared a stance suited to hand-to-hand combat, tensing every muscle in his body. "I'm sure there's no changing your mind. You know the law of Arid Retreat. Make it official."

"King Rolfe Rexharne. Your rule has failed, and I challenge you to combat for the throne." Kasibel recited as he had many times to himself preparing for this moment. The man who raised him and trained him to be who he was, standing in front of him, ready to fight to the death. The fact that he was a hybrid made no difference. The man was a monster all the same.

The first blow was struck before even an acceptance was made. Rolfe had darted across the room and hit Kasibel directly in the throat. It knocked him backwards and caused him to choke. Calvin and Laura stayed to the side as they were instructed by Kasibel beforehand. They were told this was his fight, though Calvin was starting to have second thoughts on following orders. Also, if someone had found out the battle against the king wasn't a fair fight, according to law the new ruler was null and void.

Kasibel sprung back to his feet quicker than his armour should have allowed him to. He rushed in at his unarmed opponent keeping his sword in front of him. Even with the amount of muscle Rolfe had inherited from a lion, he wouldn't be able to stop a blade without getting cut. Or, at least that's what Kasibel thought.

The moment his weapon was in range the King had knocked it to the floor with the back of his hand. The sheer force was unprecedented, but that alone wasn't what disarmed the guard captain. That was the problem with fighting your teacher. They taught you your moves. In the case where that same teacher was paranoid, they didn't teach you everything. After what felt like a blow to the chest, Kasibel keeled forward into his father's oncoming knee, knocking him back onto the floor in a daze.

Before the guard captain could even find his weapon, he found a foot on his throat. His father was almost too ready to kill him as he tried to choke for air. Calvin was having a harder and harder time listening to this. He had already turned his head away and closed his eyes, but he couldn't ignore it any longer. Despite direct orders and the fear of breaking tradition, Calvin raised his blade and rushed the king. The next thing he knew, he was against the opposite wall with his weapon on the floor, and that awful sound of choking didn't stop. It drove him to try again.

Calvin left his sword on the floor as he rushed in once again, this time attempting to tackle the king off of his commander. He could at least see his fate coming this time as a strong hand wrapped around his throat and threw him to the floor once again. Calvin had no idea how Laura could just stand there listening to this, but he felt almost too weak to get up himself. He quickly shook the negative thoughts out of his head and got to his feet again. As long as he could stand, he was going to fight.

That was until the door burst open, and someone else did just as Calvin had planned, only successfully. Drake had come in and knocked the king off of Kasibel, and Ana was there to help him up. Calvin couldn't help himself from thankfully uttering the word "Princess…" before falling to the floor once again.

"You can't…." Kasibel said weakly. "The laws…"

"Mean fuck all against a mass murderer." There was never more conviction to Ana's words. She stared daggers at her father, who was sizing up Drake, neither of them throwing the first punch.

"You can't mean that, Ana." Rolfe said, keeping his eyes on Drake. "I did what was best for the kingdom."

"No, you didn't." She said, pulling her blade out in response. "But we're about to."

Drake had thrown off Rolfe just enough by dropping the horn of his head guard on the floor. He came in at the king quickly. The two of them locked together, every muscle in both bodies tensed as they tried to overpower the other. It wasn't too long before the power of a dragon overrode that of a lion. Rolfe tried to get up a fight back, and he might have been able to if it wasn't for Calvin and Kasibel coming in and pinning down both of his arms. They weren't at their strongest anymore, but they had enough to keep him down with the help of Drake.

"I hope you feel helpless." Ana said, standing over her father, who had almost an entire body holding down each one of his limbs. "You'll at least know what they felt."

"You fools." He responded. "They hate you. They need my leadership. Whether I die or live, you'll never have the will of the people."

"We have the will of the people you ignored." Ana said, staring into her father's eyes for what she knew was the last time. "The ones you outlawed. The ones you slaughtered. What you forgot about is every hybrid you killed had a mother, a father. They had brothers and sisters. Friends and lovers. Some of them may have been ousted from their families, but many of them weren't. Remember as you make your way down to hell that those families paved your way there. It's for them that I send you on that journey." She didn't let him have a single word against her as she shoved her sword through his throat hard enough to embed it in the sandstone floor that lay beneath.

Epilogue

Ana and her brother stood on their father's balcony in the midday sun. The remaining hybrids and Kasibel's forces were finishing securing the castle, save for Drake, Calvin, and Laura. The battle was over. Countless lives had been paid to make this coup happen, which led none of them to feel they had won. The victory would have to be felt over time as the fresh wounds made their way into scars, gone but never forgotten.

Kasibel was the first to break the silence, though he did so quietly and without his usual inflections. "What are you going to do as queen?"

Ana was well aware of the loose laws surrounding taking the throne in Arid Retreat. Though there were official rulings that claimed it had to be taken in one on one combat, the victors who had played dirty had still maintained their rule in the past. It was really less of a law and more of a formality that was polite to follow. Since she had been the one to take her father's life, it rightfully went to her. She let out a long sigh before answering her brother's question. "I don't think I should have the throne. So I suppose the only thing I will do is hand the throne over to you."

"But the laws state-" He had started but was quickly cut off.

"Well, I don't plan on taking it, and I think we'd both prefer if I was alive. At least, I hope we'd both prefer that." Ana narrowed her eyes at Kasibel just to be sure.

"Of course." He responded awkwardly. "But what of the witnesses?"

"What? Them?" Ana turned to the three in the room, pretending they weren't eavesdropping. "Any of you plan on telling on us?" Drake, Calvin, and Laura all quickly shook their heads.

"Saw Kasibel kill him with my very eyes. Isn't that right?" Drake said, bumping his arm into Calvin's. It took him by surprise, so it was a moment before he could get his words together.

"Y-Yes. Of course. Clear as day. All hail king Kasibel!" Calvin shouted.

"Ease back a bit." Replied Laura, seemingly the only one who could read the room. Calvin rubbed the back of his head and quietly apologized.

"There you have it. King Kasibel Rexharne. Has a ring to it." Ana gave her brother a witty smile which she wore as a mask.

"Well, I suppose there's no arguing that." Kasibel responded, equally hiding his own feelings. Though both of them had lost respect for the man, the king was still their father. Even if their feeling of loss was small, it would bear a heavy weight as they couldn't show it to anyone. Not even each other.

"There's only one thing I request." Ana came out solemnly.

"I already know. I have an intention of integrating hybrids back into society. It will take time to get the laws changed...."

"Within the week." She said sternly, narrowing her eyes once again.

"A week!? But that's barely enough time to-"

"Would you question the rightful queen?" Ana added. Kasibel looked back to his two guards and Drake for support. Drake he expected to stay quiet. But to be betrayed by Calvin and even Laura as well? None of them came to his aid.

"You clearly have a better way with them than I do. You sure you don't want the throne?" He asked.

Ana reached an arm around her brother. Something neither of them would admit they needed right now. "Give it time. You'll get there. Someday you might almost be as good as me." She chuckled a fake chuckle. "But you do only have one week, and I'll be back to make sure of it."

"Where are you going?" Kasibel asked, sounding surprised, though he already knew that she had no plans of sticking around the kingdom she had been locked into for years.

"Henry talked about finding the hybrids that fled to Ingress. I figured I would go and help him. I do owe him, after all." Ana took her arm off of Kasibel and started playing with the hilt of her sword. "I... owe all of them."

Kasibel wanted to tell her that she didn't. He wanted to say that it wasn't her fault and there was no burden to bear for the blood her father shed, but he knew he'd be a hypocrite. He felt the same way, though he knew he himself had done nothing wrong. These people deserved to know that someone was paying attention. That someone cared. That there was a world for them to live in that didn't hate them. All they wanted was the same thing we all would, to be welcome in our own home.

"Within the week it is, then." Kasibel confirmed. "Though the nobles will hate me right off the bat."

"What's a few rich people complaining?" Ana threw that out there to calm her brother, though she understood his dilemma. "Though I think at least one of the families had a regular at Henry's bar. You'll just have to start there."

"So when are you leaving?" Kasibel asked, though he already knew the answer. It was confirmed to him by a lack of eye contact and a long silence.

"As soon as I leave this room." Ana responded honestly. "And I don't intend to stay here longer than I have to." She motioned to the body and the drying pool of blood on the floor behind them.

Kasibel grabbed his sister's hand in a firm handshake and locked eyes with her. "Just be safe, and know that as long as I'm here, you'll always have a home to come back to." He knew just as well as her that this trip was going to be more than just bringing hybrids back home.

"Thank you." She said, keeping her eyes from watering the best that she could. It wasn't very effective. "Don't run my home into the ground at least."

"No promises." He smiled, as did she in return. The two of them unlocked their hands and shared a long silence with each other before Ana walked out. Neither of them needed to say goodbye. It was already in the air.

Ana took Drake out of the room with her and gave Calvin a pat on the back before they left. For once, she could walk these halls with no fear of guards trying to get her back to her room. The ones remaining had fought alongside her and knew she could take care of herself. That day she walked out the front doors of the castle and didn't even glance behind her.

There was a whole world out there, and Ana was going to see it all.

About the Author

My name is Gregory, and I grew up in Lawrencetown, Nova Scotia. My interest in fantasy novels started at ten years old, when my mother took me to a local bookstore and I picked up the first book in the Dark Sun World series, *The Verdant Passage* by Troy Denning. I went on to read the whole series, and then found my true inspiration in the Forgotten Realms books, particularly The Legend of Drizzt series. From that point, I couldn't pull myself out of fantasy novels or Dungeons and Dragons!

I spend most of my spare time with videogames, many of which have passed stories on to me that no other medium could. There's rarely a game I'd avoid playing, but character driven RPGs have always been a forefront for me.

If you have any questions for me about my life or my books, feel free to reach out to me at;

ModernDragonPublishing@Gmail.com

And I'll try to get back and answer you as best I can!

Manufactured by Amazon.ca
Bolton, ON

27512613R00157